THE FINE ART OF DECEPTION UNDOING TIME

BOOK 1

ALYSSA RICHARDS

Library of Congress Control Number 2014942577
Ebook ISBN - 13 978-0-9792265-7-1
Editing by Book Alchemy, LLC

Sign up for Alyssa's newsletter at to receive special offers and news about her latest releases.

You can follow her on:
Instagram

Contact Alyssa at:
authoralyssarichards@protonmail.com

PRAISE FOR USA TODAY BESTSELLING AUTHOR, ALYSSA RICHARDS

A MURDER AT ALCOTT MANOR is very definitely a thrill-a-minute tale of evil trying to keep a stranglehold on the living. This is a perfect book for readers who enjoy non-stop action and suspense with a dash of sexy." FRESH FICTION REVIEW

"THE HAUNTING OF ALCOTT MANOR is a great read... an escapist read, full of secrets and surprises that caught me out completely!" —*Jeannie Zelos Book Reviews*

"Having read Alyssa Richards other books, I knew I was in for a treat, even though this was a slightly different genre. And gothic suspense being one of my absolute favorites, I was extremely psyched to read this book. Fortunately, everything that I anticipated about how good this book would be, and how much I would enjoy it, came true.

At first glance, this might appear to be your average haunted house story. But in the hands of this very capable, and highly readable author, it becomes so much more. The haunting was unique and the story revolving around the haunting was very intriguing. I totally did not anticipate the way the story was going or how it was going to end up. This was a great first entry in a new genre that I hope the author will continue. This book, as well as everything else this author has written, comes highly recommended." — DT Chantel, Book Reviewer, THE HAUNTING OF ALCOTT MANOR

"Man oh man! Alyssa Richards has seriously outdone herself with this trilogy. It encompasses love, passion, deception, heartache, reality and alternate reality. Just stunning from start to finish. This trilogy is awesome. If you're looking for a paranormal romance that's focused around psychics and time travel, definitely grab this trilogy. It's simply amazing!" —*Nay's Pink Bookshelf,* THE FINE ART OF DECEPTION SERIES

5.0 out of 5 stars "Now this is what I'm talking about...absofreakingamazing!

"It's authors like Ms. Richards that really opened up the portals to my world, and instilled/nurtured within me a love for reading. Hook, line and sinker you are pulled fast and hard into her storylines and are wrecked when you've reached the end...you just don't want it to be over. THE HAUNTING OF ALCOTT MANOR is no different and has a wonderful mix of gothic suspense/mystery with a titter of romance that will captivate you..and the end...omg I so didn't see that coming. What a stunning conclusion!" —*K. Berry, Amazon Reviewer*

5.0 out of 5 stars That ending...!? Are you kidding me?!

"Like others, I'm sure, I`ve read hundred(s) of these types of books. This was a great read, great twists and turns.

...and the end...? WOW! What's really getting me right now though? Henry and Gemma at still with me....days after I've finished the book! I cried with them, I loved with them, and they touched me deeply! Great job! (This is the first time I have been inspired enough to write a review, too!)" *T. Varianon, Amazon Book Reviewer,* THE HAUNTING OF ALCOTT MANOR

"...undoubtedly Alyssa Richards has just become one of my new favourite authors for this year." —Living in Our Own Story Blog, THE FINE ART OF DECEPTION

"This is well written with complex characters who reveal more of themselves as the story progresses. It is a great mystery with paranormal elements that make it enthrallingly different and captivating."--Splashes into Books, THE FINE ART OF DECEPTION

"I felt like I was standing right in the middle of a Movie Set of something between Pierce Brosnan's "The Thomas Crown Affair" or Sean Connery's "Entrapment". I was sucked into the story from the beginning and I could not stop reading. It was such an interesting mix between the paranormal – romance and crime elements that kept me reading and wondering what might happen next."--Jeri's Book Attic, THE FINE ART OF DECEPTION

"An intriguing read that kept my interest until the last page. Very enjoyable and definitely recommended."--Archaeolibrarian, I dig good books!

"This book was loaded with mystery and suspense. The plot was well executed and kept me on the edge of my seat. The sizzling passionate scenes between Addie and Blake were red hot." --Smut Book Junkie Book Reviews, THE FINE ART OF DECEPTION

THE HAUNTING OF ALCOTT MANOR is a fascinating tale of tragedy, ghosts, and soulmates. Mystery fans will enjoy this heroine's efforts to track down clues -- both tangible and ghostly -- while trying to find the truth about a woman's death. Romance fans will adore this match-up of a strong heroine and an enigmatic yet endearingly charming and earnest hero. I look forward to reading the next book in this tantalizing _Alcott Manor_ series." FRESH FICTION REVIEW

"The plot is unique in a way that you will keep thinking of its awesomeness for a long time after finishing this book. There was so much positives in the book, that kept me awake with my Kindle at night, in spite of my recently sleep deprived life. This book has exceeded my expectations in every way. You should definitely read it, if romance, suspense or paranormal genre suits you."-- Books are Magic, THE FINE ART OF DECEPTION

"I was very drawn to the characters. Richards did an excellent job weaving you into their world whether it was the good guy or the bad guy you just wanted to know what they were thinking, doing and their next move. I definitely recommend."--The Reading Pile, THE FINE ART OF DECEPTION

For the love of so many of my lifetimes.

1

———

The perfect life can disappear without warning. Like an elegantly designed wisp of smoke, it can be here one minute, gone the next. Then the simple, busy, normal you took for granted suddenly becomes a part of your past, while its absence fuels your obsession to find it again.

I was down to my last chance to find it again.

In slow, deliberate cadence I paced through the library of my townhome, then across the salon and into the kitchen. Insomnia gave me ample opportunity to practice my pacing routine.

There was comfort in routine. I was calm now.

But just an hour ago I'd woken up gasping, my back slick with sweat. It wasn't just a nightmare. It was a memory from my childhood—a recurring fear I couldn't put to rest.

With bare feet I took a turn and padded onto the cold, marble-floored bathroom, sat at the vanity, and brushed the tangles from my hair, giving extra attention to the mass of knots that gathered at the nape of my neck. Fitful dreams gave fitful hair.

I smoothed a few long strands behind my ears and stared into the large, round mirror. As usual, a related image of my father stared back at me. My sisters favored our mother with their thicker hair and warm, ginger skin tones, but there was no mistaking that I was my father's child.

I lifted the lid on the wooden box first and looked at my diamond solitaire engagement ring in the back left corner. Jeremy and I had been planning our wedding when he left me for my best friend at the time.

Looking at the ring was part of my morning constitution to remind myself that men often left without warning.

I closed the lid on the wooden jewelry box.

Though there was Jack...

This perfection of a man who dropped in on my dreams from some other life we'd shared together. Yes, he had been real to me at one time. Now he was only real in my dreams.

I picked up the second jewelry box. Trimmed in antique gold and coated in pink enamel, it looked like it could have belonged to Marie Antoinette. Inside was the one surefire weapon that could move me beyond all the tragedies of life. At least for a few moments. I'd found the ring in a dusty antique shop while on a trip to Paris—a cushion-cut, corn-flower-blue sapphire in a wide platinum setting. I'd known immediately that it had been my ring.

I picked it up and read the inscription which was written in English:

To Sassy, All My Love. Always, Jack. May 23rd, 1922

I knew from the first instant I touched the ring that this Jack was the same and only Jack of my dreams. The energy from the ring, and the energy from the man in my dreams, were one and the same. It was undeniable. I had jeweled proof that he existed. That we existed. I thought perhaps it was a gift from God, reminding me that I had been loved.

I put the ring back in its case, and climbed into the marble-encased tub which sat in the middle of the room, and I soaked in a hot, lavender-infused bath.

The scent that wafted off my heated skin immediately transported me back to childhood when my mother used to give me a lavender bath every morning, telling me it was "the way of the Goddess." It felt a bit like my duty as a woman in the Montgomery family to continue the tradition.

Plus, it made me feel like a figure in a Greco-Roman relief. Not an everyday occurrence for most people. Unless, of course, you're taking a scented bath every morning. There's just something so regal about it. Not the least of which is how the lavender smoothed the frayed edges of dreams destroyed and loves lost.

I DOWNED the last drop of the Italian-born espresso and stared out the warped glass of my favorite room of the house —a quiet turret nestled on the side of what used to be my grandfather's New York City townhome.

He'd vanished with my father while on a buying trip in Paris years ago.

I glanced at the black mantel clock that sat on the third shelf, and watched the second hand drag what was left of the night into daylight. Four more hours until my interview. An interview that had to go well.

I'd learned my lesson. Keep your gifts tucked away. Don't let people know what you see.

If I got the job, I knew I could make a career for myself authenticating art. No one had to know how I did it.

There really was no end to the details I could see about art, or anything else I touched for that matter. As long as I had the hunger to know the details of the object. Of course some of those details came through, whether I wanted to know or not. It wasn't an exact science.

Through the library glass, I watched a petite runner while she jogged down the street and jogged in place under the lamplight to take her pulse. Her ponytail bounced from left to right as she fumbled with what looked like an old Sony Walkman. Thoughts of how much she hated her husband pulsed through my head each time her white running shoes hit the wet sidewalk.

She'd begged him for a divorce, but he wouldn't let her go.

The not-so-funny feeling of being seen hit me in the chest and ignited the caffeine I'd sent into my system. Even though she had just been half a football field away, she was now in front of me. Her face was drawn tight, her brown eyes dark and focused, searching like heat-seeking missiles.

A tiny bullet hole was above her left eyebrow.

Though I didn't want it to happen, my own world slipped away. I had no choice but to see how the hooded man with the long face and the thin lips surprised her in the parking garage. He knew her schedule, had waited until she was pulling groceries out of the trunk of the black Mercedes. When she turned, he shot her before she knew what was happening.

She still didn't know she was dead.

Two young boys screamed and cried in the backseat while apples and oranges hit the ground in dull thuds and rolled across the parking garage floor. Dad didn't account for the boys' whereabouts when he set up their mother's death.

I went into the kitchen hoping to escape her, but she followed.

"I've been a good wife. I was everything he wanted when he was building his career. I was thin and charming and beautiful because that's what he needed on his arm so he could make partner." She leaned close to my face and my heart clanged. I abandoned the small mug and the bowl on the sink counter, slunk around her and out of the kitchen.

"When he wanted children, I gave them to him! When he had affairs? I looked the other way! All I want now is a little freedom and my sanity. Is that too much to ask?"

"I hear you," I mumbled and went toward my bedroom to get dressed.

"Why does everyone ignore me?" she yelled.

I gently closed my bedroom door behind me, but a loud clatter echoed through my home.

I knew that was my porcelain mug and dish shattering on the marble floor.

No matter how many times this happened, I never got used to self-obsessed strangers dropping into my home and making my life their own.

Ghosts had no boundaries.

As a child, ghosts stalked me at night, tormenting me, leaving me with so much terror I was powerless to move. Even as an adult, I still didn't sleep much. They were always out there. Watching. Waiting. Impossible to ignore. And because normal had always been my goal, I hated their presence in my life.

The first hint of a migraine pinged the inside of my skull.

A closed door wouldn't keep the lady away from me forever, but I hoped it might buy me a few minutes to catch my breath.

Sometimes they just drifted away, so ensconced in their own troubles they moved on. Others knew they could get to you, and hurt you. This brought them a certain amount of satisfaction, knowing they had a little power in their nonexistent lives. I wasn't sure which category she fit into.

I pulled my phone out of my robe pocket, scrolled through the short list of favorites until I got to my sister's name.

Adeline: Need a change of venue. Going to The Remedy early. Come when you can.

I needed to get myself together before seeing her. She was going to be far less than pleased when I told her I was interviewing at the same firm our father and grandfather worked for when they disappeared. But I was out of choices. The Albrecht Firm was my last option. And though it wasn't my primary goal, maybe I would find a few clues that helped us figure out what really happened to our father and grandfather.

2

I tossed back two feverfew with a swallow of water to ward off the building migraine and diverted my attention to something far more enjoyable—my closet.

I smoothed the front of my emerald, slim fitting dress, and settled my favorite bag into the crook of my left elbow like a beloved pet. I peeked into the mirror on my way out the door, everything good except for that frightened look in my eyes. I took a deep breath and tried to settle back into my body.

I paused at my bedroom door and snaked my awareness throughout the townhome in hopes of seeing that I was the only person in residence. But she was still here. I could feel her. I hardened my stomach into a cement block.

I tiptoed down the hallway and worked hard to stay off her radar. I heard her before I saw her.

"Everyone leaves a mess for me to clean up. Why is that? Jeff! Jeff!! Are you going to clean up your mess?" She stood over the broken dishes on the floor screaming for the man who was responsible for her murder.

I carried my shoes and tiptoed quietly around the corner and out the door, hoping to get past her unnoticed. I'd been running from ghosts all of my life. Apparently today wouldn't be any different.

3

The yellow cab dropped me in front of The Remedy. I looked forward to the relative busyness of the small, neighborhood restaurant. Even at this early hour there was enough activity to make me feel relaxed and focused. Quiet and alone were not my friends. Who was I kidding? I was never alone.

The smell of fried eggs and bacon soaked my senses when I entered through the double glass doors, and a heavyset man in a white business shirt passed by. I managed to avoid the lust in his wanton eyes—unfortunately I wasn't as lucky in avoiding his lewd thoughts.

I waited at the hostess stand, even though I'd never known a hostess to be present at this early hour. The green tiled walls and 1950s-style globe light fixtures made me wish I could slip back to a more simple time when people seemed to be happier. I surveyed the restaurant and picked out a remote table.

I slid onto the vinyl seat of a booth on the far, unpopulated side of the restaurant and opened my laptop. Sylvie walked by with a coffee pot in one hand, a plate of scrambled eggs and toast in another, and raised her eyebrows. "The usual?"

"Please." I smiled.

She gave me a nod and a wink and headed toward the kitchen "I'll be right back, sweetheart." She used that term with nearly every customer. I still found it comforting when she said it to me.

Sylvie started working at the diner right after high school graduation in 1979. Her bleached blond hair was twisted into a tight knot at the top of her head, where she pinned a bright plastic flower. Right in front. Today it was hot pink, and the entire presentation was a jarring contrast against her olive skin and dark eyebrows.

The homeless man seated in the rear corner wore too many layers for the weather. His greasy hair and beard showed how long it had been since he'd bathed. Sylvie put a plate of food in front of him, filled his coffee cup, and patted him warmly on his back, refusing to interrupt his ongoing conversation with someone who no one could see but him. And me. The bodiless man said something to him and the homeless man looked over at me. Recognition and understanding moved between us like a secret note.

An hour and a half later, my sister Alexa finally arrived in her typical artistic panache. Her light beige hair tossed into a messy ponytail, her naturally slender figure swathed in an off-the-shoulder Yale T-shirt with leggings. Not a hint of make-up, unless you counted the tiny smear of blue paint on her right cheek, and still she managed to draw the attention of every male eye in the place.

Alexa sashayed across the diner and I envied her for living her life among the living. "I have the best news. I had a premonition about a guy. I think he's the one. Why are you so dressed up?" She leaned in, kissed me on the cheek, and slid into the opposite side of the booth.

"Good morning."

"You look amazing! When did you get that dress?" Alexa adjusted her ponytail.

"I have an interview today."

"Really. Where?"

"The usual?" Sylvie appeared out of nowhere and placed water in front of Alexa, rescuing me from answering. My hands had a white-knuckle grip on one another under the table.

"Actually, I'll have a chocolate macchiato today, please, Sylvie. With whipped cream. I'm celebrating." Alexa winked at me. "I'll tell you all about it. And then I want you to look at this psychically for me. Tell me if I'm right." She winked again.

"I'll have one more when you bring her macchiato." I tapped the rim of my cup.

Sylvie patted me affectionately on the back before disappearing again.

"Lex, don't say those things in public."

Alexa waved me off. "Why are you here so early? I'm guessing it wasn't an earthly problem, like your electricity went out or something."

"No. My electricity did not go out."

"Would be nice if you could have a few more normal days once in awhile," Alexa said as she adjusted the positioning of her silverware.

Sylvie took our food order in between Alexa telling me about her premonition in excruciating detail.

"I know he's out there. But I don't know where. You know what I mean?"

I thought about the man from my own dreams.

Alexa had several gifts, but her strongest was pushing. She could convince just about anyone to do just about anything by pushing their thoughts in a particular direction. You could be completely convinced of your perspective one minute, but once Alexa got hold of you, you'd change your mind completely. She once convinced an ex-boyfriend to propose to her...even though he was engaged to someone else at the time. Not one of her more shining moments.

Now I felt her about to push me into doing a reading for her, even though her pushing didn't work on me. Years of fending off her gifts kept me aware. Still, old habits died hard.

"How about if you—"

"I'm interviewing at The Albrecht Firm today," I said quickly.

Our drinks arrived. Alexa's lips parted, and for one eternal moment nothing came out.

"Anything else?" Sylvie asked into the silence.

"No. Thanks, Sylvie." I tucked a long, loose curl behind my ear.

"Addie, why would you do that?" Alexa said. "Our family has such bad history with that place."

"We don't know that that has anything to do with the firm, Lex."

"We don't know that it doesn't, Ad. Our grandfather and our father both were connected with that firm. Both of them disappeared."

"I've thought this through." I stared into my espresso, bit the inside of my cheek.

"There are so many other places you could work. Other things you could do. I know you love art, but—" she snapped her fingers and pointed at me. "You could go back to your marketing work.

You were really good at that career."

I stirred my espresso with a piece of biscotti.

"You could! Addie. Listen. You don't have to do this." She inched toward me.

I had planned on patience this morning, knew that she would try to talk me out of this. But she was now firmly on the hairy edge of "I Know Better," which was easily my least favorite tune.

"How many interviews have you been on?"

"Counting today?"

"Yes."

"One."

She blanched for a brief second before she answered. "Well, there's the problem, honey. How many résumés have you sent out?"

"Three hundred fifty-four."

Now Alexa's lips that pulled tight. "Because of Centaurian?"

"Somehow the word has magically gotten out to every worthwhile agency in town that I might not be a good hire."

"Patti?"

I nodded. "She's good friends with Claire in Centaurian's HR department."

Alexa and I stared at each other.

"You two used to be such good friends," she said.

"I should never have told her that I had a gift." I put my head in my hands.

"You didn't really," Alexa said.

"Well, she guessed and I confirmed it. I should have laughed at her. Told her she was ridiculous."

"It wasn't wrong to think you could trust her." Alexa reached out and rubbed my arm. "She was supposed to be your friend."

"You never know how good a friend really is until they know you can see their secrets."

Alexa sighed.

"She's done some pretty horrific stuff. Apparently she never planned on anyone finding out," I said.

Alexa watched me sympathetically.

"Let's just say that considering some of the things she's done to other people, I'm lucky all she did was ruin my career and steal my fiancé."

"That doesn't surprise me, honestly. If you look closely at her—"

"You know, she spent months asking me questions about everyone in the firm. Months. Pulled everyone's darkest secrets out of me, things I couldn't possibly know. Then told people what I knew about them and made it look like I'd spread it around. She moved through the company strategically—enemies first, and then friends, and finally my boss. In less than a week, I became the most feared and hated person in the company." I exhaled hard. "Then Jeremy—"

"You should file a lawsuit. It's illegal for them to keep you from future employment. I know an attorney—"

"I just want to move on." I put my hand on my churning stomach.

"Adeline, you need to stand up for what's right. You need to protect your career—you worked hard for that!"

"There's nothing left to protect. Besides, I don't even want to work in marketing. I never did. I just did that to placate Isabella and Grandmother Grace. All I want is a modest space where I can work with art, and maybe find some quiet purpose for my gifts. I think I might do well with authenticating. Maybe being there will lead to some new clues about Dad and Grandad. I don't know. I can't go back to what I used to do, and no one in the city will hire me without experience."

Sylvie placed our food in front of us and disappeared without a word.

I moved the eggs around on my plate. "Work is all I've ever wanted to do. I need to work."

"You need to look at your future, Ad—"

"I am looking at my future. It's sitting in the back of the diner. If I don't work, if I don't get a focus for my mind, I'm going to lose sight of how to separate the only reality I can see from the one everyone else lives in."

I stared at my plate and fought the angry tears that burned to let loose. Alexa looked at the homeless man, who was laughing at a joke his invisible friend told him.

"Everyone in here thinks he's crazy. But is he? Or did one reality just finally win out over the other?"

Alexa swallowed hard.

"I need this. You have your art. You have success, passion, and focus, and that—whether you realize it or not—allows you to ignore a lot. On a good day I can ignore very little, and when I'm not working, I can't ignore anything at all. Plus, your gifts aren't like mine. Pushing and premonitions are different from being empathic. You don't have to—"

"Addie, I would give my eye teeth to have gifts as powerful as yours."

I had known she felt this way, but was surprised to hear her say it aloud. "Right now you spend your time trying to see more. If you had my gift, you'd spend all your time trying not to see at all."

Alexa stopped arguing and exhaled. She grabbed her macchiato and took a long sip. "Your gifts aren't all bad.

Sometimes they give you helpful insights and peace of mind. Like when you sold your apartment? They were quite useful to you then."

I smiled a little. I knew what she was doing.

"You know, you are impressive," Alexa said as she maintained her stare, cream cheese at the corner of her mouth. "When you put your mind to it, you can see whatever you want."

I felt a burst of pride, the kind I used to feel about my abilities when I was a child.

Alexa sat up straight with a jolt, her green eyes sparkling with an idea. "What about doing what Dad did? You could travel the world, search out rare and interesting artifacts. You wouldn't have to work with The Albrecht Firm—the museums and galleries would beg to work with you, and you love travel. You could shop the markets in Paris—you love Paris!"

"I don't have the network set up for that. And Dad spent a lot of time traveling alone. I need a lot less time alone." Our eyes met as we stumbled over the memory of our dad, how he failed to return home from one of his many buying trips. His disappearance was very cryptic, and Isabella never recovered from it. None of us had.

Alexa gave a sigh. "No. I guess not. You should go get the job you want. I'm sure everything will work out." She covered her lie with a sympathetic smile and pushed the strand of hair into her ponytail. "You're smart. You're gifted. You'll be fine." She reached for my hand and gave it a squeeze. Alexa's encouragement sent my guard pooling around my feet.

"I'm not trying to be a pain in the ass. I just don't know what I'd do if I lost you, too."

My chest clenched and I squeezed her hand in return. "I'll be careful. I promise. I just—I have to work. I can get a job with a different firm as soon as I have some relevant experience to put on my résumé."

Alexa threw on a smile. My older sister knew she'd harassed me enough for one day. "Okay, then. Let's go. I've got shooting practice today." Alexa patted her bag.

"You do not have your gun in your purse."

"It's not like it's loaded.," she said as she grabbed the check.

I shook my head at Lex as she rose gracefully and headed toward the cash register. She gave me another wink, her signature move for distracting people from whatever it was she really felt.

I hated making her worry, but I didn't have any other options. I didn't have any quantifiable experience in the art world. No other firm would be willing to hire me without experience. This was my last chance at a career, my ticket to freedom. I was calling in a favor and hoped the owner would be willing to help.

A dark-haired, pear-shaped woman entered the restaurant with a slight waddle and waited at the hostess stand. She cleared her throat in a high-pitched sound as she adjusted her black-rimmed glasses.

"M-m-m-m-m-hmmmmm."

Less than ten seconds later she did it again. When she did it a third time I decided to wait for Alexa outside.

But it took me a minute to gather my things, and I didn't realize she was now headed down the aisle next to my booth. I dropped my phone into my purse, stepped out of the booth, and we collided. Her unzipped tote and most of its contents clattered to the floor.

"Watch where you're going!"

"Oh! I'm so sorry!" I reached down and picked up her bag, holding it up for her as her hands seized at her belongings. She chased after a rolling tampon and I picked up her phone, a prescription bottle, and an odd black pen that looked like a Greek column with two snakes encircling the top. It's hard to say which item spoke to me first. They all had a something to share. Some confidence to betray.

"You're all alike," she grumbled as she reached at something under the booth. "Waif-like idiots—"

I didn't hear what else she said. The unedited visions of her life clamored at me more loudly than she did. Damn it. Her husband was older, or at least he looked older. He didn't give her any attention, hated being around her, actually, but he did give her money. More than enough to do what she wanted with her time.

His straight black hair was combed too far from the side, heavy bags from stress and age pulled under his eyes, and his nose was aesthetically too large for his face. He bore an odd resemblance to an aging Adolf Hitler. He cheated on her whenever he could.

"Sorry," I said and handed the belongings over.

God bless her, I thought as I looked into her eyes.

And then it happened. The very thing I tried never to let happen. But when our eyes met there was no way to stop her. She felt revealed. She didn't know how, but she did know that her secrets were on parade and out of her control, and her hatred flared instantly. She stormed away.

Sylvie sat her at a table near the homeless man, who broke out in a fit of laughter after leaning in for the Cliff's Notes from his spectral friend.

Ghosts missed nothing.

I rubbed my chest, the saddened spot where the woman's hatred had run through me.

Alexa reappeared and we walked outside.

I wiped the spot of cream cheese off her cheek, gave her a kiss, and headed for a cab. I had no idea how I was going to fake normal today.

4

The air in the warehouse was cool and damp, which was why he had built the special room inside. A vault. Small, but big enough. He could walk inside, inspect his investments, spend a little time with them.

He congratulated himself on how well he had managed the construction of the vault. He'd had it built elsewhere and brought it here using a nondescript moving company so its exact location would be harder to trace.

He walked around the outside of it. The vault was temperature-controlled, fireproof, and waterproof. The warehouse could be engulfed in flames or swallowed by a tsunami, and the vault and its contents would survive.

It was hidden. Not in the back of the warehouse, but right in the middle. In plain view, but hardly noticeable among hundreds of similar looking crates. The occasional inspections by warehouse security would reveal nothing.

Because 9/11 had given Homeland Security reason to search the contents of warehouses, he had protected himself against that. Each original masterpiece was surrounded with several brilliant forgeries. Any uninvited visitor to the mobile vault would not see singular pieces of priceless art. Rather, they would assume some amateur had painted a bunch of good-looking copies to sell at the local flea market. Or maybe on the Internet. They might question the security, but strange and worthless things were often kept under lock and key.

He punched in the code and stepped inside. The familiar release of air pressure and the clean, cool scent brought a smile to his face. He glanced once at the cameras, knowing he was on film. He decided this just strengthened his aura of responsibility, and reassured his partner that he was taking care of the precious works.

He thought he could tell which were forgeries, and which were the originals within each collection. Honestly, he'd done such a good job painting the forgeries, he wasn't sure which were which. They were all identical. He couldn't authenticate them. And he couldn't bring anyone in to authenticate. Not these pieces.

He used to have a partner who could authenticate.

Now each canvas had a number on the back to identify which piece was an original work of art, and which ones were the forgeries—a system that he had designed, and his new partner implemented. Now he would need to get the key chart from him so he could appreciate the real masterpieces.

Though he did nearly burst with pride that his pieces were indistinguishable from the old masters' work. He had studied art all of his life. He simply had a knack for knowing how the masters created their work. And he emulated them beautifully.

Unbeknownst to others, he had shared his talent on a few, select occasions. Even though sending his forgeries into the open market could have set a chain of events in motion that would ruin him for life. Except the validation of their admiration was too tempting. Too irresistible to have proof that he was *that* good.

He walked by each grouping, admiring them with—was it? Yes. Love. Nothing made him feel the way that fine art did.

It was right that only he should be able to appreciate them. He understood them as no one else could.

For a while, at least, he had them all to himself.

$$5$$

The firm's brick building appeared exactly as it did when I visited as a child, an upward event reaching for the clouds. My grandfather used to keep a photo in his office of him and Otto shaking hands in front of the building on opening day. The firm was Montgomery and Albrecht then, and it had been my grandfather's dream come true.

The cab driver tapped the meter and stuck his hand out. He didn't pause his phone conversation.

I reached for my wallet and noticed wave paranoid energy. Everything tightened and contracted, and I started to feel very...unsafe. I dropped a crisp twenty in his palm, opened the door with a creak, and placed my platform shoe on the already-warm pavement. A few yards from the front door, recognized him. Not his face, but his vibe. He was the sender of the paranoia.

He was an armed plainclothes man with a buzz cut, standing just to the side of the front door. He stared at me from behind his dark glasses. Bodyguard. Tall, broad shoulders, bizarrely large frame.

He must have been connected with someone who was in with a significant collection.

I flashed a smile, none was returned. His energy was a stone wall

I reached the door, pulled hard on the glass door, and nearly yanked my arm off.

Locked.

I took an awkward step back and searched for a call box. I looked around the hulking muscles barely contained by the black T-shirt and noticed the corner of the box peeking out from behind.

"Excuse me," I said.

He stared at me without moving.

"I need to get to the, um—" I pointed to the call box behind him. "Box. Please."

I expected him to move at my request, but he just stared at me. Several cars passed and still he didn't move. His G.I. Joe face was immovable.

Finally he took one small, reluctant step to the side. I pressed the button and tried hard to ignore him eyeing me from the corner. Tried not to read him. But even without touching anything of his, I had the impression that he was untrustworthy. Maybe that was the reason for his paranoia.

I tried little energetic trick I learned from Isabella and Grandmother Grace. I tuned in to his energy and mentally tried to move it off me. An exercise that often worked, but today it felt like pushing a cement wall. I wasn't as talented at that skill as some of the other Montgomery women.

Grandmother Grace had harped at me for years to do my protection exercises before leaving the house each morning, and to get so good at them that I could do them quickly, in response to any dynamic. Of course, I had not taken the time to tune in this morning. Or most mornings.

Truly, I just wasn't very good at it. No matter how much I tried to insulate myself, my gifts made me too aware and I was often lost in a sea of someone else's sensation.

The only protection lesson they taught that I performed well was seeing the traces of someone else's energy work. The little flashes of light didn't last long, but they were always there, for whoever had the insight to see them. Unfortunately, that didn't help me much in this moment.

This man pushed his energy right through my barriers. The shallow ones I had, anyway.

"Yes?" said a female voice on the speaker.

"I have a nine o'clock with Otto Albrecht?"

My statement came out like a question, my voice sounded a bit high and pinched. Annoying.

"Would you mind facing the security camera?" asked the voice from the speaker.

I searched for the camera. "Of course." I flashed a smile at the lens, wondering who looked back at me, and why fear was the name of the game on this particular corner of New York.

The bodyguard's vibe got darker, more foreboding. His sheer will to overpower crouched around the perimeter of my mind.

The buzzer on the door hummed.

I grabbed the handle, and pulled. I scurried into the small, glass room, too quickly to appear nonchalant, and tugged on the next door. But it was locked as well. Security cameras flanked the upper corners over the second door. I turned. The bodyguard looked at me from the outside of the first door, and a wave of relief washed through me.

When the first door closed behind me, there was a pause. Then the lock on the second door opened with a heavy *thunk* and another buzzer rang. I pulled on the door and it opened.

The second door closed behind me—*ka-chunk*.

Once inside the ornately decorated, dark-paneled room, my energy naturally climbed, and I shook him off. I let out a heavy exhale and hoped on a wing and a prayer that the next few hours would be easier than the last few.

Extraordinary gilt-framed fine art hung around the room, and I searched for anything recognizable. When my grandfather worked here I'd spent my childhood roaming these halls. The shape of the room was familiar, though its decoration had changed since I was here last.

Other things seemed to have changed, too. I didn't remember the presence of bodyguards or the undertow of distrust I felt flowing in and around the building.

An energetic current ran down the wall panels from top to bottom. The building was bulging with secrets. I stepped closer. Another wave billowed from top to bottom, growing larger as I got close, its information awakening something deep and complicated within me. As I lifted my hand toward the wall, the surge of energy reached out to me. The building knew me. It was literally reaching out to me.

6

———

A seductive crest of energetic information rolled from the paneled wall and reached for my outstretched fingertips, desperately pulling me closer to it with its complex and dreamlike layers.

"Adeline," a woman's voice projected from the memories trapped in the wall and echoed around me. The familiarity of her voice carried me back to childhood. I turned my head away, but my eyes were locked on the wall. I pushed against the invitation inherent in her tone.

I stepped away from the energy. "I can't—"

Memories weaved around this woman's voice in a tangled mess. Whoever she was I had to walk away from this. I could not relive complicated childhood memories in the lobby of my much-needed interview. Anxiety pulsed through my hands.

"Adeline," she said again.

I took a deep breath and turned away from the wall. A blond woman in her fifties, wearing a tailored gray suit, stood in the foyer with me. She wore a multi-strand, white pearl necklace with matching earrings.

"Hi, yes—yes!" I nearly choked.

"I'm Ellen Browning. Mr. Albrecht is expecting you. Won't you come with me?"

"Of course," I said. I blinked my eyes several times to shake off the trance-like state. "It's good to see you again." I gave Ellen my warmest smile.

But her lips only pulled into a horizontal line. "It's good to see you, too."

My stomach flopped to my feet and lay there in a sick heap. It was her voice that had called to me from the knotty past.

Without speaking we made our way down a long corridor and into a paneled elevator, just big enough for two or three people. Ellen punched a code on the keypad, swiped her access card, and then hit the top button. The elevator began to rise, and she silently watched the climbing numbers, the warm and subtle spiced vanilla scent of her perfume expanding in the small room.

Her thick hair was parted to the side and pulled into a classic, elegant French twist. With her neutral pink lipstick and her lined eyes, she looked a little like Catherine Deneuve. It had been a long time since I'd seen her. She now had that slightly-heavier-with-age look. The kind of look that reeked of too much disappointment. So many years had passed, I didn't know if she'd still be here. But this was definitely her, though she used to be far more welcoming.

Her laughter used to ring out like a chime when I ran through the carpeted hallways with the sons of some other employees. And there was the endless supply of butterscotch candies that she kept in her desk drawer just for the three of us.

Now there was only a sense of active hostility about her.

I smiled and pretended I wasn't aware of what she was feeling. No one liked it when you noticed their secrets.

"It's good to be back," I said, trying to start a conversation. Over the years I'd honed my ability to pretend normal. I could be very talented at it. At least for short periods of time. My hope was that I could build an entire career on the appearance of normal.

"We're glad to have you back," Ellen said. Her eyes never left the climbing numbers on the wall. She ran her hand along the side of her hair to smooth imaginary strays.

The elevator stopped, and when we exited, I felt Ellen's vibe shift into a steely exterior.

A walkway cut through the open work area below. I looked down and spied stacks of canvases leaning against the walls, statuary stood on tables and pedestals, and about fifty people hovered quietly over their work. Restoration of exquisite art was in progress.

Halfway down the carpeted walkway we took a sharp left and Ellen led me into a large executive lobby. Male voices could be heard through the door that stood guard on the far side of the room.

"If you'll wait here." Ellen gestured toward one of the plush armchairs. "I'm sure he'll be out in just a moment. May I offer you some coffee? Cappuccino? Espresso?"

"Espresso, please, thank you." I smiled at Ellen again but she walked away without returning the gesture. I watched her all but glide out of the room. Why she didn't care for me I didn't know. The walls knew.

The espresso arrived and I quietly cautioned myself not to spill anything. Always a distinct possibility when I felt nervous. I lifted the tiny demitasse to my lips, my hand shook a little bit.

Ellen disappeared, and I sipped my espresso with two hands.

7

"I need you to keep a close eye on Addie. Show her some interest. Develop a steady relationship with her. From the little bit I know, she's spent a lot of time alone lately. I doubt she'd refuse you," Otto said.

"Doesn't sound too hard," Blake said. "What's your plan?"

"I think she could be very useful to an art business I keep on the side. First I want to see if she takes the job. Then I need to know if she has the same uncommon talents she had years ago. You need to keep her close. If anything goes askew between her and the firm, chances are I'll still need access to her. Your job will be to keep that avenue open to me."

Blake nodded. "I'll take care of it."

8

____

After several minutes, I heard male voices from the other side of the door. I recognized one that had Otto's distant Welsh accent. I couldn't identify the other one, but his commanding tone sent a current through me.

Ellen reappeared, rounded the desk outside of his office, picked up a telephone from the side table, and punched three numbers onto the keypad. "Adeline Montgomery is here, Mr. Albrecht... Yes, sir."

I placed the tiny porcelain cup on the table next to me and smoothed my dress.

I reminded myself of my agenda: Meet with Otto, and claim my birthright. Charmingly, of course. This had once been my grandfather's firm, too. Surely I still deserved a job here. Then I would ingratiate myself to him, and work hard to make him proud he'd hired me. Get a couple of years' experience for my résumé, and a good reference. Then move on with a great career. Or stay here with a great career, if it worked. Either way, I would stay tucked away, hidden and happy.

A strange sensation worked on me, like someone was pulling my strings. I could feel it in the bodyguard, Ellen's resistance toward me. I could feel it in the walls. Something was off in this place. But I didn't have another choice. If I wanted this career— if I wanted to *work*—I had to move ahead with my plan.

9

———

The door opened but it wasn't Otto who walked out.

Morning light poured behind him and he looked like a walking Calvin Klein ad. Thick, dark hair, chiseled features, athletic figure. And stubble. He was young, early- to mid-thirties, maybe. And straight. That I picked up clearly. Not a common phenomenon in the art community. He reached into the small pocket of his waistband and pulled out what looked like an antique pocket watch to check the time. *Extraordinary good looks* and *old world charm*. I felt faint.

"Forgive me for taking so much of your time this morning, Otto. I'm sure I've ruined your schedule." His voice was refined and smooth, with an undercurrent of undeniable power. Determination and strength.

"Not at all, Blake. We appreciate you thinking of us, and we're excited to help your clients however we can." After a firm handshake, Otto Albrecht, one of the most powerful men in the art world, escorted the male model out of his office.

Calvin Klein looked at me with his sky-blue eyes, something shot right through my midsection, and I felt light-headed. He flashed a brilliant white smile and I was immediately rendered stupid. Unable to speak.

I should have said hello, should have introduced myself. But instead I just stood there swooning. Like an idiot.

Fortunately, I had a smile I could use as well. And though I couldn't say whether mine held the power that his did, at least it was one part of me that I could still control.

"Ah, you're here, Adeline." Otto welcomed me with a somewhat possessive hug and a kiss on each cheek, and then pulled back to look at me like a grandfather inspecting his grandchild after a long absence.

Despite his sixty-odd years, youth and genetic good fortune favored Otto. His silver hair, strong jawline, light gray eyes, and smooth, tanned skin gave him a comfortable elegance. His regal demeanor made anyone feel like a royal subject—well taken care of, and just a little curious of what unknown privileges he might be enjoying.

His worldliness was always evident in a shared story of a prestigious trip taken, a rare artifact examined or appraised, or a meeting with an esteemed dignitary in the art community. You could just about hang a frame around Otto. His whole life was picture perfect.

"It's hard to believe, but I think you're even more beautiful than the last time I saw you." He looked me over from head to toe, and I could tell his educated eye approved of my choices.

He smiled his grandfatherly smile, and I gave him another hug.

"I'm so happy to see you, Otto," I told him. And I meant it. My family could think what they wanted, but Otto had always been good to me.

"Well, I don't know what she looked like the last time you saw her, but she's simply stunning today," the male model said from behind.

Annoying butterflies banged at the walls of my chest.

"Well, that she is. That she is…" Otto trailed off admiringly while still gazing at me with his loving smile. "Blake Greenwood, allow me to introduce a close friend of the family, Miss Adeline Montgomery."

Blake smiled his winning smile as recognition fluttered across his eye. "Montgomery…as in—"

"One and the same. She's the granddaughter of my former partner, John Montgomery, the founder and former CEO of our firm when it was called Montgomery and Albrecht."

"Ah, yes, of course." He spoke slowly, as if pieces continued to click into place. "Your grandfather had quite a reputation in our community. He was a brilliant man."

"Thank you…" I paused, realizing I'd been so entranced by his looks that I didn't remember his name.

He flashed his provocative smile again, holding my gaze just a second too long as he waited for its effect to reach me.

He wielded that smile like a weapon.

He took my hand and gave it a firm squeeze. Actually, it was more of a hand hug than a hand shake. I felt a sudden urge to meet his grasp, pull him into a full embrace, and ask him why it had taken him so long to find me.

"Greenwood. Blake Greenwood. I'm an art dealer here in town." Chemistry stirred between us and I had to look down for a minute to get my bearings.

"Are you new to the city?" Blake asked, his hand still holding mine.

"I've been here a few years," I said.

"All the same, I hope you'll let me give you a personal

behind-the-scenes tour of New York. I like to think of it as *my* city."

"That's very kind, thank you," I said.

"Will you be working with the firm?" he inquired.

The smile lingered on his lips, and I had to pull my eyes away from his mouth.

"I guess that's what we're here to discuss." I glanced at Otto.

"Perhaps we ought to get on with that, then." Otto placed his hand under my right elbow as if he were taking possession, and Blake finally let go of my hand.

I felt my head clear instantly. "Pleasure meeting you, Mr. Greenwood."

"It's Blake, please. Nothing formal with me. And the pleasure is all mine. Perhaps we'll have the chance to work together. Here's my card."

I took his card carefully, making sure I didn't touch his hand again, and then slipped it into my purse so whatever energy it contained wouldn't hold me hostage. I wanted my full brain at my disposal. Otto tugged my arm slightly, pulling me in the direction of his office.

"We'll talk again soon." Otto smiled and waved good-bye.

Ellen reappeared, her smile resting on thinly drawn lips, showing ever so subtly that she was ready to usher Blake Greenwood out.

I glanced back at Blake as he walked out. A small movement caught my eye. A tiny blip of an image. One minute it looked like someone was there. But on a double take, nothing.

Most people would have written that off as their imagination. As if they were seeing things.

But I knew differently. Even through the haze of Blake's

energy, I could feel someone there. Someone besides Otto had been watching our exchange. And when Blake left, he left.

10

O tto guided me down the opulent white and gold marble corridor that led into his office, but all I could think of was the short discussion with Blake Greenwood.

"Water?" Otto asked.

"Yes, please, thank you."

"Make yourself comfortable. I'll be right back."

I was left standing alone in Otto's office. The same office where he and my grandfather undoubtedly had countless meetings. The morning light from the floor to ceiling windows cast an extraordinary glow on the white and beige tones. The views of the skyline were the perfect art to fill one of the large walls, and it gave the space a heavenly look, though I couldn't ignore its contrived feel. Appearance is everything in the world of art.

The wall behind Otto's desk was painted black with specks of gold, which must have made him look something akin to Zeus when he sat at his desk. The shelves on the dark wall were filled with his own affectations. A familiar looking bronze eagle with outstretched wings oversaw the office from its roost on the corner of the crowded middle shelf. Silver-framed pictures of family and friends smiled from their perch next to the eagle. I recognized Otto's wife, Marilyn, in an older picture taken on a trip to India, his daughters and sons on a family ski trip, and several grand-children with semi-toothless smiles.

There were other pictures toward the back and I walked around his desk to get a closer look. There was a small, black and white frame that showed a young Otto with who must have been his father standing behind him, hands on his son's shoulders. Next to it was another photo of Otto's family in Paris—they were all standing together in the inte-rior courtyard of the Louvre. Otto and his wife were in the center with their arms around each other, their four then-young children crowded in front of them. Our families had been so close when Grandpa and Otto were partners. The Albrecht children were like cousins to Lexie and me.

Otto and Marilyn gave effervescent smiles for the camera, and I placed my fingers on the photo to reconnect with the family I used to know and love. But Marilyn's quiet, punishing anger at Otto ripped through me. Otto's loneli-ness was an undercurrent that ran through the family. His heart ached for a love he'd lost, and for a child he knew he would never see again.

I took my hand off the photo.

I looked up at the gold-flecked walls and noticed how they, too, breathed with memories—arguments, laughter, successes, failures...secrets. They undulated, and I bit my lower lip, wondered if I ought to do a quick probe for a clue or two about my grandfather. My family would definitely want me to.

I thought about it, and leaned on the edge of Otto's desk. Without warning another surge of Otto's private world streamed through me. He was sitting behind his desk, working feverishly, obsessed with having the best and being the best.

Then a vision of a young Otto appeared. He sat behind the desk, his father towering over him, criticizing, pointing his finger at the drawings in front of them. Nothing the child did was good enough. Tears ran down the boy's reddened face, but the scolding continued. "This is *pathetic*, Otto. Nothing original," the father chided in his European accent. He smacked the boy across the face, and I felt Otto don a protective layer. His humiliation passed through me, and tears welled up in my eyes.

I decided I needed a very different vibe to wash through my circuitry. Something that would get me back to neutral.

On the side wall was what looked like a copy of Giovanni Bellini's *Madonna and Child*. Just as I'd been taught to reach out for the story when I was a child, I quickly walked over and placed the tip of my middle finger on the bottom right of the canvas. That tiny bit of raised paint would be enough to speak to me.

Images of 1480 Venice launched, pulling me into the artist's life. The noise of the bustling crowds of San Marco's square, the pressure the artist felt to be different, to be unique, the competitiveness he felt with his father and brother—

Otto cleared his throat as he walked into the room, and I jerked my hand away from the canvas. I hoped my body had blocked his view of my finger touching his artwork.

"It looks like the real thing, doesn't it?" Otto said as he made space for me among the stacks of papers.

I swallowed hard, and looked at him as ancient scenes of Venice faded gently from my mind. "It isn't?" I asked, donning my best sardonic smile. Beneath the flippant remark, my heart pounded so hard it hurt, and I worked to catch my breath.

"No, no," Otto laughed. "The real one's in Glasgow now. Or maybe the Met still has it on display. I don't remember. Anyway, this piece was given to me by an art student." Otto walked over and studied my face. "It's an amazing copy, don't you think?"

I tried to look innocent, even passive.

"It's extraordinary. If I didn't know better, I would think it was the real thing." I stared at the art. It wasn't a replica. I didn't know if Otto knew that, and now was not the time to bring it up.

"I had the opportunity to help the Met with their authentication of Bellini's original. I have several close friends there. They call me in occasionally," Otto said as he walked back to the rosewood table at the corner. He placed a coaster under the glass of water. "Sorry for the delay this morning. I didn't realize he was going to be here today."

My heart still beat too quickly, but I acted casually and followed Otto across the room. *It's a mistake.* I told myself. *A mistake. Someone at the Met made a mistake and somehow Otto got the wrong painting.* Although I didn't think The Met made those kinds of mistakes.

"It's no problem." I smiled, thankful for my corporate training. If I learned anything at Centaurian it was how to smile and be professional in the face of nearly anything. "It gave me time to collect my thoughts and enjoy a little espresso. I've traveled all over the world, Otto, but I think *you* have the best."

All men love a good compliment and Otto was no different. His chest swelled with pride, and as he focused on himself, I cautioned myself not to touch anything else in his office.

"I have it shipped direct from Italy," he said with a sly grin. "You know we specialize in the best of the best around here."

"Yes, I know." I detached a little more from the shock of seeing an authentic Giovanni in Otto's office.

The buzzer on Otto's phone went off. "Mr. Albrecht, Elizabeth is here."

"Give us just a moment, Ellen. I'll be right there."

Otto put his hand on the table directly in front of me. "Adeline, before we get started, I'd like you to meet someone very special."

I anticipated the next curve in the road and leaned into it.

"Her name is Elizabeth Morton, and she's the new head of the Antiquities Acquisition Department at the Metropolitan Museum of Art. We have clients who donate pieces from their collections to the museum from time to time. Elizabeth helps to get them placed by directing the authentication and the acquisition processes. She would just be a good person for you to know."

Otto gave me a wink as he took a sip of his espresso from a small white cup and then walked across his office toward the marble hallway. In that short span of time his energy, his presence, amped up considerably, like he tapped a hidden reservoir of influence. I watched him change from the caring, approving grandfatherly figure I needed him to be—to an aristocratic, authoritative, forceful character who would greet the person on the other side of his door.

"How simply marvelous to see you, dear." Otto's voice bounced off the Italian stone. He gave Elizabeth Morton a grand hug and a kiss on each cheek, and immediately she was under his spell.

"I know you're busy," she said.

"Well, I always, *always* have time for you. You know that." Otto's enchanting demeanor could have warmed the heart of a corpse. He understood the value of charm.

Elizabeth Morton walked in like a breath of fresh air, her shoulder-length brown hair curling up at the ends, making her look a bit younger than she might have actually been. I pinched and rubbed the fabric of my dress again to try to distance myself from the crosscurrents of Otto's world.

There was something so familiar about her, like she was an old friend. And I relaxed immediately.

"Gorgeous dress. Hermès?" she asked.

"It is, thank you. Chanel?" I asked, waving at Elizabeth's vintage suit.

"I'm a bit obsessed, I'm afraid. Though it's hard not to be when you live in this city. So many temptations. I'm happy to finally meet you. Otto talks about you like you're his own daughter. He says you have an amazing eye for art."

I melted. I'd been unsure about how Otto really felt about me since my grandfather was no longer around, and our families didn't spend much time together. He could be hard to read.

"Thank you, Otto." I flashed him a heartfelt smile.

We chatted for a little while, all the time standing in Otto's celestial office. Otto bragged on my intuitive sense for fine art. Elizabeth thanked Otto for all his good work. It felt like the headquarters of a mutual admiration society.

"I hope the two of you will have the opportunity to get to know each other—"

"Definitely," Elizabeth responded before Otto could finish. "How about drinks next week, Adeline? I'll email you to set it up. Otto, here are the contract originals you needed." She placed her hand on his arm, giving it a little squeeze before she let go. He leaned in for the European-style kiss on each cheek, working his gift that made Elizabeth feel endearingly loyal to him.

Otto escorted Elizabeth to the outer office. I took a seat at the round table in the corner to catch my breath while they talked. I sat with my hands in my lap and didn't touch a thing.

Otto rushed back in, his wavy, silver hair making him look as though he'd been caught in a fierce wind.

"Elizabeth is wonderful, though, isn't she? Now the job I have in mind for you is a research position, though there's always room for growth..."

We talked about my career, what I'd been doing for the last year, and what I wanted next. He asked only briefly about why I'd decided to leave Centaurian after being there for so long. Fortunately, a brief answer about wanting a career around art sufficed.

"So, I think I'm particularly well suited for this position, and I think I could become invaluable to the firm," I said confidently in spite of some jangling nerves.

Otto's eyes twinkled as I spoke. "I think you're right, Adeline. The job is yours if you want it." He had switched from the larger than life celebrity who greeted Elizabeth, back to the kind patriarch who gave me a soft place to land.

He meant what he said. I could feel it. Of course I also felt a roll of possessiveness from him that made me wonder what he had in mind for me.

"I would love that, Otto. I really would. You know, art has always been my biggest passion."

"Then let's do it."

I smiled from ear to ear as we shook hands, and Giovanni Bellini's *Madonna and Child* came into focus just behind Otto's head. I hoped it wasn't an omen. Either way I couldn't worry about it. Not now. I needed this opportunity.

"There will be lots to learn, but you'll catch on quickly, no doubt. It's in your genes." Otto smiled brilliantly and placed his hand on top of mine with a heartfelt pat.

Behind my smile, my heart startled at the phrase.

It's in your genes...

My mother had often told me that things didn't "just happen." That there was a reason for everything. I wondered if she was right.

11

M y heels clicked on the marble like metallic notes, as Otto escorted me into Ellen's office, and she handed me a folder thick with tax forms and employment papers. Her area was small and windowless, with a row of metal filing cabinets along one of the side walls. It didn't at all match the finely detailed design reflected by the rest of the firm, but it did hold the spirit of secrets and control. She and her office were power centers. I doubted that Otto could have run the business without her.

"You'll want to complete these at home and bring them back in with you on your first day. Which is...Monday?" Ellen avoided eye contact and smoothed more imaginary strays along the side of her French twist.

"It is, yes."

"Where do you live now?" she asked and shuffled through papers on her crowded desk.

"We kept my grandfather's townhome on Riverside Drive after he—um. Anyway, my grandmother is letting me live there."

Ellen stopped shuffling. It was the first time she had softened toward me since I arrived. "I remember several Christmas parties there from years ago. The views of Riverside Park and the Hudson River were exquisite. Which architect designed that space again?"

"Clarence—"

"Clarence True," she interrupted. "Right, I remember now. Clarence even lived there after it was built. I remember the round corner turret windows he designed and how the sunlight poured in throughout the day. He rented the house to Marc Chagall in the sixties. Well, you probably knew that." She waved me off before I could answer. "Do you still have *Paris par la fenêtre* hanging on the wall?"

"It's still there, yes. Perhaps you'd like to come by for a visit once I get myself organized?"

But Ellen managed not to answer, even though she walked me all the way to the elevator.

~

I TEXTED Alexa from the top floor elevator lobby.

Adeline: Got it!

Alexa: Shirl You go! :) oxox

Adeline: Who is Shirl?

Alexa: Stupid autocorrect. I meant Girl! Girl! Go Girl! We'll celebrate!

I was sure that the news made her more nervous for me than happy, but she gave a good show of support. Alexa would tell the rest of the family. In fact, they would all probably know before I stepped outside the building. Alexa was the grapevine in our family. If someone was talking about something—or shoot, just thinking about it—Alexa would pass it on. Tele-graph, tele-phone, tele-Alexa.

12

Blake stared out the window of the limo that was now parked in front of The Albrecht Firm. His right hand periodically squeezed into a fist.

Thomas sat in the driver's seat and looked at Blake's face as it reflected in the rearview mirror. "Something happen while you were in your meeting?"

"No. Nothing. And, well—something that complicates everything."

"I saw your nothing when she walked into the firm earlier this morning. I tried to discourage her from going inside, but she seemed pretty intent upon it. Otto knows her?"

"She's the granddaughter of his former partner, John Montgomery," Blake said as he looked at Thomas' eyes in the mirror. "Otto wants me to date her, keep her distracted until he figures out what to do with her."

"That job shouldn't be too hard."

"No, probably not."

A phone rang from the center console. Blake pulled a

key from his pocket and unlocked the lid. "William," Blake said.

"What did you get from your meeting with Otto?" William asked.

"He's bringing in a new researcher," Blake said.

"No leads on the Gardner art?"

"I think she's the best lead on the art. He said he wants to use her for the art business he keeps on the side. I'm sure it's all related. He's asked me to develop a relationship with her, to keep her close. I'm going to pursue that right now."

"You really think she's a lead to the Gardner pieces?" William asked.

"I do and I'm all over it," Blake said.

"You'd better be. The FBI is running out of time on this. When the statute of limitations run out on this theft, we won't be able to touch him. If you're not into this—"

"If I'm not into this? Who else would you bring in that would be more into this?"

"I'm aware of your family's history with Otto, and I'm glad you have that motivation. But if you don't get us some proof or some leads on these pieces soon, we'll lose him and the art."

"Right now there's no one closer to him than I am. If he's going to confide in anyone, it's me." Blake silently dared William to challenge him on the job he'd done on this operation. No one on William's FBI Art Crime Team could have done any better. No one wanted Otto Albrecht in jail more than him.

"I'll call you when I have something," Blake said.

"Make it soon," William said before hanging up.

Blake shook his head.

"William's not happy?" Thomas asked.

"Not even remotely," Blake answered. "Though, neither am I."

Thomas turned around to face Blake. "You could leave the investigation. Follow up on your personal interests on your own time. Your mother has moved beyond this."

"She may say she's over it, but she's not. She used to travel the world for her work. But now she lives under a false identity, afraid to step foot outside her front door for fear that he finds her. She has not moved beyond this.

"The only way she has any peace in this life is if Otto is dead or in jail. And I'm the man who's going to see him in one condition or the other," Blake said.

"I just meant—" Thomas tried.

"I know what you meant. But she's not happy. No one is happy without their freedom."

Thomas nodded and turned around.

"Here she comes," Blake said. "Raise the divider so she won't see you. Whatever you did to intimidate her this morning probably didn't make a great impression."

13

I slipped on my black Chanel sunglasses and strutted out the front door of the building. A black limousine waited on the street and my eyes were drawn to it like a magnet.

The sun landed on my face and I stopped as the back window lowered. Blake Greenwood appeared, the shine of his smile reaching me before his words.

"Is it too soon for that tour?" he said.

Common sense told me to head on down the sidewalk and hail a cab. Whatever the entanglements of his life, I didn't need to be a part of them. But the silkiness in his voice wrapped around my heart and pulled me toward him.

"Hey." I walked toward him. He struck me as the type who always had a plan. I wondered what he was up to. "I probably have too much to do today..." I waited for his response while I enjoyed a swim in the current of flirtation that flowed out of the limo. "Thank you, though." I looked at his hand that rested on the lowered window and was tempted to reach out to touch it.

"How'd the interview go? Well?"

"Yes, I'm starting with the firm next week."

"Really? Well, that's reason enough to celebrate, don't you think? Why don't I take you to lunch? It will be a homecoming celebration."

I paused for another moment, bringing my right hand to give my arm a little pinch.

"How about French? Balthazar's isn't far from here," Blake said.

I felt the unmistakable sensation of someone watching me. I turned and saw only a ripple of energy, like heat rising. It was the same person's energy who had been in Otto's outer office, and he was angry. Hostile.

"Adeline?"

I faced Blake, his blue eyes sparkled hypnotically.

"Hmm?"

"Let me help you celebrate. Come on." Blake's smile was infectious, dreamy even. He was a present-day James Bond right here in New York City. He opened the door and slid to the other side of the backseat.

Getting away from an angry ghost seemed like a wise idea. Maybe getting to know Blake would be a good thing for my career.

Blake kept a respectable distance in the limo but the heat between us left me feeling inextricably connected to him.

He was professional and charming.

A little too charming, though. I had to keep tightening my stomach muscles to keep the nerves in check.

Balthazar's was busy, and the wait for a table was an hour. But the maitre d' greeted Blake by name and seated us immediately. He even seemed a little intimidated by Blake, who emanated authority and dominance without even opening his mouth.

"May I order for us both?" Blake asked me when the waiter arrived.

I was dumfounded. No man had ever ordered for me. Not since my father when I was about eight. Blake had the waiter bring fresh salad with escarole, warm bread with butter, and a large platter of *fruits de la mer* and a bottle of wine. It was rather perfect.

"Tell me how you chose to work with The Albrecht Firm," Blake said and leaned in.

"Well, I guess I decided it was time to honor the family tradition." The words left my mouth and I prayed he wouldn't ask me what happened to the patriarchs of my family. "Ultimately, I guess Otto was the one willing to give me a chance. I'm new to the community."

"With your genetics you probably have the right touch for understanding art."

"You have no idea." I buttered a thick piece of crusty bread. "Sometimes I think art is all I really understand. People are—complicated."

"I know what you mean. And yet art is drawn from the human experience. Doesn't really make sense, does it?"

I laughed.

"Are you planning to build a career in our little incestuous art world?"

"Hopefully."

"You'd be surprised how the art community is a lot like Hollywood. No one is who you think they are, and once you're in, it's very hard to get out." Blake's tone turned cautionary around the edges.

"Well, not Otto," I scoffed. "He's helping me out just when I need him most. And I guess our choices are somewhat limited by what we love," I said as I felt more of the effects of the political underpinnings from The Albrecht

Firm. Blake nodded but it didn't seem to be agreement. More of an acquiesce.

I hoped I wasn't walking into trouble. After the political fallout at Centaurian, I wanted nothing more than a quiet corner to do my job and live my peaceful life. I didn't need power or position. Just purpose. And normality.

"I'm attending a private show at the Met tomorrow night," Blake said as he stabbed a shrimp. "Perhaps you'd like to come with me? I could introduce you around."

The Met. That was quite an offer. I wasn't much on society gatherings, but a private showing at the Met did have cache'.

Blake gave a sideways glance that was camera-worthy. "Maybe the event would be a good respite for you. It's seventeenth century Greek sculpture."

Ohhh. I never tired of Greek sculpture. Translation: I never tired of the story that Greek sculpture offered. Once on a private tour through the Louvre with my father, I managed to touch an edge of the Winged Victory of Samothrace. I stepped right back in time to ancient Greek society. Absolute nirvana to pull those stories from the past.

The opportunity to be networked, certainly had its value, too. But Blake's glance was now a handsome grin that made me cautious.

"I'm not, um." I started to say not dating, but this wasn't a date. I didn't think so, anyway. And did I just um? "Going out much right now."

Blake put his fork down. "Husband? Boyfriend? Girlfriend?"

"No." I grinned. "None of those. I just have a busy schedule"

"That's a relief," he said as he ran his hand through his silky hair. "I'd hate to have to challenge someone to a duel."

My belly laugh caught me by surprise.

"Busy with work, and not dating. That must mean there is a...bad breakup in recent history?"

"Something like that, yes." I shared.

Blake nodded but didn't press.

"Suffice to say that my former fiancé—is now my former best friend's fiancé," I offered.

"Well, with friends like that...I understand why you're busy." Blake raised his hands in surrender. "Just don't stay out of the game too long. You might miss out on something you didn't realize you were looking for."

Such an odd thing to say.

Blake filled my wine glass for the second time. I took the opportunity to accidentally run my finger against his phone for information. Strangely, I couldn't get much of anything. It was as if there were walls upon walls that kept me out. I also had the distinct feeling that our professional lunch was coasting into date-land, which made me feel uncomfortable. Not necessarily uncomfortable with *him*. In fact, I felt a little *too* comfortable with him. Like I could sync my life right into his. And *that* made me uncomfortable.

"Adeline?"

"Yes?"

"You seem to have traveled somewhere else."

"Oh. Too much to get organized before Monday. This has been so wonderful. I hate to bring it to an end." Part of which was true. "But I should probably go."

"Promise me we'll see each other again soon." His eyes stayed with mine as he lifted my left hand from the table and slowly grazed my knuckles with a gentle kiss. His lips sent a wave of electricity through me.

"I hope so," I finally answered. Though I knew as soon as

I said it that I could never spend time with this man. I needed to focus on my new job and my career.

Without hesitation he dropped our hands to my bare knee, his thumb giving my skin a near imperceptible stroke.

"Check, please, Jean-Luc," he said as the waiter appeared by his side.

"Oui, Monsieur."

"You are most beautiful, Adeline," he whispered almost imperceptibly. "I look forward to our next moments together."

I inhaled his energy, strong and masculine, swirling with power and intrigue.

Blake's limo pulled up in front of the restaurant, and he held the door open for me to get in. "You know, it's such a gorgeous day, I think I'll walk." Blake's eyes took in my four-inch heels, then climbed their way back to my face. "Looks like you forgot your walking shoes."

I nodded once. "I'll be fine."

He leaned in and pressed his warm lips firmly against my cheek, his good-bye kiss just a hair slower than was professionally acceptable. "Until the next time," Blake said.

I nodded. "Thank you for lunch, Blake." I tried to sound casual, but it's difficult to do that when you've been holding your breath.

I waited until he was out of sight before I hailed a cab. Sitting in the back seat of the taxi, I wished I had walked away from Blake's limo earlier that day. Even though it would have meant having to deal with that horrific ghost.

14

———

Back in the safety of my turret overlooking the park, an open bottle of merlot and leftovers on the coffee table, I snuggled under the faux lynx blanket on my couch, and enjoyed the tranquility of early evening. For me, the girl who could see anything but wanted to see nothing, it was a rare time of quiet stillness. Between the last minutes of sunlight and the onset of darkness, crowds began to turn inward, to find their way home. They retreated from the day's events with a willingness to start a new page tomorrow. When my eyes closed and my barriers to unwanted information collapsed with them, it occurred to me that the momentary happiness I felt today might have been the calm before the storm.

Like a vision out of 1920, Jack, the beautiful man from my past, wears a pale blue button-down shirt that sets off his striking blue eyes and blond hair, slicked and styled with a side part. On his face is a rakish grin. Light pours in from beyond the French doors, surrounding his head like a heavenly aura, and the red-and-gold silk curtains frame his figure. He is like a figure from a John Singer Sargent painting.

I look forward to my regular visits from him. The dreams vary, the scenery changes, our discussions evolve, though he is always deliciously the same.

Today we're at a garden party, but we're inside. The sounds of chatter and laughter filter in from outside. We're alone, together. The rest of the world ceases to exist. The heat coming off him warms my skin, even though he stands across the room.

I look down and see that I'm wearing a blue silk Delphos dress with Venetian glass beads on the sides—my favorite color and material. He's walking toward me, my breath catches.

The love Jack emanates is all-encompassing and it makes me dizzy.

I feel safe, understood, and loved.

"Did you see it?"

"See what?"

"How could you miss it?" He chuckles at my cluelessness and he circles me, wrapping an arm around my midsection. I lean into his embrace. His warm cheek touches mine as his other arm slides beneath my own, raising it to point at a portrait over the fireplace.

I gasp. A large oil painting of myself hangs on the wall. I'm wearing sapphire blue, my own blue eyes staring back at me. I feel the rise of his cheek against my face. His smile is brimming at his success in taking my breath away. The colors in the painting vibrate, the rough brush strokes alive with memories. It pulls me forward through time. My companion fades, and my chest aches with the emptiness where he once had residence. His absence is too painful to remember.

Years pass in blurred strands of color around the edges of my vision. I hear crowd chatter, and a distant, slightly warped record of Duke Ellington playing "It Don't Mean a Thing" serenades me as the painting comes to rest in the overcrowded stall of what appears to be a swanky Paris flea market.

My portrait sits atop an antique bombe chest. The frame is gone and the soft canvas edges are frayed. But there is something mesmerizing about the portrait, as if it has a soul, as if it has a part of me inside of it. The canvas rests near an oversized, gilt-framed mirror. In its reflection I see an impatient shop owner speak to a handsomely dressed young man, his features obscured by a sunbeam on the mirrored glass. And an older woman in heavy dark glasses, a scarf wrapped fashionably around her head, stands beside him.

"*Alors*, you vant eet or no?" the shop owner asks.

"Yes," the woman answers softly. "I believe we do." She smiles at the young man and kisses his cheek. His eyes never leave the painting. The details fall away as I start to wake up, the cool darkness of my room dropping a veil on the sunny afternoon of Paris past.

Then, from somewhere outside my conscious world, I realize he's back. It's *him*. The man with the steel-blue eyes and the cream-colored suit is walking slowly toward me. I stand up to greet him. He reaches me and runs his hand over my hair, brushing it lightly off my face.

"You're here," I say.

"I *am* here," he says, his fingertips grazing up and down my bare arm. "We don't usually meet *here*. We usually meet *there*, where we used to be."

He says nothing, a slow smile widens across his face. The love I feel for him spreads throughout my chest.

"We're going to meet *here* from now on," he says with a smooth voice, a knowing look in his sparkling eyes.

"Why?"

"Because it's time."

"Time for what?"

"It's just time. You ask too many questions."

"You give too few answers," I pout.

He simply smiles again, and the glow in my chest intensifies.

"Are you coming for me?" I dare to ask.

"One can only hope," he chuckles.

"You'll never change." I laugh and lean into him, noticing how good the hardness of his body feels against me.

"I've missed you," I say, my hopes dangling on a string. My heart aches at the foggy memories of our life together, and a tear slides down my cheek.

"I've missed you, too, Sassy." His eyes and fingertips trace the contours of my face.

"*Sassy*," I say with a laugh. "You haven't called me that in a long time."

His fingers frame my face, and he kisses away the tear.

"You left me," I say, my heart splitting in two, hands rubbing against his chest, testing to see if he's really here now.

His soft lips brush against mine. "I'm here now. And I'm never leaving you again," he says, his fingertips gliding down my neck. "You're still so beautiful. Time changes nothing."

My eyes fill with tears, and they spill onto my cheeks faster than he can catch them. "Time changed *me*, Jack. It's nearly destroyed me to be away from you for so long."

"I'm sorry." His face shows regret and concern. "I'm so sorry. I didn't want to leave you."

"I had to handle everything alone," I choke out, my voice thick with tears. "You don't know how hard it was. After you left, they...they..." I try to finish but can only make frightened gasps.

"Oh, Sassy." He pulls me close. "No one is ever going to hurt you again, not while I'm around." His hands wipe away my tears and caress my face.

"And what about you? Who's going to protect *you*?"

"It's going to be okay, I promise."

"You promised me that *last* time."

He winces at the anger in my words.

"Don't ever leave me again. *Please*. Don't ever let them take us away from each other again." I kiss his neck again, and again. His skin is warm and salty, real. He's here.

My kisses find his. His lips crush mine, as if he could erase what happened, as if he could ever really make me forget. I pull at him and feel his muscles flex beneath my fingers.

"I need you, Jack," I breathe as I stare into his eyes, my hands cupping his face. "Come back to me." His beautiful blue eyes fill with tears.

A truck rolls by and startles me awake.

I sat up on the couch and looked around, confused to have found myself alone in the dark.

I put my hand to my lips, remembering his kisses. Remembering his touch. The details from that life were becoming clearer, though no less painful.

I laid down and curled into a ball.

15

Ellen stood at the kitchen counter of The Albrecht Firm looking like Kim Novak from Alfred Hitchcock's *Vertigo*.

Glamorous and full of secrets.

"Good morning, Ellen," I said and walked through the kitchen on my way to my office. I'd been at the firm for several weeks now, and discovered that work was a fabulous outlet for my insomnia. Unable to sleep, as usual, I had arrived early and was grateful to have an office to go to. A quiet office, a cup of caffeine, and a pile of work could heal the soul.

"Good morning, Adeline." Ellen studied my face and she dipped her tea bag into a ceramic mug of hot water. She looked as if she prided herself on being a few steps ahead of everyone else.

The lines around her gray eyes crinkled as she forced a smile. "How about some espresso? I was just about to make a cup for Otto's guest."

"I—uh. Sure. Thank you." I kept moving, laptop bag

over my shoulder, files and resource books in my arms. "I'll be back for it. I just need to drop these in my office."

My office. My office. What a lovely ring. I was well on my way.

"No, you go ahead." Her words lilted with a somewhat vapid, hostess charm. "I'll bring it by."

I almost stopped mid-step. Ellen never offered me kindness. "Thanks," I said. My guard rose to attention.

I hiked in heels through the maze of stairs and hallways. Whatever Ellen's reasons for coming to visit me in my office, I was sure it wasn't good news. I was pretty adept at softening people when I put my mind to it, but Ellen was as cold to me today as she was the day of my interview. Nothing seemed able to change that. Maybe it was because of the history we shared. I didn't remember much of it, but unconscious connections were often the strongest.

Or maybe it had more to do with the fact that I was John Montgomery's granddaughter. Maybe she hated him, and therefore me. I didn't know. There was something complicated in our long-ago history, but I hadn't looked at it, and I wasn't going to.

I passed a large, plate glass window that framed the rising sun as it graced the tops of the buildings. Whatever the trouble in my life, I always found hope in the rising sun of a new morning. "No matter what," my father used to tell me, "you can always begin again."

I was counting on that.

I tucked an old pang of sadness behind my heart, the one that always came with missing my father, and walked down the last hallway that led to my office. Fingertips of energy curled out to me from the walls. I leaned away from their constant invitation. This building held more information than a D.C. insider.

"Keep it to yourself," I muttered.

I stepped onto the thick pile of my office rug and kicked my shoes behind my desk. I dropped the books and laptop bag on my desk, turned on my desk lamp, and began to organize. Ellen's coldness was confounding. Otto's possessiveness was alarming in a way I didn't understand.

At least the work had been great. Challenging. And that was the reason I was here. I had made it a point to learn their systems, and memorize their procedures quickly. I was happy to do it in exchange for the three things I wanted most: an insulated work environment where no one would harass me for who I secretly was, the opportunity to build a career, and the opportunity to engage with precious works of art.

My intuitive sense gave me the connection to see the art's story, to watch the moving picture of its life. It was fascinating, and satisfying to me like nothing else.

To watch how and why great art came into existence, to see artists take ideas and develop them into something extraordinary, enthralled me. As Picasso said, "I begin with an idea and it becomes something else." Artists spoke the language I understood—the unspoken language of energy.

The processes that the firm used to authenticate and appraise were certainly not as intuitive as my own. They were slow and clunky. They took time and patience, whereas I could tell you everything about any piece of art inside of an instant.

To get through it, I viewed their processes as a different language. A different way of getting to the same information. And since it was the language that was spoken in the art world, I learned it to legitimize myself and my take on art.

But it would never replace my native tongue.

I had quickly learned how to authenticate and establish value, and I had watched the restoration techniques closely. Of course, I had been learning these processes all my life from my father and grandfather. Although this was an education I could put on my résumé.

Each time I could, I found a way to touch the backing of the print, the edge of the sculpture or the surface of the jewelry so that I could access its story. Partly because of the Giovanni painting I had read in Otto's office on the day of my interview. I wanted to know what I was getting into with the art in this place. Though I'd not found anything else suspicious. And partly because I just loved the story inherent in each work of art.

Like plugging a cord into a socket, my touch would release a flow of energy from the object and the movie would begin. It was hard to predict what information would present itself first. Most often it was the secrets that were tied to the artist's story. His or her personality, how they viewed the world, how they thought things through, how they approached the work, their struggle with the people in their lives. I couldn't get enough of their stories.

Of course the stories weren't always what I expected them to be. Sometimes the artists weren't, either. Nevertheless, whatever I saw, I made a promise to myself that this time I would keep my findings quiet.

Ellen slid silently into my office with my espresso and placed it on my desk. The tinkling of the porcelain cup against the saucer shook me out of my head.

"You have a minute?" she asked.

"Sure." I eyed her over my reading glasses, picked up the tiny cup, and brought it to my lips. "Wow, this is good. If I ever lose my job, I'll probably stand on the street corner with a sign that reads Will Work for Espresso."

Ellen leaned against my round table and almost laughed. "Tell me, what's the name of the perfume you wear?"

"Uh...Bulgari."

"Right." Ellen snapped her fingers. "I've been trying to place it since the day of your interview."

"Thank you," I said. Then I realized that she hadn't actually given me a compliment.

"Adeline, I have a friend who works at the Stephens Appraisal Firm. You're familiar with them?"

I nodded.

"As you know, they're an established firm, they work on a fair number of high profile pieces each year, and they're looking for a new researcher. It's a rare opportunity. One that could launch a career, really. The position won't be advertised and they're only going to talk with a few candidates. I thought I might tell you about it in case you knew of anyone who might be interested." Ellen eyed me over her mug when she took a sip of her tea, like she waited for the hook she'd tossed to land in my cheek.

And there was something in her tone that I didn't like.

"I would be happy to give my personal referral. On the QT, of course. No one would need to know about this. I understand what a delicate situation interviewing can be. Especially when one already has a job." Ellen's cheek muscle twitched near imperceptibly.

I nodded slowly and took a quiet sip of my espresso to mask the fact that my heart was punching both fists against my ribs in a fit of fury.

"That *is* an opportunity," I looked at Ellen. Waited for a forked tongue to slip through her lips. "I'll have to give that some thought. I could ask Alexa. Maybe she'd know of someone. Do you remember Alexa?"

"I do, yes." Her lips pursed like I missed the point.

"Who's in this morning and sharing my favorite espresso?" I sucked down the last ounce of my espresso to medicate my temper.

"That would be me." Blake Greenwood waltzed in my doorway and his wide grin crashed into me.

16

———————

"Hi, Blake," Ellen said as she wrapped both hands around her mug.

I waved but had to take a minute to clear the coffee I'd inhaled into my windpipe. Ellen's lips pulled into her signature thin line.

Blake's presence filled the room with temptation and he wedged himself into Ellen's and my conversation. He worked it and he amped up his smile, leaned forward, and tapped his long fingers against the high back of the guest chair. "I'm not disturbing the two of you, am I?"

"I was just leaving." Ellen nervously ran her hand against the side of her chignon. "Adeline, remember to return those signature pages from the paperwork I gave you." When she left she cast a familiar side glance to me before she disappeared down the hallway. The kind of look that said she wondered who let the farm animal into the room.

Blake's eyes twinkled, like he was happy to see me. "Did I interrupt?" Blake said.

I wondered how he made his eyes sparkle on command

like that. "Ah, no." I coughed again. "Well, maybe a little. But it's all right."

"You seem to be hard at work." Blake was considerate enough to ignore my apoplectic fit and he took in the piles of books and folders spread across my desk.

"Well, I try to give the right impression."

He laughed, and right on cue I slipped my reading glasses off, twirled them in my hand. I caught myself and put my glasses on the desk.

He walked behind my desk, and it felt like I'd let wild animal too close. His scent surrounded him like an aura and my stomach tightened. Spices, woodsy outdoors, and something subtle that reminded me of a vineyard.

"Do you have time to go over these this morning?" Blake held up two file folders. "Mrs. Jefferson wants to finalize the value of the Martin Heades before agreeing to her divorce settlement. Henri said you had the research completed on them."

"Oh." I rubbed the back of my neck. "So these Heade landscapes will go to her? I thought he wanted them."

"Looks like Mr. Jefferson has decided to give his soon-to-be-ex-wife everything she's asked for. He's hoping he can pacify her into keeping his affair with his secretary out of the society pages. Not to mention the news of his illegitimate son."

"Ah." I nodded.

A brick dropped right in the middle of the small espresso lake residing in the pit of my stomach.

I'd met Jordan Jefferson when he'd brought the Heades in last week. And right or wrong, I knew I wouldn't lose a wink of sleep if I stayed quiet about what I knew about the paintings. Not that I slept anyway. But that really wasn't the point. Now that Mrs. Jefferson was getting the Heades, my heart twisted on itself.

"How much will they go for at auction?" Blake asked.

I flipped open my research file and pushed a press release toward him that covered a recent sale. "One Heades landscape just went for a little over a million last week in Boston."

"She'll be happy to hear that," Blake said. He looked at the article, and rubbed his stubbled beard.

"Is she auctioning them or keeping them?"

"They will go to her in the settlement. But she's confided in me that she's going to pass them to his older sons from his first marriage. She doesn't want them."

I fingered the vintage diamond necklace my father had given me on my sixteenth birthday.

Blake sat on the edge of my desk and his presence crept right past my boundaries. "Adeline, Henri mentioned to me that you seemed...concerned somehow about the Heades when the two of you were looking at them last week."

"Um, no—not really." *Did I seriously just um again*? "She's not his first wife?"

"No. His first wife died about thirty years ago. Sad story, really. If you have a concern about the Heades, I'd like to hear more about it."

"I'm not an expert, Blake, I'm just the researcher. "What happened to her, exactly?"

"She was murdered in the city. They think the killer must have been looking for drug money since he just emptied her wallet, took her jewelry, and ran. Even if it's a minor concern, you should share what you know about the paintings. Subtle feelings are sometimes our best guides in these situations."

"I don't *know* anything." A shiver ran through my body.

My heart began to keep pace with my mind. Back and forth, back and forth. Something wasn't right about the first wife story. And then it hit me.

The ghost mom with the walkman who had visited me. She had two boys, and she'd been murdered in the city. Maybe that was why she was still around? To make sure her boys didn't get cheated out of their inheritance?

Blake looked at me like he already knew what I knew about the Heades, and he was waiting for me to say it.

I looked away and felt my guard being replaced by an overwhelming urge to tell the truth. The wave of compulsion started in my gut and spread to my chest, leading me to confess, demanding I tell the truth. The whole story. What I knew and how I knew it. The sensation worked on me until telling him what I knew felt like the safest option.

Even though I didn't want to, my lips began to form the words. "I, um. I know you won't believe this, but—" And then I recognized it. The energy.

He was *pushing* me the way Alexa could.

Did he know what he was doing? It was possible for someone to have a gift for pushing and not know about it. They might just be considered a good salesperson or a persuasive personality, someone with charisma. Someone people wanted to please. But he was strong. He wasn't just pushing me for an answer—he was pushing me for the truth.

I'd grown up with Alexa pushing me to give her everything from my deepest secrets to my dessert from the dinner table, and to take the blame for the vase she broke in my grandmother's living room. Pushing wouldn't work on me. At least I didn't think it would. My protection was knowing when it was coming, so I knew how not to get sucked into it. You just had to let the intensity and the pressure pass on through without grabbing its hook. It was harder than it sounded, but practice helped. And thanks to Alexa I'd had a lifetime of practice.

"I mean— Do the Jeffersons know the provenance of the Heades?" I watched the flashes of white light dance around Blake's upper half.

Blake's eyebrows climbed. He was obviously accustomed to getting what he pushed for. "He purchased them at auction through an auction house about thirty years ago for about a hundred thousand each. Theodore Ebingham authenticated them before they went to auction."

My heart sank. Theodore Ebingham was the foremost Martin Heade expert in the country. If he said they were real, then everyone else would follow suit.

How the forger had been able to fool Ebingham, I didn't know. I did know that these pieces weren't authentic Martin Heades. And if Mrs. Jefferson kept them, she and the sons were going to get screwed. Again.

Maybe I could lay out a few bread crumbs for Blake to follow.

"This may be nothing. Or it may be something. But there were some pretty impressive Heade forgeries that hit the market about thirty years ago. Theodore Ebingham authenticated at least one of them."

"And you think these Heades are forgeries?" Blake's eyebrows rose.

"I'm not going to say that," I said honestly. "It's just that, there's a story circulating that one of the Heades from that time period, that had also been sold through Christie's and authenticated by Ebingham disintegrated during a fairly recent restoration effort. The restorer cleaned the painting with the standard acetone and it fell apart. The owner had paid over $700,000 for that piece. It could just be a rumor.

There is a lot of money at stake. And there are some freakishly talented forgers out there."

"I'll talk with her about it."

Like a storm dying down, the pressure to confess left me.

With Blake's ability to push, I knew the second Mrs. Jefferson would have no choice but to have the cleanings done. Then she and the sons would have a more fair settlement. And the first Mrs. Jefferson might be able to move on to the Other Side.

"I'd like to know more about this research you've unearthed on the Heade forgeries. Are you free for lunch today?" Blake asked.

I gave his invitation a moment of thought. "I wish I were, but I have a tight schedule this week and a mountain of work to get through. I don't think I can."

"You sure?" He flashed a handsome *GQ* sideways glance, and like a teenager I ran my hands through my hair, and a nervous laugh escaped my lips.

"I have so much work."

A devilish smile spread across Blake's face. "Well, how about drinks tonight? I'm sure you won't be working all night."

His natural cologne encircled me like a wreath of laurel. I rubbed the sapphire stone of my ring that I'd spun to the inside of my hand. His focused attention had the ability to make me feel blissful and weightless, completely forget my worries. A vision of him kissing me felt so real I thought it might actually happen. Or did happen. I could feel his warm cheek against mine as he nestled in behind me. Spun me around and kissed me like we'd always have each other, like today was all we had.

"How about I pick you up at eight?"

"Yes. How about eight?" A cold, flat voice shook me out of my fantasy.

The ghost I'd seen when I first met Blake appeared beside him, brown eyes harshly fixed.

"You might want to think twice about who you spend your time with," the ghost said. He circled behind me. His uncomfortable chill coated my skin.

"Rain check?" I said. My leg shook hard under the desk. I sprang up and walked to the other side of my office.

"I'll try not to take it personally," Blake said.

"No... It's just...all this work, and...Elizabeth has invited me to an event next week that I need to go to." I tried to rub the chill from my bare arms. "I'm serious, though. Rain check?"

Something mysterious scampered across Blake's face. "Okay. I'll get you next time."

Blake walked out the door and the ghost disappeared with him. I rubbed the ache in my chest.

I waited a few minutes, then I broke my gifts out of bondage for a quick energetic scan of the office, searching to see if Blake and his ghost was still around.

I stumbled on someone unexpectedly. The first Mrs. Jefferson appeared in the doorway of my office, the ghostly mother I had met in my townhome. She gave a slow nod then turned and left. And she was gone. Really gone. As in gone from the planet. I couldn't sense her.

Her boys were protected from their father now.

I took a deep breath, then headed to the kitchen for more espresso.

17

Blake tapped his fingers on the car seat as Thomas drove him back to the gallery.

"Something bothering you?" Thomas asked.

"No."

"You tap your fingers like that when something's bothering you."

Blake stopped the tapping. He ran his hand over his face and he looked out the window. "No, just realizing that I'm going to have to solve this problem with her a little differently than I originally planned."

18

____

A new week—a new adventure in New York. This time it was Old Masters Week at Christie's, and Elizabeth had invited me to attend as her guest. The chance to connect with Renaissance-era works was rare.

Weekly outings with Elizabeth had become a regular event, and last week over drinks she confided that she hoped to acquire one of the more extraordinary *tondi* from Fra Bartolommeo.

She had her eye on a particular *Madonna and Child* that had been painted in the 1400s.

"It will probably cost the museum fifteen million, but it would be the perfect addition to our Renaissance collection. It's quite unusual to find a piece like this in its original frame."

Original frame. The phrase echoed in my head, and my thoughts rolled with excitement.

What were the chances that Elizabeth might let me get close enough to that exquisite *tondo* to touch the frame? For just a second. That's all I would need. Literally one second.

It would be an odd request, but maybe Elizabeth would allow me access somehow. I could come up with an excuse. Participating or assisting her team. Hovering close by while they worked. I could download the story on the artist and the painting. I'd bet it was extraordinary.

Elizabeth and I were ensconced in comfortable chairs in the Christie's sale room at Rockefeller Plaza, insulated from the rest of the world by the deep, mahogany walls. Well-dressed men and women stood under the Christie's sign, a bank of phones on the wide desk in front of them. They stood poised to connect with their client buyers, ready to help them claim new acquisitions.

The currency conversions sign up front read, Welcome to Old Masters Week at Christie's. Like it was a direct greeting for me. I thought about how it must have felt to see Elizabeth Taylor's jewelry or Princess Diana's dresses in this room, and a smile warmed my face.

Every significant museum, gallery, dealer, and private owner was represented in some capacity. I caught sight of Otto across the room, wearing a navy suit, in serious conversation with two dark-haired, dark-suited gentlemen. Together the three of them looked rather mafia-esque. One of them turned to the side and I recognized him as Jordan Jefferson. I wondered if he knew about his fake Heades, yet. I wanted to walk over and whisper in his ear that I knew he was a murderer. I decided against it.

Everyone who was anyone in the New York art community was here. Now I was here, too.

And with someone who worked for the MMA, no less.

"They've added a new piece to the auction." Elizabeth

leaned in, looking stunning in her vintage Yves St. Laurent suit. "It's a piece by Agnolo Bronzino. Watch for it. I think it will probably go for eighteen million. The Museum should have that one as well."

Agnolo Bronzino. Yes, I knew him. His pieces were in the National Gallery, the Getty, and other prominent museums. My heart rate climbed and a smile crept across my face.

Sitting in the middle of Rockefeller Center, surrounded by great works of art and people who appreciated them. No one knew about my gifts. I used them privately. My career was taking off. I had finally achieved my blissful normal, anonymous in the crowds of NYC.

Life was good.

Centaurian, Jeremy, Patti and the rest were so far behind me today, I couldn't even see them in my rearview mirror. A shiver danced across the upper part of my spine. Someone watching me? I rubbed the goosebumps that appeared on my arms.

Cold? No, I wasn't cold.

Excited? Maybe.

What *was* that feeling that just ran across me? I looked away and tried to disengage from my immediate surroundings while I figured it out. People were milling about, their conversations dotted with warm laughter that bounced off the taupe-colored walls. Elizabeth and I had arrived early, and it would be a while before the auction began.

I'd felt this before...like...like someone had just noticed me too closely. It was a bit of a vulnerable feeling. Not entirely unpleasant.

I looked around the room, and the feeling drifted away. Probably nothing.

But then it came back. That feeling of being noticed. Of being watched. Of being wanted.

It snaked behind me, slithering up and around my back. My skin tingled, and gooseflesh stood up.

Whoever he was, he was behind me.

I turned. Casually. Searching as nonchalantly as possible. But I could not spot the source of the energy. It was moving fast, hitting me in waves.

I worked to push away the energy. I was, after all, in front of the world's most exclusive art community.

I lowered my head and rubbed a finger up and down the bridge between my eyes. I exhaled.

"Are you okay?" Elizabeth leaned in, her signature Chanel scent traveling ahead of her voice.

"Yeah. Just a...migraine, I think. Must have been something I ate. Is the ladies lounge close by?"

"Right through there," Elizabeth said.

I scooted out of the aisle, snaked my way through the sea of dark suits and balding heads, the largest demographic of the crowd, and tried to remain unnoticed. But every eye seemed to land on me as I wiggled around each mini-grouping.

19

———

The sensation subsided when I was out of sight.

This was more powerful than just being noticed. Whoever he was, he was able to push his focused attention right through my invisible barricade.

Wait. Pushing. *Blake.*

My breath kicked up a notch.

I began a slow walk back to my seat and scanned the faces I passed. Looking for Blake. I wanted to see if he might sport the inevitable white sparkles that would trail any recent energy work.

Buyers were finding their way to their seats. Others quietly studied their auction catalogs. No one revealed the sign I was searching for. That is, until I rounded the corner and approached my seat next to Elizabeth. There was a pillar at the side of the room with little flashes of light, like the twinkle of stars dancing around its edges.

Whoever was on the other side of the pillar had been my psychic admirer.

I backed out of the aisle and walked around the pillar,

hoping I didn't find Otto or Jordan Jefferson. Or worse, Blake's not-so-friendly ghost.

There was no one. I stood alone in the crowd, searching through a mass of people. No one bore the energy traces that were fading next to me. The room that had felt so enchanting earlier was now disorienting.

20

—————

I had no idea if Blake knew just how much he had affected me. Or even if he had intended to. There was a chance that I had been sensitive to his all-too-focused energy. I'd seen that with Alexa before. When she wanted something she could slip into pushing for it.

The other possibility was that he knew exactly what he was doing.

Either way, I wanted to figure him out. He affected me like no man ever had. And I didn't think that was the result of his gift. Or maybe not entirely.

Of course, there was that advanced technique that Grandmother had also told me about. She had seen a shaman clean up all the energetic residue of the magic he had worked on a person. There were no sparkles, no remnants of energy left on him. She had watched it happen, and no psychic had been able to pick up his trace.

Was Blake gifted enough to do that?

"You feel better?" Elizabeth asked.

"Tons. Thanks." I sank into my seat.

"Were you able to take something?"

"I was." I smiled and nodded at Elizabeth.

"Hello, ladies." Blake Greenwood slid into the seat next to Elizabeth, his arm rested on the back of the chair in front of him. His dark gray suit jacket fell open, the last four letters of the Brioni label visible, as well as the black cap of what looked like a Mont Blanc pen in his pocket. The gold chain of his pocket watch was just visible on his waistband and he looked ever the part of the art dealer.

Elizabeth was exceedingly charming, greeting Blake as though he were a long-lost friend, kissing him on the cheek and immediately engaging him in conversation about his business. She was the master. Had it not been for my ability to see beneath the surface, I would never have known how he stirred a little fear within her. He seemed to command this reaction from everyone.

While the three of us talked, I searched Blake for any hint of sparkles of light.

Nothing. Not even a glimmer. Too much time had passed.

Then he looked at me and just to the left of the side of his head, was a tiny ping of light. It had been Blake.

"Let me take the two of you out to dinner tonight, to celebrate the exquisite acquisitions I know you'll make today, Elizabeth." Blake smiled his most charming smile.

I let Elizabeth handle the conversation since I felt too distracted to give a political answer. Then she declined due to previously made plans, and I was caught unaware. No preplanned excuse, no way out. And so I was on my way out to dinner with Blake that evening.

"Be careful, Adeline," Elizabeth warned after Blake had left. "I get a strange feeling around him. I mean he's drop-dead gorgeous, incredibly wealthy. Obviously successful.

But something's just not right about that picture. You know, it just might be a little too perfect."

I was surprised at how perceptive Elizabeth was.

"Yes, I get a strange feeling from him as well."

"Then why spend any time with him?" Elizabeth was a fearless New Yorker in many ways, and would question anyone about anything, putting them right on the spot.

"I actually didn't mean to put myself in that situation. Next time I'll have to have an excuse tucked away just in case."

"Sorry about leaving you out there like that." Elizabeth looked contrite. "And yes, you definitely need to carry a good excuse with you at *all* times." She laughed. "Just be careful. Blake seems to be a very...powerful man. He has a way of...influencing people."

"What do you mean?" I whispered. She knew more than she was letting on.

Elizabeth eyed me carefully, and I stayed quiet, hoping she would sacrifice some of her political grace and spill a few beans. She lowered her voice and leaned in. "Peter Campbell, my predecessor, told me before he left that I should watch out for Blake."

"Why?"

"I don't know specifically." Elizabeth lowered her voice even more, looking around as she whispered in my ear. "All he said was that whatever Blake Greenwood wanted, Blake Greenwood got. Maybe Peter lost out to Blake in some acquisition battle. I couldn't say. We never talked about it. But I always get this feeling around Blake that he just makes things happen. Whether or not you might want them to happen."

"Is that why you refused Blake's invitation for tonight?"

"No, I really do have plans tonight. But even if I didn't, I probably would have found some reason to bow out." Our eyes met, and I nodded.

Elizabeth gave me a near-motherly smile that told me the conversation was over. She faced the front as the auction began. She was ready to claim her pieces.

I settled in my seat. Blake's energy continued to spin through my mind. And the memory of it still waltzed through my body.

Elizabeth's comment that Blake *just made things happen* knocked around in my thoughts.

Blake did have a bizarrely powerful presence. And he could push someone more powerfully than I had ever seen Alexa even attempt. I wanted his story.

I knew there was one way I could get it. I'd just need a few moments alone with that Mont Blanc pen.

21

Traffic and heat were co-conspirators, like Greek gods toying with the humans on this New York afternoon. They each added frustration until my cab driver hung out of his window, screaming and cursing at the other drivers. I'd meant to, but still hadn't made arrangements with a car service. Some part of me liked the *Matrix*-like gritty reality of a New York cab. It was like being part of history. But today there was no a/c and the threat of a storm made the heat feel wet. Everyone was tricked into believing that patience was a fool's choice, and I was rethinking my choice in transportation.

When I arrived in Greenwood Gallery, I lifted my long hair off the back of my sticky neck, the quiet, chilled air was a welcome relief from the chaos and the tension in the streets. I stood in the lobby and stared out the window, wished the dark clouds would just put an end to the angst.

From around the corner an über-thin brunette in a translucent, white button-down and an ultra-short skirt emerged. Her blunt, angled hair and darkly lined eyes fit with the sophistication of the surroundings, though she was less than welcoming.

"Are you Ms. Montgomery?"

"I am." I dropped my hair.

"Blake—um, Mr. Greenwood is expecting you," she said with a slight French accent. Her voice was cool. "He's just finishing a meeting, and he'll be out shortly. Have a seat." As she ushered me to a seating group she put her hand behind my back and my hackles went up. I wasn't wild about being touched by strangers, and I wasn't particularly curious to know her story. I scooted ahead and out of the way.

With an inelegant look in my direction, she walked away, stooped behind the front table (no small feat considering the heel height), and picked up her clutch from under the front desk. She eyed me as she sniffed the white gardenias held in the peacock blue Tiffany favrile vase. Then she walked out the front door, locking it behind her.

Apparently I was in for the evening.

And clearly, New York allowed too many models into the city. There should be a limit.

Sit and wait was not in my skill base, so I decided to tour the gallery instead. I walked into the first room whose warm, red walls and crafted wainscoting surprised me. In fact, the walls in each room were a different warm color, and reminded me more of the museums overseas than the pale white or gray walls of the galleries of New York.

The collection was impeccable. Five large rooms filled with classic art, framed not only by baroque-styled gold, but also by ornate crown molding and pillars that clung to the wide doorways. Several artists' names were immediately recognizable and I was so transported by the beauty of their work that I lost track of time.

When I finally looked at my watch, I realized I'd been

waiting thirty minutes for him to finish whatever he was working on. Probably buffing his nails to a fine gloss. Anyone that gorgeous had to be narcissistic. At least I hoped he was. It might be too much for me to handle if he was also emotionally evolved.

I thought of Blake sitting in his office staring at his watch while he waited for enough time to pass. Enough time to pass for him to seem importantly engaged.

I guess he could have been doing something important. Actually, probably not. Something about him just smelled sinister. And warmly pheromone-like.

Also, who was that ghost shadowing him at the firm? Not that I wanted to know. But still. To have a ghost attached to you like that was odd.

I stopped in front of a Picasso and stood with my hands on my hips, mesmerized by several sketches signed and dated 1901.

The Calvin Klein model had Picasso in his art gallery. Interesting.

A drawing by Picasso wouldn't exactly be the main focal point for a gallery that specialized in classical paintings, but a piece from Picasso would be hard for any art dealer to walk away from.

Probably a guaranteed sale. At some point, anyway.

Every part of me ached to touch the frame. Just one little finger to the back of the mat, and I'd have a very personal story about Picasso. He probably still had some fascinating, unpublished secrets.

I raised my hand to touch the edge of the drawing.

22

———————

Blake walked quietly into one of the rooms of the gallery and found Addie staring at his Picassos. Her hand was lifted and ready to touch the canvas.

But he wasn't alarmed. He wasn't even surprised him.

Blake had recognized her distinctive energy when he first met her on the day of her interview. He'd been around psychics all of his life, and so he could spot the trait immediately.

He had family members who could tell you the history of an object, and even all about its owner, just by giving the object a touch. He knew about psychometry.

He watched Addie hesitate. From his experience with his own gifted family, he knew she must be struggling between her desire for Picasso's secrets, and a need to keep her gifts under wraps. She might also worry that some emotional trauma might accompany his secrets that she wanted so badly. Sometimes getting the story wasn't worth the pain the reader had to ingest along the way.

Blake walked back to his office, and wondered if Otto knew about Addie's abilities, and if that had been the real reason he hired her. Because Otto really wasn't the kind of guy to pay it forward and give a gal a shot at a new career. Otto was in a perpetual, winner-take-all kind of life-long contest where anyone could be a pawn. If Otto knew about Addie's gifts, he wouldn't let an opportunity like this pass him by.

Nervous sweat bloomed on his skin.

If Otto knew, this wouldn't work out well at all for Addie.

23

————————

Thunder rolled outside in an apparent warning, and I looked up. A security camera in the corner of the room caught my eye. I couldn't imagine Blake would approve of me touching a piece of their price-less art.

I stopped myself mid-effort and decided to touch my chin instead. As if that's what I intended all along.

I wondered if Blake was watching me somewhere behind those camera controls. I found that idea just a little bit thrilling, and then was disturbed that I felt that way. Oh, how I wanted to be unmoved by Blake Greenwood. But it was impossible. I was seduced by the power running beneath his exterior—breathless when he looked at me with untamed sensuality like an animal recognizing its mate.

I rubbed my chin for a few moments to make my movement look authentic, and then I straightened my fingers and examined the sapphire ring on my right hand. I turned my ring from left to right, the facets inside the sapphire shining as Blake's brilliant museum-quality lights penetrated it. The diamonds sparkled and the emotional electricity in the ring seemed to charge and jump when I focused on it.

I held my hand to my chest and let the love that still lived in the ring run through my heart.

I looked at my watch again.

Forty-five minutes. I was tired of waiting and tired of being tempted. Left alone and surrounded by all of this gorgeous art and yet not able to touch any of it.

Lightning flashed and thunder rolled four seconds later. I counted. A habit left over from my childhood spent living at the beach. I liked tracking the speed of the storms as they rolled in over the water.

Electricity hung in the air as I turned and walked down the private corridor toward the heated energy I had come to recognize as Blake's. It was a steady mix of pulsing heat and a cool glass of Scotch that burned on the way down. Intoxicating. Enticing, yet bad for you.

I followed the trail, feeling my way toward him as my Manolos clicked slowly through the hallways.

He would know I was coming.

Taking a few more steps, I felt Blake's awareness land on me. He must have heard my heels on the marble. I stopped in my tracks and turned to the wall, pretending to look at a painting. I felt my cheeks flush hot.

24

———

I rounded the last corner slowly, and found Blake talking on the phone and staring out floor-to-ceiling windows.

"*Va bene allora. Fammi sapere quando hai tutti i documenti completati, e noi organizzare il trasporto. Sì, le mie guardie di sicurezza scorteranno l'Canalettos in persona.*"

And speaking Italian.

What little bit of Italian I knew was rusty, but it sounded like he was arranging international transport. And didn't he just say "Canalettos"? Plural? Those went for about $10 million a piece.

He turned around when I caught his eye, his mouth broadening into a sexy grin.

"Sorry," he mouthed, then moved his hands like he had a real chatterbox on the other end of the line.

He waved me in and gave me the *just a minute* sign with his hands. He stood there, hands on his hips, white shirt unbuttoned just enough, his gray suit jacket's sheen complemented his skin.

He motioned toward the bar at the other end of his

office. The amber Scotch seemed to glow in the crystal decanter.

Out of the corner of my eye I admired the giant Ruhlmann desk and I tried not to be impressed with the picturesque elegance of the scene.

I cautiously eyed the items on his desk as he looked out the opposite window.

There they were.

His pen.

His pocket watch.

His leather-bound notebook.

Everything I would need and more. I sat quietly and waited for my chance, making a mental note of how each object was evenly spaced and arranged so that they were straight up and down.

"Sì, aspetterò di sentire da voi." He took off his telephone earpiece, tossed it on the desk, and put his hands on his hips. "Well," he laughed. Actually, he kind of glowed. He shuffled through the neatly stacked papers on his desk and looked up at me with a handsome sideways glance and devilish half-grin. "A rather big deal I'm working. Sorry you had to wait so long. I'll make it up to you, I promise."

I noticed the black clouds now filled the windows from end to end, making it look much later than it actually was. With only a few table lamps to light the prematurely darkened office, a yellowish-white glow surrounded Blake, and I waited for the angels to start singing.

I waved him off. "Oh, don't worry about it. I enjoyed looking around your gallery. You have an exquisite collection."

"Thank you," was all he said as he flipped through more stacks of papers. He knew he had an exquisite collection. He knew art. And he knew what would sell. I appreciated the confidence that came with that insight. My father and grandfather had the same acumen.

He stood over his desk making notes with the Mont Blanc Meisterstuck I'd seen earlier—a silver pen with ridges from top to bottom, a gold band around the middle, and the signature six-pointed star with rounded edges on the cap. *Perfect.* He put the pen down, grabbed his notes, and rounded the desk, heading for the door. "I'll just be a few more minutes, and then we're on our way. Please help yourself to a drink. I'll be right back."

This was my chance.

"Take your time. Do what you need to do. May I borrow your pen for a moment? I just need to write down a few reminders." I held up a small, crocodile-encased notebook I'd pulled from my open purse and held my breath again, hoping that he wouldn't offer a different pen.

He stopped in his path and tensed as he took a step back, his model-quality smile fading slightly. But then something flitted across his face and he relaxed again. "Sure. Help yourself. Whatever you need."

I paused for a moment in the awkward quiet. Then took three quick, tip-toed steps to Blake's rosewood desk and grabbed his pen. I might have only a few moments, but that would be enough time for me to delve into the hidden places.

I turned my back to the door and held the pen lightly, preparing myself for Blake's energy to rip through me with a story as with any other object.

Then, oddly...nothing happened.

In fact it felt as if I were holding nothing. Like it was fake. Like I went to pick up a piece of antique Wedgwood and found myself holding a piece of Chinet instead.

I moved the pen to my left hand—the feminine, receiving side of the body. Maybe that would help.

The energy finally poured out smooth and slow, like honey from a sticky jar in an old pancake house. I nearly popped a vein out of impatience.

Drip by drop it came forward. There was his extraordinary desire to make money, his career goals, his extensive knowledge of art—

It read like a commercial. Like marketing copy.

Something was wrong. I picked up more about him by just looking at him.

A shot of anxiety dashed through my nervous system, and I felt sweat forming on my pale skin. Nervous sweat. Panic.

Getting nothing when I read someone had never happened before. Everyone had a story, a history, and motives that were simply lying there, contained in their familiar objects, waiting to be seen. It was impossible not to leave that trace.

How could Blake have blank spots in his story? Murky details that I couldn't access? His story was there, somewhere. It had to be.

Lightning flashed outside, and in the background I heard the rain beat against the glass. But I definitely didn't count the seconds until the thunder erupted. Like a soundless bell clanging, fear rang through my body, setting my teeth on edge. I replaced the pen to the spot where I'd found it on his desk and glanced at his pocket watch, which sat neatly beside the pen.

It was yellow gold with a handsome white face, about two inches in diameter. The black numbers were crisp and clean, styled in the Art Deco fashion. The second hand clicked along its own dial, loudly enough that I could hear it easily.

I held my left hand over the top of the watch for a moment to feel the energy. The story in the watch was strong, and energy emanated from it a good four or five inches. Blake's story was in there. I felt it.

I turned toward the doorway and sent my awareness out into the hallway and around the corners to see if anyone was coming.

No one was.

I came back to the pocket watch and stared at it for a few moments, biting my lower lip as I debated. If the story was too strong, I would completely leave my body to channel it. And if someone walked in, well, I wouldn't be able to feign normal. I'd be lost to whatever history the object held.

I checked the gallery again. No one was coming. Everyone seemed to be focused on something else.

I took a breath and grabbed the pocket watch. Immediately I was sucked into what looked like the 1920s, a flash of gardens attached to an elegant home, and then two men in period attire yelling, fighting. A gunshot is fired. I can feel myself struggling against the firm grasp of a man's hand on my upper arm, trying to pull me away as I scream.

Horror ran through me and his pocket watch slipped from my hands, hitting my foot and jarring my eyes open. My breath was heavy, my heart twisted into panic, nausea spun in my stomach. A slick sweat had formed on the back of my neck.

I rubbed my arm where I'd felt the man grab me and looked down at it. To my fright I saw the red bruises of his handprint. I was channeling too deeply. I couldn't hand myself over to this experience right now. Blake must have purchased a vintage pocket watch with a significant history.

I stared at the watch lying on what looked like a Voysey rug and my head spun. Holding on to the edge of the desk, I bent gingerly, picked up the watch, and placed it back on the top of the desk, careful to put it in the exact spot where I'd found it. I stared at it for a moment, and then turned. My heart ached with sadness and loss from this story I didn't want to see.

I walked over to the soft leather chair that was positioned next to the three-cushion leather couch and sat down. I looked around Blake's office for something else to focus on. I needed to ground myself back in present time, which meant I needed a different story to latch onto. Something benign.

I ran my hand over the Macassar ebony wood on the arm of the chair, stroked the alternating bands of black and tan. I expected the porous material to offer me some information on Blake, or maybe a few stories from clients who'd sat in the chair. But nothing came forward.

This just wasn't possible.

I looked around. Blake's office reflected all the trappings of his success—expensive, vintage furnishings and decor, a gorgeous view from a prestigious office. There should have been loads of story and attachment. And yet it was all vapid somehow.

For me to attach to something in the here and now, it had to have a story or a sense of meaning or attachment. Something that meant so much to their owners that their vibration would be imbued in it, and the story would permeate the object. Then I could read it and free myself from where I had just been.

But the energy in Blake's office didn't reveal itself in stories as it should have. The objects were empty.

Wait—

Not empty.

Sealed.

I jumped up and went back to the pen on his desk. I picked it up, intensified my focus, and looked at it psychically.

There it was. A thick gel of energy surrounded the pen, completely invisible to the human eye. And only evident to those who not only had the ability to see it, but who knew what to look for.

The energy worked like Teflon, keeping the object free from being saturated with the details of their owners so that identities could be kept secret, and confidential information contained within objects could remain hidden.

Energetic sealing was a little-known method that got some publicity just after World War II. A true believer in the occult, Hitler had been afraid that gifted spies would learn his secret plans by touching his personal belongings. So he hired shamans to place energetic sealants around his things. The energy in the sealant was misleading, so that spies would see only what Hitler wanted them to see. Everyone had discounted the technique as rumor. But my grandfather had learned it from his father, who worked in Intelligence during the war. *It was real.*

Nothing in his office had any readable authentic information except for maybe his pocket watch, and that information wouldn't answer my questions.

The distraction I'd searched for earlier finally came, though not in the form I had expected. I felt his stare before anything else. Before the chill, even.

Blake's ghost.

Two eyes in the corner of the room that glimmered with hatred. My boundaries were completely down and his cold, venomous torment cut through my body, slicing a path from left to right inside of me. The chills spread across my back, and my insides turned to ice. I couldn't move out of sheer terror, and my breathing shrunk into tiny, kitty breaths.

I stood paralyzed, the terror leaving me with the same default approach I had used as a child: close my eyes, sit perfectly still, and hope that the ghost would leave. But the overpowering scent of liquor hit my nose, and I knew I needed to open my eyes. I had to.

A glass shattered against the wall behind me and my eyes flew open. He drifted right in front of me and the air left my lungs as his lips curved into a wicked smile. His cold, dead eyes stared at me.

He was younger than I had expected, barely over thirty, if that. His brown hair was swept to the side in a youthful cut, and his simultaneous malevolence and immaturity confused me.

"Did you think I was going somewhere, *pretty girl?*" he said in his hardened Brooklyn accent. "I'm not going anywhere yet, doll. I've got a little payback to give to someone first. They take from me—I take from them."

He turned his face close into mine, the whiskey on his breath burned the inside of my nose.

"Such a shame." He clicked his tongue against the roof of his mouth three times. "You didn't know what you were getting into, did you?"

He ran a cold hand down my face to my throat, where he suddenly tightened his grip and cut off my air. I gasped and tried to capture his wintry hand to pull it away, but there was nothing to grab onto. He laughed and slowly strengthened his grasp until my senses dulled, the edges of the room went blurry, and the slowed ticking of Blake's pocket watch echoed in my ears.

25

Without warning he jerked toward the door and loosened his brace on my neck at the same time. I bolted away and hotfooted it out of Blake's office, sputtering, coughing, and gasping my way into the hallway. If I ran into someone I'd have to tell them I was having an allergic reaction or something.

Once on the hardwood floors of the hallway I slowed my steps, and started making my way toward the front area of the gallery in search of safety. I wasn't sure why the ghost backed off, but I was relieved he did. I looked up and down the hallway before I stopped again, my heart hammering so loud and hard against my rib cage that my chest jumped with every beat.

My legs felt like they were made of wet noodles and I coughed and barked until the air was flowing almost naturally again.

Thunder shook the building and I hoped it had been loud enough to cover my choking noises.

If only I wielded my gifts more powerfully, more like my grandmother and mother. Maybe then I could push ghosts away. The matriarchs of our family were on top of their gifts. I was used by mine. My only protection from ghosts was to pull up stakes and run. Assuming I could.

My bones still clattered inside my skin, but I thought I had my appearance together enough to make it back to the lobby. I paused for a few more breaths to gain a sense of steadiness, and then began to walk on my own.

My purse. I'd left it on the floor of Blake's office. I couldn't—I just couldn't go back. I clenched my fists in front of me.

Lightning flashed as I turned around and—

"Whoa!"

Blake grabbed my arms to keep me from falling off my heels. I hadn't realized he was so close behind me.

He laughed and steadied me. Then he studied my face and his expression clouded.

"Are you okay?" he asked.

And that was all it took. I leaned in and wrapped my arms around his neck as he pulled me close. Like a magical spell he calmed me, his hand holding strong against my back. His arms comforted, and tears burned in my eyes.

"What happened?" he asked.

I took a step back. Carefully. And smiled. "It's nothing. I just—it's nothing. I'm fine."

His eyes showed a growing concern just before they glanced down at my arm where he saw the red handprint on my pale skin.

"Oh, Adeline. Did I do that?" He ran his palm over the handprint.

I took another step back and looked at my arm as I rubbed it. "Oh. No...it's okay. I'm not hurt. It's just because my skin is so pale, it shows everything." My voice was raspy and I tried to clear my throat.

"I just didn't want you to fall." His eyes focused hard.

"I'm fine. Really, it's okay." I pushed a lock of hair behind my ear.

He touched my arm, gently rubbed his fingertips over the imprint my channeling left behind, and butterflies took flight in my stomach. "Can I get you some ice? Or—I didn't think I grabbed you that hard." His eyes looked up at my face and a tear chose that moment to slip out in an effort to make a run down my cheek. I caught it but not before he saw it.

"You didn't. It's okay. I've just had a—really odd day," I said with a shaky exhale, and tried to force a pleasant smile.

He reached a hand up to my neck and I took an immediate step back, leaving his hand in the air. The rain battered the windows in the quiet. I had to look away and opened my mouth as I struggled for a deep breath.

"Adeline. Your neck—are you sure you're all right?" he asked with a frown.

"It's probably from the heat today." I swallowed against my still-sore throat. "Heat rash, probably." I rubbed my throat. We both knew he didn't believe me.

His eyes scanned the features of my face, my cheekbones, the lines of my jaw, and finally my lips, as if he were seeing something. His gaze locked with mine, and I felt the air leave my lungs. Again.

Our eyes stayed locked on one another, and I saw something clear and recognizable that skipped across the waves of time. Something that began long before today. His eyes closed gently in a blink that lasted a second too long, which told me he felt something that was nearly too strong.

"Shall we go?" I said in that 'I don't want to talk about it' voice that tended to be enough of a warning for any man.

"Actually I need to get my purse from your office." I smoothed my hair and felt my hand shaking.

"I'll take care of your purse," Blake said and he noticed my hand. He put his hand on mine to comfort me. His thumb moved back and forth and my mind moved with it like a pendulum, until I realized what he'd said. Someone would bring my purse out to me.

Before or after they had a chance to run through it?

"I'll just grab it, I won't be a minute."

What was I saying?

"Nonsense. Let's get on with our evening. Maybe it will take your mind off things."

"Okay," I acquiesced.

Blake left his hand on mine while he pulled his phone out of his pocket. His thumb continued back and forth, ever so slowly, soothing me, and I was beginning to feel fractionally better.

I took the opportunity to feign interest in a painting. Which meant I had to step away. I needed to think. I had to assume that Blake was somehow responsible for the energetic sealant that was in his office. It was too improbable to think that he had nothing to do with it.

If it had just been on his furniture, and then maybe. Ruhlmann furniture had been around for 100 years—anything could have happened to it in that amount of time. But his furniture *and* his pen? He had to have had a hand in putting it there. Or at least have been aware of it. Why had it been put there? Was someone after him? Did he have something to hide? And what, he was afraid that some psychic someone was going to see these secrets by touching his things? Was he afraid *this* psychic was going to see his secrets? No. It couldn't be.

"Thomas? Ms. Montgomery left her purse in my office.

Bring it to the back lobby. We'll pick it up there. called?" Blake stepped away.

I continued to stare at the painting. Recognizing a person from a past life was like seeing someone for the first time and yet instantly knowing there was never a time when you didn't know one another.

Past life memories were tricky in that they brought a sense of familiarity, which bred comfort, but not necessarily clarity. Our memories are very unreliable in that we forget important details from one life to the next. We might only remember the passion from the love affair and completely forget the fact that our lover killed us in the end.

"Thomas will bring it up, and that will save you some high-heeled steps."

I wanted to cancel our evening and head home for a hot bath and a glass of wine. However, I couldn't risk being alone. Not right now. I could sense the ghost nearby, keeping his awareness on me, though staying away while Blake was close to me. That had to have been the reason he turned away—he must have sensed Blake coming in our direction.

I stared at Blake without really seeing him while I studied my catch-22. If I went home, I'd have to deal with a life-threatening ghost. If I stayed with Blake, I'd be safe from the ghost, still I'd be trusting someone who had more secrets than a Freemason.

Jagged lightning danced in front of the plate glass windows just before a loud crash of thunder vibrated through the floors and walls and shook me, body and soul.

The lights flickered, then went out.

26

"Well," Blake said after a few seconds, "I knew we should have gotten that generator replaced." I heard his shoes come slowly toward me, where I had been looking at a small eighteenth-century painting of a nude woman. The plate had read Reclining Nude. Jean-Antoine Watteau, French, 1684-1721.

I felt his hand on my arm.

"Ah, there you are. Are you okay?"

"Yes. I'm fine," I said.

"The storm must be directly over us. Let's just wait here a minute and maybe the lights will come back on."

I hated the dark like most people hated snakes. "Does this happen often? With the lights?"

"Now and then. The electrical system in the building is outdated and overloaded."

I heard a heavy door thud in the back of the gallery and I jumped.

Blake's hand rubbed my arm. "It's all right. That's just Thomas on his way down to the basement to check the generator. If he can get it going we'll get some emergency lighting here in a minute.

"At least you were able to see the Watteau before the lights went out. It's extraordinary, isn't it?" Blake said and he dropped his hand. He spoke to me as though nothing were wrong, as if we weren't standing in the pitch-dark, as if he hadn't noticed how unnerved I was.

"It is," I said. My eyes moved around the room but I saw nothing but the black in every direction. It was my living nightmare. Stuck in the dark with an angry ghost nearby. I inched toward the heat I felt from Blake's body.

"Are you familiar with Watteau's work?"

"Oh. Yes. A little."

I thought he might touch me again, just to comfort me. I thought I might feel his hand on my back or my arm. But I didn't.

"Though I thought this piece had been placed in a museum in Pasadena," I said, my breath touching his.

"I'm impressed." He said. "We had it in the Norton Simon on loan. But my client wants to sell it now. He has his eye on something else."

"Well, it's stunning," I said.

Several sirens wailed outside, along with the winds of the storm.

"Yes, it is," he said. "Watteau does an excellent job of creating a question in the mind of the viewer. We wonder if her lover has just left, or if she's awaiting his arrival. Her pink cheeks would suggest that he's just left, or perhaps that she's watching him leave. Are you okay, Adeline?" Blake said as his hand found my arm again.

"Yes." I reached out and felt him step closer still. "It's just —so dark."

"I'm sorry about that." Blake moved his hand to my back and pulled me to him, our cheeks touching in the quiet.

"It may be that her smile shows us both scenarios," I said as his lips gently brushed over my cheek.

"Both?" he asked, his whisper thick with anticipation.

"Perhaps she's looking forward to him *and* basking in the glow of the love they've shared."

"I hadn't thought of that," he said. His hand tangled into my hair as he pulled me to him. His lips were strong and soft, his kiss intoxicating.

27

There was a loud *ka-chung* from the distant area of the basement and two warm, orange emergency lights came to life at the end of the hallway. They gave Blake's god-like face a coral glow.

Without words we stared at one other.

The back of his hand gently grazed the side of my face, his thumb traced the edge of my bottom lip, and my heart tumbled. My eyes closed against the heightened sensation of his touch, and when I opened them again, I was staring into the bottomless depths of his eyes. Eyes that pulled me into a space where only the two of us existed.

He ran his thumb down my spine in a delicate stroke like a water droplet falling, and my heart fell with it, into the depths of careless abandon. I couldn't stop myself.

Blake's signature strength and sensitivity streamed through me, and my heart just fell open. In spite of my better judgment.

When he reached the lower part of my spine, he held me close and enchanted me with a slow kiss.

But the heels of a man's shoes clicked in the distance of

the near dark hallway. "The elevator probably isn't working. Come on, we'll take the back way through my office."

When my heels hit the floor I stopped.

His office.

Would the ghost be there? I psychically scanned that area of the gallery as a crowd of endorphins giggled together in my brain. No, he wasn't there, but he was still here, and not far away, either. The thought of him being close and even watching Blake and me would normally have been enough to frighten me. Blake had his protector vibe in full swing, which kept the ghost at bay for some reason.

Blake turned around and reached for my hand. "Are you okay?" he asked.

"I'm just slipping my heels off," I fibbed.

We walked hand in hand through the dark gallery. But when we cut through the lobby, the antique Tiffany vase that normally sat on the front marble table was shattered on the floor. Gardenias and small puddles of water lay among the fragments.

"Watch it." Blake pushed me back from the broken glass. He stared at the shards on the floor then cautiously looked around the room.

The ghost. I felt the remnants of his rage in the air, smelled the faint scent of liquor. Broken glass must be his tell, his way of letting people know he was around. And angry.

We turned the corner, went through a private door that was camouflaged in the wall, and then down a quiet hallway. We arrived at Blake's office through another private door that opened into the back of his office. He held his office door open for me and then shut it behind us, locking the deadbolt with a key from his keychain.

One small security light lit the office from the corner. I

looked across his shadowed, elegant office and stifled a shiver as the memory of Blake's ghost and the energetic sealants came back to me.

Blake turned on his phone flashlight. We stared at the broken glass on the floor that the ghost had smashed earlier. I watched his reaction closely but he didn't give any clues, other than to shake his head slightly. He moved the chunks of glass aside with his shoe as casually as if someone had left a pen on the floor.

I slipped my shoes on.

"I have reservations for us at Daniel this evening," he said.

Footsteps echoed outside of the main door to Blake's office, the one I didn't think was locked, and my heart stopped. I didn't know if the ghost had noisy footsteps or if it was the man Blake had spoken to on the phone.

When the knock came I relaxed. Ghosts didn't usually knock.

Blake opened the door halfway. "Thomas. Only you could pull off vintage Chanel and not lose your masculinity."

I recognized him. It was the bodyguard from the front door of The Albrecht Firm all those weeks ago. He wore his signature black, this time a button-down with a dark blazer and dark pants, a gun tucked off center into his waistband. His appealing good looks kept his darkness from making him look too thuggish, but his steeliness made him fierce.

I looked down at the purse. The top was zipped. Something I never found time to do.

"Thank you, Thomas," I managed in a small voice and smiled. But no smile was returned and he walked away.

"Thomas is a little short on social graces, but he keeps

things safe and running smoothly here." Blake flashed a grin.

Now I knew who had been on the other side of the gallery's security cameras.

28

———————

Magical bubbles rose and burst from my champagne, the subtle fruit and floral scent filled the air between us while we sat in the back of Blake's limo. I struggled to keep my glass completely stable, the day's events still jangling me into a low-grade fret. I finally just put two hands on the delicate glass. I hoped I didn't look like a three-year-old hanging on to a sippy cup.

"To new beginnings. And of course, Elizabeth's newest acquisitions for the Met." Blake raised his glass, a cocky half-smile spread across his face.

"To new beginnings," I said softly.

Our tulip-shaped glasses were perfectly cool to the touch and we clinked them together while the limo pulled out of the parking garage and into the driving rain. The velvety bubbles were like tiny, exotic pearls, and seduced my senses in a single sip.

Blake watched as I swiftly downed the golden-blond nectar from my two-handed grip. "Tough day, huh?" he asked and refilled my glass.

"Definitely not my usual day." I waited for its effervescence to slow.

"I hope that whatever has you bothered doesn't have anything to do with us," he said and returned the bottle to the silver wine bucket.

"No," I lied again, and hoped there wasn't any lightning in the immediate area. I attempted a smile but only half of my mouth rose and I thought it showed more like a slight sneer. Exhaustion washed over me, along with the effects of the bubbly.

The traffic moved slowly through the remnants of the storm, and I decided not to drink anymore champagne. I needed my wits about me tonight, presently they were in a tipsy dance with my other emotions. For someone who saw so much, I sure had a lot of blind spots when it came to my own life.

Blake must have felt the walls going up around my heart, because his protectiveness wafted across the car like a warm breeze at the beach, wrapping around me in the fashion of a well-loved security blanket, and sent any fearfulness skittering in search of another host.

Just like that my muscles relaxed, my shoulders dropped, my heart softened, and I drank in the comfort that no one had made me feel before.

My head had a different reaction.

You've already forgotten what you saw tonight? my head warned.

When was the last time anyone was able to bring us into a sense of peace? my heart answered. *We need to be around him tonight anyway. A few minutes of relaxing into the connection isn't going to hurt. Leave us alone.*

Blake leaned in and extended his left arm across the back seat, probably well aware of the effect he had on me.

His deep exhale morphed into a sly grin, although his vigilant eyes told me he was anything but carefree. "Adeline, I didn't plan on kissing you tonight. Though I'm not sorry I did. I hope you're not." He lifted my hand and kissed it gently.

"No, I'm not," I said honestly. "But ..."

"I guess that but was inevitable, wasn't it?"

I laughed gently. "My life is a little complicated right now."

"I specialize in complicated." Blake smiled, but the disquiet in his eyes told me he was more aware of what was astir than I was. Curiosity pushed my awareness to tune in for clues.

"Maybe I could help take your mind off whatever's bothering you. At least for tonight."

"I think the champagne is doing a pretty good job of that," I said.

"Maybe I can do better."

Intimacy threaded between us. Blake reached down, slipped off my shoe, and began to massage my foot.

"May be."

My heart melted into a small puddle.

I relaxed into the warmth and electricity that traveled from his hands. There was only comfort, no demands. So unusual.

"You have the magic touch," I assured him.

Not now, Addie. Especially not him. You don't know what you're getting into with him. My head said.

Heart got jumpy and demanded to be heard. *But read him. Really read him. What do you feel? Something to be wary of? Or something to lean into? Explore...*

Feel? Explore? Seriously? How about what you saw? Hello? Was I the only one paying attention when we landed on the ener-

getic sealant? And the ghost who tried to kill you—ever notice that he's always where Blake is? You may need him for tonight, but you still need to protect yourself from him.

My head and heart were always at war these days.

I looked out the window. It was legitimately dark outside, and the lights from traffic signals and passing store-fronts highlighted the streaks of rain on the glass. The lights caught the gold in the chain of Blake's pocket watch that shone in plain view on his waistband. I thought about its history and wondered why it wasn't sealed the way the other items were. Regardless, it meant Blake's story had to be in there somewhere. Somewhere beneath the tragic tale that spoke to me more loudly than anything else. I wondered if I could try to read it again. I let my eyes wander back to his face and I found his watchful eyes.

"That's a handsome pocket watch," I said. "Did you find it here in New York?"

Blake pulled the watch out of the pocket in his waist-band and eyed it proudly. "No, it was a gift."

I nodded and waited for the inevitable, *from my girl-friend/from my wife, but we're separated...* My heart brought out the brick and mortar and began building.

"From my mother, actually. A long time ago."

From his mother.

My heart put away its building materials. Leaned into Blake again.

I laughed. Vintage?"

"It is. Yes."

"I thought so," I said.

His hand intertwined with mine. I searched but there was no ring. No bracelet. The watch was probably my only option if I was going to delve into Blake's secrets. Though on some other day, apparently. I would just have to find the space to wade through the past life that held onto the watch so powerfully.

I winced. That particular past life wasn't one I was anxious to travel through.

"It's gorgeous. I love antique pieces."

"Thank you." His gaze traveled across my face. "Whatever happened at the office—before I found you—are you sure you're okay?"

"It was nothing." I looked down at his pocket watch and physically leaned back from it.

"It's going to get better," he offered. Another current of safety and freedom ran through me.

See? My heart jumped up and down and got caught in my throat.

It will get better when you let me read your pen, my head argued.

"Thanks," I said. "Listen, it might be better if Otto didn't know that we've been out. Together." I decided that if we were going to have anything between us, even for a short while, we would have to keep it quiet. My heart sank a little at my suggestion.

Blake nodded. "I doubt he would mind."

"It's just that Otto is hard to read sometimes and I'm usually more comfortable keeping things low key," I said, worrying about a repeat political nightmare.

"That's fine. We'll keep it out of the firm altogether."

"Sounds good," I said.

My heart bounced gently between disappointment and relief, and finally landed in a plash of confusion.

29

———————

The car arrived at the restaurant and we stepped out of the limo as the doorman held the umbrella for us. Blake held out his hand to help me from the car. As he turned toward the restaurant he left his hand around mine then pulled me close under the umbrella. My body nestled perfectly against his. I dismissed all other concerns to a future moment so I could swim in the protection he gave. If I could bottle the effect he had on me I thought I could rule the world.

We walked into Daniel on East 65th, and his energy shifted. The softness I'd seen in the car disappeared. He became more insulated, more in control, and a surge of power flowed through him. All eyes turned to Blake. Both women and men were mesmerized by him. All were under his spell, just as the other diners had been at Balthazar's.

It wasn't just his looks, though every woman and several men sat poised to move on his command, and I doubted any of them would have resisted him. No, it was something else. Somehow people were ready to do whatever he asked. They wanted to make him happy and seemed almost afraid that he might not be. Elizabeth's mention of Peter's words came to mind: "Whatever Blake wants, Blake gets." My mind stirred with more warnings.

He was clearly pushing everyone in his path, but I'd never seen anybody push like *this* before. It blanketed the entire restaurant. Alexa's abilities had always been limited to one person at a time.

Did he know he was pushing? Or was it an unconscious effort? I could ask, but I risked making a fool of myself. "You've really got the world in the palm of your hand, don't you?"

"Tonight I do." He took my hand in his and gave it a squeeze.

My heart swooned.

We sat in a private room with cream-colored walls, coffered ceilings, and pillars on each side of the doorway. Soft, elegant lighting accented the room with white candlelight. The air was redolent of warm bread and spices, and I realized how hungry I was.

When the maitre d' left, I opened my menu and eyed Blake over the top edge.

He knew I was looking at him. Because without missing a beat he took my hand.

My heart picked up speed, and it knew that the walls I'd been determined to keep between Blake and me were now a crumbled mess.

The wine steward poured us each a glass of the Domaine Serene Pinot Noir from the Willamette Valley Evenstad Reserve. A bewitching bouquet of raspberry, cinnamon, and cherry rose from the glass; the scent wrapped around my head, and effectively silenced it. I welcomed the quiet.

"To new discoveries, acquisitions, and friends," Blake

raised his glass. "May the joy of their company last us at least a lifetime or two."

"Beautiful." I raised my glass and drank to his toast. The complex flavors rolled across my tongue and I wondered if his new discoveries and acquisitions were the Canalettos I'd heard him reference.

We chatted and laughed as if we'd been together for years, as if our relationship were well-rooted into the ground of shared experience, shared memories. And it was, though I couldn't remember yet what those were.

The waiter arrived with my sea bass with syrah sauce, and Blake's red snapper in a salt crust. It was impeccable. As was the rest of our evening. As was Blake.

I tried to be guarded, not impressed. But he knew art the way my father and grandfather had, the way I had been taught to appreciate it. Where art is the language you under-stand, the reality that connects you to the past, the present, and the future—the pathway to understanding the world and its people. The evening flowed like the wine through my glass.

Blake looked at my right hand and stared at my sapphire ring when I twirled the stem of my wine glass. The air hung still in the room. I felt his energy spin off-kilter. He raised my hand and brought it closer.

"I don't remember seeing this before, Addie. It's beautiful."

My heart skipped two beats at the sound of Blake using my nickname. "I have a habit of spinning the stone to the inside of my hand. Too many years of riding mass transit after I moved to New York."

He held my hand gently, and stared at my ring.

"Did someone give it to you?" His face seemed to lose years and vulnerability crept into his features.

"I gave it to myself, actually. Found it in an old antique store in Paris."

Blake nodded and lowered my hand back to a resting place on the table, letting his thumb drag slightly as it left my hand. "It's beautiful. And it suits you."

"Thank you."

Blake continued to gaze at the ring, and I watched his thoughts whirl within.

"It's a Ceylon sapphire. Or so the shop owner said," I offered, trying to rescue him from whatever was pulling at him from inside.

"May I see it?" Gone was the confident man about town. In its place was a man humbled by something I didn't quite understand.

I slipped the ring off my finger and placed it on his outstretched palm.

Maybe he thought another man had given it to me, and he was jealous. Ha! Yeah. No. I doubted Blake was ever jealous. The man had double of everything any man could ever want.

He held it gingerly, staring at it for a long moment before turning it to the inside and reading the inscription. He nodded smoothly and with a degree of certainty.

When he went to return it, I thought he would place the ring in my palm. But instead, he turned my hand and slipped it on my ring finger. The tenderness of the moment washed over me, and the familiar comfort grew between us.

"Does it mean something special to you?" he asked and his eyes found mine.

"Well, there's an inscription inside the band. I don't know if you saw it—"

"I saw it," he said quickly.

I lowered my head and nodded quietly at his sudden

intensity. I wasn't sure where the strength of his focus had come from, but the energy had shifted with his response. I looked up slowly, and met his direct stare.

His eyes were in sharp focus now, looking beneath the surface. The sensation of being seen surprised me. Living in a house of intuitives, I had grown up with that feeling on a daily basis.

But rarely did I experience it in my everyday life. It's kind of like a punch to the gut if you're not expecting it. What he saw in me I didn't know, and I had a sudden empathy for anyone who had been on the receiving end of my knowing looks. I searched for words to keep things moving and hoped he didn't see me for who I really was. I wasn't ready to watch him run just yet.

"Well, it reminds me to believe in the possibility of true love. To have hope that love could survive the test of time. I guess that must sound silly these days—"

"Not at all," he said.

I held his gaze, and my soul passed beyond the confines of my head and heart to be with him for just a moment, a timeless moment.

"Have you ever received impressions from the ring? As in—psychic impressions?" Blake asked.

I felt my mouth fall open. My insides suddenly felt slippery. Greasy. Like important organs might just slip out.

Blake's stare became magnetic. "It's called psychometry. Some people can gather information from an object through touch." He said it as though this could be a positive thing. A compliment, even.

"Yes. I've heard of it." I couldn't look away. Couldn't even blink. This was a bad neighborhood that we had just wandered into. "But, no. No impressions."

"Are you sure?"

"Am I sure?" I finally managed to pull my eyes away and I attempted to mock his question. But I just sounded shifty. Definitely guilty. "No, I—I mean, yes, I'm sure. What a funny thing to ask." I picked up my glass of wine, but my hand shook. I worked hard to look nonchalant while I slid the glass along the tablecloth in my direction, then used two hands to pick it up.

Blake shrugged. "It's a vintage piece. Vintage always has a story. It might be interesting."

I couldn't bring myself to look at him. So I looked at the wine as I swirled it in my glass. "I don't really know about those things." I desperately wanted to appear calm and take another sip of wine. But now both hands were quivering. So, I gave my head a subtle shake to move the hair off of my face, and I smiled at him, instead. My lips remained sealed in that smile.

Blake scooted his chair toward me, sidled up against my face as if he were going to share a secret. "I know," he whispered.

I swallowed against my closing throat.

Blake pulled back to look at me.

I shook my head. "I don't...know what you mean."

"I know about your abilities."

I kept my face still while I scrambled through the time we'd shared, through our time at the gallery. *What had I done? How did he know?*

"It's okay. I think it's wonderful, actually. I have family who can do things like that—so it's not hard for me to recognize it in someone else." His smile was welcoming. Kind, even. Nothing to fear was the impression he gave.

I nodded and crossed my arms. I might not be able to stop myself from falling in love with him, but I wasn't going to make the same mistake twice.

"You must be gifted as well, then," I said, trying to turn the tables.

Blake gave a shrug. "I like to think I have a gift for persuasion."

"I've heard it's called pushing."

Blake leaned back in mock surprise. "So, you do know about these things."

"I read—a lot."

And then *he* happened. I felt his presence just outside the room. The waiter entered through the doorway with our desserts in glass dishes on a small tray. I watched the ghost extend its invisible hand and he upended the tray toward the marble floor in the hallway.

Glass burst into pieces on the hall floor, and the ghost's laugh trailed away.

Blake turned and scanned the general area. "You've met our dearly departed friend, too, haven't you? And I'm guessing he wasn't your first?"

His comment kicked the air out of my lungs. I calmly looked over Blake's shoulder and waved at the Italian waiter, who was bellowing apologies and wouldn't stop until we forgave him. It was just the moment I needed to put myself together. Where these questions came from I didn't know. Though I decided I didn't have to tell him. Or anyone. He didn't really know anything.

"I don't know anything about the supernatural, ghosts, or otherwise. I'm sorry."

"No, I'm sorry. I just thought—" Blake took my right hand and twisted the ring around my finger. I heard his voice, but a dark memory of baby-faced Jeremy placing my former engagement ring on my finger hit to the front of my mind. He asks me to trust him with my heart, and my life.

Then there's his betrayal, the crash and burn of my career, my life. And that did it. I shook my head to clear it.

"I'd better get home, Blake. Why don't I take a cab? I'm sure you have someplace you need to be this evening."

"No, I'll drop you." Blake waved his hand, and the restaurant staff flew into action. The check appeared, the table was cleared, and we were quickly on our way.

I pulled away from him just before we walked through the revolving door, but once inside the glass I felt his hand on my back. His thumb moved against my skin, and I felt my eyes glaze over.

The limo promptly drove around as we stepped onto the sidewalk. I noticed Blake putting his phone back in his pocket.

Once in the car I crossed my legs and bumped up against his hand, which was resting on his knee. His little finger twitched against my crossed leg.

Whatever the reason for his curiosity, at least I'd learned from my mistakes. I'd done what I should have done with Patti and Centaurian so long ago. I'd laughed at the suggestion that I was psychic. I denied it.

I surprised myself by making no effort to move my leg away.

I felt captivated by Blake. Captive, even. I had too many doubts to pursue anything with him, but I couldn't find the willpower to let go of how I felt about him.

He was like an unfinished story that begged for more.

The unending rain pelted against the roof and the windows and a low rumble of thunder gave notice to the frustration that still hung in the air. The storm continued to build.

I raised my head, looked away from my ring to thank Blake for dinner, and found his face far closer than I anticipated. Before I could think his fingers touched my chin and he brought my face to his.

His kiss was so tender and slow, so passionate and strong. The scent of his skin ran straight through my senses and down into my heart. He pulled back slowly, his gaze mesmerizing.

The rain continued like a shroud, protecting us from the outside world, obliterating distractions. I breathed him in, fascinated by his feral look as he leaned in again.

Our connection—it wasn't just his kiss, there was something inside of him pulling at me.

He drew my hair behind my shoulders and grinned his all-too-perfect smile that sent me traveling into other worlds with him. I smiled through the tension, and ran my fingertips along the strong frame of his face. In this moment he was mine to touch, to experience. I loved the feel of his subtle beard against the pads of my fingers.

His normal guard, which kept me from seeing too much of him, dropped and a vivid insight burst open, an unexpected doorway pulling me into all things Blake. It rose up through my hand like a private confession, piercing the magic spell that had brought us together. My mind flew through the portal and I prepared myself to see steamy scenes between Blake and other women, perhaps in his gallery, perhaps with the brunette I'd met earlier in the day. But what I saw was not at all what I expected.

Blake sits at a long conference table with three other men, each dressed in white starched button-downs with ties and suit coats or blazers. The room's canned lighting creates dark and cold pyramid shadows on the solid gray walls, the air is thick and vault-like still around them.

"Remember. For as long as you're a part of this, no one can know you're involved," the man with the brown hair says. "If anyone finds out, well, let's just say it seriously limits your life expectancy. And once you're in, there's no out until this over."

Blake nods in return, some mixture of fear and rage flickering across his eyes.

My mind chose that exact moment to wake up and panic and fury warred against my heart. This man wasn't who he pretended to be—he wasn't the sophisticated dealer here to broker art. I pulled my hand back.

"I can't—I can't do this."

"Addie," he said.

I looked out the window—the limo was parked in front of my home. "I can't." I opened the car door as he reached for me. I ran down the wet sidewalk to the outer door of my townhome in record time. I didn't dare to look back.

30

———

I stood under the burgundy awning at the arched entryway of my townhome and tried to catch my breath. Rain knocked against the canvas and the engine of the limo was still running. Part of me needed to waltz through the doorway and never look back.

"He's not who he said he was," I said as I stared at the lock on the door. "Whatever he's involved in, I don't want any part of it. I can't make room in my life for people who use energetic sealants, who are followed by ghosts, and who run around pretending to be someone they aren't. I'm keeping my life simple."

Then I realized. I didn't have my purse.

I spun around— "Oh! Blake..."

He chuckled, grabbed my arm to keep me from falling off my high heels, and I held on to the outside of his arm to steady myself.

"I love that we keep meeting like this," he said with a wide grin. There wasn't any sign of his needing to convince or control. There was only quiet confidence, as if nothing was wrong. As if he was content to let me fly away if that's what I needed to do. Despite my better judgment, little bits of peace began to warm the layer of icy fear around my heart and mind.

"I didn't know you were there." I was stunned to have the emotional space. And he wasn't dancing to hide his secrets, or pushing me to reveal mine, which was so uncharacteristic of any man I'd known.

"I believe this is yours." He handed me my metallic clutch and held my gaze. My heart was stricken, and my mind was filled with fierce warnings.

"You know—I, um... Actually, thank you. For a really lovely evening," I extended my hand for a handshake.

Blake looked at my hand like I had just offered him a duck or something equally strange.

He took my hand, turned it over, and laid his lips on the inside of my wrist.

Then he brought my arm around his waist and slowly pulled me to his chest. His mouth opened slightly, and I thought he was going to say something. Instead, his hand cupped my face, his thumb dragged softly against my cheek, and he kissed me.

When he finally pulled away he smiled, leaving me with that one last tender kiss. I stood there, watching him go, until finally, I went inside.

31

Blake was silent while the car pulled away from Adeline's residence, he ran his hand through his hair in frustration. He watched her through the tinted glass, standing under the building's outdoor lights, planted on the sidewalk where he left her, until she finally drifted inside.

It wasn't hard for him to see into the future with Adeline. If he wasn't careful, she would build new walls around her heart. New barriers of distrust that he would have to find a way through. That could be a huge step backward.

"The timing isn't right," he said aloud. She wasn't ready to trust him with her secrets..

He let out a long, rocky breath. Felt the blood pulse through his veins in a tempo all its own. He knew he'd never find any peace until he could hold her in his arms without any reservations between them, and know that she was completely his. But how and when she would get there, he didn't know. Blake slammed his fist against the armrest of the door.

Once home he sat in the burgundy leather of the quiet

library in his pre-war penthouse, staring at the paintings that hung on the walls. These framed pieces were among his very favorites. Sitting with them was like visiting with old friends. And friends were good company when you couldn't sleep.

He sipped his Scotch from the crystal rocks glass, one of an antique set his mother had sent him as a house-warming gift. Even though she hadn't wanted him to move to New York, she was ever gracious. He enjoyed the slight burn as it poured down his throat, felt the warmth as it spread through his body.

Blake stared at the largest piece of art, a gilt-framed portrait that hung over the fireplace. He'd stumbled upon it years ago while strolling through a Paris flea market with his mother. Although only a teenager at the time, he was already gifted at seeing past lives. When he saw the woman's face in the painting, a memory awoke in his soul. She was once the love of his life, and he knew she would be again. That was the moment that started the searching. And the waiting.

The past life scene played out in his mind, as it had so many times throughout his life—how he lay dying in her arms from a fatal gunshot to the chest. Then, with his last breath, he promised her that no one would keep them apart, that he'd find her again.

Now he finally had.

It took only a glance, and he knew her immediately. The color of her hair was lighter, and the style was different. He had expected that. Styles changed with the times. But he didn't expect everything else to be quite so...exactly as it was in the portrait. Her light blue eyes with the white starburst around the pupil, her smooth, ceramic-like skin, her thin frame and slender arms, even the outline of her face. She was an exact replica of the woman in the picture. She took his breath away.

Blake had always known he would find her one day, though he wondered how he would recognize her. However, Addie Montgomery walked right into his life bearing every possible clue of their last life together, obliterating the necessity of any guesswork.

Even the ring was identical. Blake studied the ring in the painting as it graced the left hand of the woman he'd once nicknamed Sassy. The sapphire and diamond ring was the biggest surprise. Somehow, Addie had managed to find it again, which gave him hope.

BLAKE WAITED FOR HER CALL. It wasn't scheduled, but he knew it was coming. He'd missed two from her so far, and knew the third would be coming today.

When his cell phone finally buzzed, he checked the caller ID: France. It was her. "Maman, what are you doing awake at this hour?" Even though he wasn't remotely surprised to hear from her.

"It's not terribly early here. Besides, I had a dream the other night."

Blake knew that at her hour in the morning she would be wrapped in a blanket, sipping freshly pressed coffee and curled up in her favorite oversized chair. He heard a bird chirping in the background and knew the doors to her garden were open. Inside was her least favorite place to be, so she did whatever she could to bring nature in.

He waited patiently for the other shoe to drop. His mother's dreams and insights had never allowed any space for secrets between them.

"You've met her, haven't you?"

Blake laughed softly. He'd known this was coming, and he waited a beat before answering. She already knew the answer, of course.

"I have." He could almost hear her smiling on the other end of the line.

"And?"

Blake let out a long, heavy sigh. "She doesn't remember me."

32

———

A warm bath did little to calm me after my night with Blake.

3 a.m. and I was still awake. The feel of his kiss lingering on my skin.

He wasn't who he said he was. And he was involved in something that reeked of the underworld. The information ran in circles on my brain, and I began to wonder if I would sleep at all.

But at 4 a.m. I began to feel a little drowsy, and at 4:30 my body finally gave in to sleep.

I feel him before I see him. He peeks around the corner with a broad smile and leans against the doorway to my bedroom—dashing as always in his cream-colored suit.

I curl against the coolness of my pillow and smile at him. "Hi."

"Hi, yourself." He smiles back at me, and I melt. The air conditioner clicks on, and I assume it's the heat of our chemistry that sets it off.

"You're making a habit of this," I tease.

"My mother raised me to have good habits, Sassy." He

crosses his arms casually, and one leg over the other. "And *you* would be a very hard habit to break."

"I hope you won't."

"You hope I won't what?"

"I hope you won't ever break this habit. I don't know what I'd do if I didn't have you to look forward to." A heaviness gathers in my chest. Several cars drive by, and I mentally time the pace of their tires swooshing through puddles.

"I told you I'm here for you now. I'll never leave you again. Don't you believe me?"

"I have my doubts. I have a lot of doubts these days." My thoughts wander, and I think of Blake. I feel guilty for thinking of him while I'm with Jack.

"Well, let's talk about that, shall we?" He pushes off the doorjamb and walks toward me. I lay very still, fearing that he'll disappear. When he sits on the bed next to me and the mattress sags under his weight, I'm flooded with joy and relief.

"You're really here, aren't you?" I reach out and run my hand along his suit-covered thigh.

"I'm always with you."

"Not always," I correct, sadness twists inside me.

"What do you want?" His fingertips brush the outline of my face.

"I want you here. I want you with me," I fuss at him.

"So what's the problem? I'm with you now."

"Really?" I'm getting frustrated. I don't want to be with any man but him, but being with him wasn't a real option. "Maybe you're with me in spirit form or you're with me in another time, but you're not with me in the present, Jack. I want you with me now!"

"You can have that. Whenever you want."

The calm sincerity in his tone takes me by surprise, and I soften. "Tell me what I need to do to make that happen."

"You need to remember." He kisses me, his breath pure. "Can you do that for me?"

I nod and the alarm on my phone chimes in the background.

I SAT up and looked around. I was alone again.

"Remember?" I fell back down and put my hands over my face. "What does that mean?"

33

When the cell phone rang Otto hesitated. He didn't want to be distracted this morning. But something pushed him to answer the phone, that little urge from his sixth sense that he had been taught never to ignore.

"I still can't find it," the voice said abruptly.

"Philippe—"

"I've retraced my steps and looked under everything. My notes aren't there. I'm leaving the warehouse now."

"Do you realize what you've done?"

"Yeah, but I'm sure you'll tell me anyway. Look, I can't find it. Why don't you just get one of your people to tell us which ones are the forgeries?"

"And how will that work, Philippe, when they realize they're admiring an authentic Manet? Or Renoir? What do you think they'll do then? These pieces aren't exactly unrecognizable in the art community."

There was only silence on the other end of the line.

Otto threw his phone across the room. He'd planned this

heist a lifetime ago, pulled it off flawlessly, kept the art safely hidden from the FBI. And Philippe managed to screw everything up by losing a single piece of paper.

34

"Careful," Blake said. "Move the packing material out of the way."

"How did you come by these pieces again?" Thomas asked.

"Lillian Van der Burke. She left these for me in her will," Blake answered. "She was close with my mother. She and her husband were huge collectors. Their favorite find was an obscure piece. Always looking for an undiscovered treasure." Blake's focus drifted and he sipped from the porcelain doppio espresso cup and examined the two canvases that he thought were original Canalettos.

"Did you see them the last time they were in New York?" Blake asked, distracted.

"Briefly, yes. But I remember them."

Despite the excitement of the arrival of the paintings, Blake figured this wouldn't be his last double espresso this morning. With too much on his mind, sleep had not come easily for him the night before, and when it finally did it was short-lived.

He stood several feet away from the canvases, but even at

this distance he thought they were authentic. There were the evidential signs of the artist's naturalistic details, his color choices, the subject matter—and, of course, they had been found in Venice. Sometimes, though, Blake just felt it in his bones. Despite all his years of study and training in the art of detecting a forgery, sometimes his body knew before the proof could be revealed.

Blake squatted and looked closely at the details and smiled at the memory of Lillian, her Christmas and birthday cards, her emails and phone calls. She always saw the best in him. Wanted the best for him. After her passing, he had found the handwritten note she left for him:

There are two of them. You'll find them in the attic. If they are what we think they are, you should use them for your escape, to create a new life for yourself. Let the past be done.

"These pieces were tucked away in their attic in Venice."

Thomas shook his head. "They never knew?"

"They may have known. Though it would have been like Lillian to gift something extravagant and unexpected. Especially if she thought she was helping someone."

Thomas stood quietly.

Unable to summon any enthusiasm for the Canalettos just then, Blake turned solemnly and walked back to his office, stopping in the kitchen to make another double espresso.

"What are you going to do with them?" Thomas asked once they were in Blake's office.

Honestly? I don't know."

"I thought you might be lining up some bait for Otto," Thomas suggested. He crossed the room and sat on the soft leather couch.

"Yeah, I thought about that, too," Blake said. "But I'm not convinced it would work."

"What did Lillian want you to do with the Canalettos?" Thomas asked.

Blake raked his hands through his hair and worked to get hold of his rage. He picked up his espresso and stared out the window. "She wanted me to use them to make a fresh start, to get out of New York and away from Otto. Maybe move back to Paris."

"So why not just drop all of this and go?"

"Because someone made an unscheduled appearance in my life."

"Which is what you've always wanted," Thomas offered.

Blake ignored him and downed half of the espresso.

"You know, sometimes things don't work out exactly the way we plan."

"Except that I never lose at this game." Blake glared at Thomas. "In all the years you've known me, name one time, when it really counted, that I failed to persuade someone to do what I wanted them to do... My mother aside."

Thomas looked down.

"I'm up to my eyeballs in this now, and if I don't find a way to shut him down for good, I won't be the only one who'll get taken out. It'll just be a matter of time."

"So, you won't leave..."

"I can't. Not now that she's here. I can't leave her in Otto's reach."

Thomas nodded, the pain of conflict crossing his face.

"Any way to get her away from him?" Thomas asked.

"I tried to warn Addie about Otto on the first day we met. But she wasn't interested in hearing it. She's completely enamored with him. So it's not hard for Otto to fool her."

"Maybe there's some way to get Addie to wake up and see what Otto is up to." Thomas stared at the ground and seemed to be searching for ideas.

"I tried last night to—" Blake stopped.

"Tried last night to what?"

"Just to get her to see, to be aware. Though she's pretty attached to her own agenda right now. Even if I could find a way to get her to see who he is, if we ran, the only life we would have where we could be truly safe would be a life of exile. A life in hiding, always looking over our shoulders. I can't ask her to live that kind of constrained existence. That goes against the very reasons why I'm here. I never should have come here."

"Then you never would have found her, Blake."

"And a lot of good that does if I can't find a way out of this trap." Blake's anger spiked again.

Thomas indulged his nervous habit of repeatedly stroking his beard.

The text alarm went off on Blake's phone.

"Speak of the devil."

"And the devil appears. What does he want?"

"To meet this morning and talk about some new opportunity," Blake said. Ice shivered down his spine.

Thomas disappeared through the door and Blake looked out the window again. He prided himself on his undeniable ability to get people to feel what he wanted them to. With concentration and will, he could inspire them to be frightened enough to run, passionate enough to fall in love, or guilty enough to reveal their sins. He could easily motivate someone to believe that his plans were in their best interests. Of course, it wasn't a slam-dunk with everyone. And Otto had a way of rebuffing his efforts, meeting them with an equal force that caused Blake's plans to fall flat. He had his suspicions about why that was, but the problem remained.

"The thought of her in his office every day," Blake said

while he studied the skyline. "She has no idea what's going on there and she's walking right into the middle of it. No matter what I've tried to do to take him out, nothing works." The double-walled espresso glass shattered in Blake's hand, sending glass and the remains of the espresso exploding into the air.

35

It took forty-five minutes for his limo to take him from his gallery to Otto's offices, but to Blake it felt like one long moment. He downed several ounces from a chilled water bottle while he stared out the window. Then he waited to feel the hatred that always motivated him when he was on his way to Otto's offices. But it was only barely there.

He'd like to think that the vendetta he'd held against Otto was finally slipping away, bit by thorny bit. Though he knew better. Knew it was just being temporarily iced over by a sick feeling that something bad was about to happen. He tried to let that threat motivate him. Though it seemed insurmountable.

Otto really was too good at his game to be caught. Karma was apparently the only force that could take him down the way he deserved.

As his limo pulled into the parking deck, Blake remembered his mother's pleadings. *Why waste your life chasing an aging art thief?* Not wanting to see her son in harm's way, she had been against his trying to trap a dangerous criminal.

That was unnecessarily dangerous, and she had a bad feeling about it. Only a fool walked into a lion's den, she'd told him.

Blake entered through the back entrance, each step of his Berluti shoes echoing while he walked down the empty hallway. He stood in front of the silver service elevator, looked at his reflection. And that's when he saw it in his own eyes. He was scared. Now that Addie was in the picture, he'd gone from fearless to frightened. Something bad *was* going to happen. He could feel it.

Blake adjusted the fit of his blazer while the elevator climbed the levels. He wondered if there was any way he could get her away from Otto before everything went to hell. He might still have a chance, but he would have to work fast. If Otto didn't know about her yet, it was only a matter of time.

36

———————

Blake arrived in the outer lobby of Otto's office, raised his guard, and reinforced it several times before he walked in. He sat at the rosewood table and immediately felt a chill cross the back of his neck. He knew it was the ghost. He knew who the ghost was. It wasn't a surprise that he showed up when the two of them were together. Blake raised his shoulders against the coldness, then looked around briefly for anything made of glass.

"So, what's this about a new opportunity?" Blake asked.

Oblivious to his shadowy visitor, Otto placed a book in the bookcase, and then leaned against the mahogany shelving. The coldness in his eyes wasn't lost on Blake. Otto was working a plan. "Word on the street is that the pieces from the Isabella Gardner Museum heist are hitting the market."

Blake paused to give the news the respect it deserved. "The Isabella Gardner heist?"

"I have an arrangement with the seller to see the pieces next week. I want you to look at them. Help me decide if they're authentic."

"How many of the pieces?"

"All of them. So I'm told."

"All thirteen pieces—Rembrandt, Degas, Vermeer, Manet—*all* of them?"

Otto nodded quietly. The rest of his body as still as a snake lying in wait.

"I think it's the deal of the century," Blake said.

"If they're real. We won't know for sure until we see them."

Blake nodded. "Where are they?"

"Here. In New York. We'll head out to see them as soon as I bring in the last team member."

"What other team member?"

"I'm going to bring Adeline in on this one."

Blake's insides jarred like broken glass. "Adeline? Why would you bring *her* in?"

"Insurance. This deal is too big to blow. Is there some reason why you wouldn't want Adeline involved in this?"

"Well, she hardly has any experience. For another, I don't think she'd do it."

Otto walked across the room and sat down at the table with Blake, like he was a friend. "I've seen the way you look at her."

"For work, Otto. *Your* work."

Otto smiled, but it wasn't warm, and it wasn't evident in his words. "I've seen the two of you together. I don't guess you're spending all of your time discussing work."

"I thought we agreed I should stay close to her?"

"We agreed you should pretend to be close to her. I have my doubts that you're still pretending."

"I must be doing a good job, then. Appearance is every-thing," Blake said.

Otto adjusted the cuffs of his sleeves. "You might want to

be careful, though. There's a lot you don't know about her," he said.

Blake sat still, his anger silently eating away at his heart. "If you want my help on your projects, Otto, you ought to think twice about telling me how to handle them."

"She's not one of your typical women. That's all I'm saying."

Blake watched control and power dance behind Otto's eyes. It was his favorite thing to fight for.

The chill in the room had become so intense Blake thought he might be able to see his breath, and a familiar uneasy feeling crept up from within. Blake took a quick glance around the room, but as usual, saw nothing amiss. Though he could feel him. And the ghost was always around when he and Otto were together. Listening. Watching. Almost as if he were planning something.

"Then why don't you tell me what I'm getting into here." Blake pushed out of his chair and walked across the room.

"Adeline has a...unique talent for picking out forgeries," Otto said.

Blake's temper shortened his breathing. His mind moved like lightning. Otto was dancing way too close to the truth.

Blake noticed Otto's eyes scanning his features for a toehold, a weakness to hook and drag him by. He deliberately slowed and lengthened his breathing, shoved his anger behind his mask. "She doesn't have enough experience to discern a forgery from the real thing. Much less have any talent at it."

"It's more of a hidden talent. The kind that doesn't come with training," Otto said.

"I'm not sure what you mean by 'hidden talent,' but I doubt her talent could rival my experience and trained eye. Plus, the fewer people involved in this, the safer you'll be."

Blake pushed hard for Otto to back down and to lose interest in involving Adeline. But he felt Otto deflect his suggestions as offhandedly as shooing a fly from his lunch.

"Well, I suspect it's one of those things you have to see to believe. It's not so much a skill as it is a gift. Something you're born with. She sees."

A loud rushing sound flooded Blake's ears and he began the speech just the way he'd practiced it. He could barely hear the words he spoke, but he'd planned them out ahead of time. Just in case Otto stumbled across the unfindable truth.

"I don't trust that new age psychic baloney, Otto. It's a crutch for the unintelligent." Blake sat confidently and crossed his legs. "There's no reason to have us both there. She's a great researcher, but my skill is what's needed for this job. You need to go with tried and true on this one."

Otto strolled away and sat behind his desk, and the position of authority wasn't lost on Blake. "It's not baloney. She's like the woman I told you about. The one I knew years ago, who helped me with several black market deals. She went with me to the purchase meetings and was able to tell me if the art was authentic or a forgery, whether the deal was a good one or a set-up. We made several million on some of those deals."

"How could you possibly know that Adeline has this same type of 'hidden talent'?" Blake cast his most dubious expression.

"Because I've seen it in action." Otto gave a quick glance at the painting of the *Madonna and Child* hanging on the wall. He took his phone out of his pocket and sent a text. "The gods are shining on me, Blake. They've delivered another seer right into my hands." He took a long pause as Blake stared at him. "These pieces from the Gardner

Museum theft are only going up for sale now that the limitations for prosecuting the thieves have expired. Those pieces are worth several *hundred* million. Of course that also means that forgeries will be flooding the market. But I can't lose with someone like Adeline in my corner. We can all make a fortune on this deal."

Blake watched Otto studying his face, like he was trying to read him. Although Blake was the better master at that game. He could be unreadable whenever he wanted to be.

Otto broke the stare and looked out the window. "I think she would be the perfect addition to our team."

Otto's words were delivered as a suggestion, yet Blake knew they were a threat. He could join the effort and help Otto get what he wanted, or Otto would move him out of the way. He knew Otto wouldn't let anything come between him and his newest golden goose.

Blake didn't have a card to play. But now he was more determined than ever to see Otto burn in hell.

37

———

I passed Otto's office on my way to Ellen's, delinquent paperwork in hand. The testosterone and fury exuding through his office door made me scurry. I didn't know what was going on in there, and I didn't want to know. I promptly put a random song in my head to keep me from picking up on anything. Unfortunately, it was a commercial jingle, and I figured I might need surgery to have it removed.

Ellen's office was empty and her door was uncharacteristically open, so I walked in and looked for a vacant spot on her desk to drop the paperwork. Her desk was full of papers and projects, and I hesitated to put anything else on it for fear it would disappear. The last thing I wanted was for Ellen to have a new reason to harass me.

Post-It Note. That's what I needed. And a paperclip. I walked behind her desk and noticed the small drawer to the right was slightly open. I reached for it, pulled it open. Pushed aside a few butterscotch candies, lifted a pad of Post-It Notes and a few colored paperclips that were looped together. If she found me digging through her desk she'd have me publicly drawn and quartered. And in New York she could probably get an audience for that. I figured I only had a couple of minutes, so I worked fast to disconnect the clips.

Not that I was looking, because I wasn't. But I had left the drawer open a good distance, and photographs always caught my eye. There it was, in the back of her drawer, the edge of an older photo peeking out from under a few envelopes. I couldn't resist. I had planned to know more about Ellen anyway. I lifted the envelopes and pulled on what turned out to be three photographs. Each were of Ellen and my grandfather in a tropical setting. In the first one they both smiled relaxed, loving smiles at the camera, my grandfather standing behind Ellen with his arms wrapped around her.

The next was more candid, and they laughed together, Ellen looking down with a wide smile. In the third they were kissing. Lip to lip. No mistaking what their relationship was when you looked at their embrace.

Did I dare? He was my grandfather. I touched the face of the photo and their feelings for one another flowed through my heart.

She loved him. Truly loved him. She knew when this photo was taken that there would never be another man for her. It was him or no one. He loved her, too, even though he hadn't meant to fall in love with her. His wife had left him, for a while or forever he didn't yet know. And in his wife's absence his love affair with Ellen had blossomed.

Without questioning the astonishing information I received, I allowed my fingers to touch the next picture. This was a trip they had taken on a whim, a trip to Mexico to be alone with each other. It was a place where they no longer had to hide their feelings, and even so, Ellen spent most of the trip worrying that the dream would end too soon.

I lifted my fingers off the photo. I stared at their faces for a minute longer, and slipped the photos back into the side drawer under the envelopes where I had found them.

Closing the drawer, I looked at it for just a moment. She hadn't set out to fall in love. It had happened naturally, growing out of her admiration and respect for him and the pleasure of sharing their common interests. I knew what it was like to lose someone you loved and the pain of seeing him with another woman. Even though I loved Grandmother Grace dearly, and was sure this situation couldn't have been easy for her, I understood Ellen more clearly now and why she regarded me with a little extra venom. Like so many others, she worked to keep me at a distance, afraid that I would know and reveal her secrets.

I pulled a Post-It off the pad and wrote Ellen a note about the paperwork. I thought about Grandmother Grace leaving my grandfather at that point in their relationship and wondered what that had been about. I knew she had been fairly wild in her younger days, and wasn't surprised that I hadn't known about her leaving. The women in our family had so many secrets.

I looked up and jumped when I saw Ellen standing in her own doorway. I did a lightning-quick two-step away from her desk. "Ellen...I was just leaving the signature pages you asked for."

"Adeline, you—" Ellen was stopped by a text on her phone, and we both looked out the door as Blake stormed from Otto's office and through his private lobby without as much as a glance toward us.

With Blake's temper driving him forward like that, I

didn't think I would be seeing him today, which made me feel more than a little sad.

"I need to get this, actually." Ellen waved her phone and backed up in the direction of Otto's office.

"Oh. Sure." I hurried out of her office and paused at the outer doorway that led to the hall. I looked to the right and saw that Blake's path had left an energetic trail of heat and anger that hung in the middle of the hallway. I followed it, even though there was no logic in doing so. My heart simply ached to be with him.

But after two steps I stopped myself. I turned the other way and walked slowly to my office.

38

———

Ellen eyed Otto behind his desk when she tentatively entered his office. "You needed to see me? I got your text."

"Oh, Ellen, I didn't think you'd be here so early this morning. Come in and shut the door."

"I was just catching up on some things before next week's auction—"

"I'd like you to have this painting moved into the vault either late tonight or tomorrow before we open for business." Otto pointed at the painting of *Madonna and Child*. "From now on, only the replicas are to be exhibited in the office. Originals will be held in the vault until they're moved out."

Ellen's stomach clenched. A thread of fear snaked its way up, effectively closing her throat. Otto was fanatical about surrounding himself with the best of the best. If he was putting the replicas up, something serious must be going on.

"I won't be able to get the movers here until tomorrow, but I'll take care of it."

Otto smiled reassuringly at Ellen, then walked around his desk and dialed a number on his cell phone. "In fact, after you put that one away, why don't you bring out an entirely new piece?"

"Of course. Which one would you like?"

"Surprise me." Otto crooked the phone against his shoulder, opened the small drawer on the left side of his desk, and popped a small pill into his mouth.

Ellen walked to her office, sat at her desk, and closed her eyes. She could spot the telltale signs. She could see it in his eyes, feel it in his mood. He had a new plan he was about to put in play. The feel of it was eerily reminiscent of earlier plans that had gone wrong.

She remembered when Otto had met someone whose knowledge and passion for art rivaled his own, someone who had a gift for seeing things that other people couldn't. Someone he fell in love with from the near moment he met her.

Now, as before, Ellen could see the characters and situations begin to take shape. She could feel it.

The past was beginning to repeat itself.

39

D riven purely by blind fury and adrenaline, Blake plowed his way through the firm, didn't stop until he reached his chauffeured car. "Get me to the gallery," he barked. "Now!"

He pulled a set of keys from his front pocket, unlocked the side console, and took out the cell phone he used for only one purpose. He tapped the call memory icon and redialed the only number that had come in or gone out on that number.

"Yes?"

"I need to see you. Now. At my office. I'm on my way."

BLAKE WATCHED William Calhoun enter his office with a gait that nearly swaggered under his considerable intellect. His caramel-colored eyes took in every detail of the office—including the broken glass on the floor at the far end of the room—but revealed nothing. It was this ability to notice, and yet pretend as though he hadn't, that allowed him to navigate the undercover art world with ease.

"Blake," William said with an outstretched hand.

"Good to see you. Thanks for coming in."

"Hand okay?" William asked as Blake winced.

"Yeah, just sliced it on some glass."

Blake guided William to the seating area as Mira waltzed in with two white demitasse cups of fresh espresso and placed them on the coffee table in front of them. Blake watched William discipline himself and look away when she bent over.

"Thank you, Mira." Blake gave her a reproving look for flirting with William. "Bring me a Band-Aid or something, would you?" He turned his palm up and examined the cut.

"So, what's on the table, Blake?" William said after Mira had left. He took a calculated sip of the espresso and watched Blake over the rim. William's no-bull attitude swam closer to the surface than usual.

"Too much time and not enough results, William. I'm getting out."

William gave a slow nod. "I see." He grabbed several thick file folders from his soft-sided briefcase then dropped them on the coffee table with a heavy *slap*. He flipped one of them open and pulled out an 8x10 black and white photo and slid it to Blake. "I'm guessing this is the reason you're out?"

Blake swallowed hard when he looked at a photo of him and Addie walking into Daniel with their arms around each other. He looked William dead in the eye. "Does it matter?"

"If she's the reason you're doing this, then I'd say it matters because you're probably about to get yourself killed."

Mira walked in with several bandage options on a

round, silver tray. She placed it on the coffee table, eyed the photo, and left.

"If anything I'd say my focus has been rejuvenated." Blake reminded himself of his personal policy against pushing friends. "It's sharper than it has been in a long time."

"You sure about that? My guys shot you and Adeline going into the restaurant that night, not because we were tailing you, but because we were following Otto. I'm guessing you missed seeing him at the restaurant."

Blake dropped his eyes on the photo. The fact that William already knew Adeline's name wasn't lost on him, and an icy feeling washed down the back of his neck. The reality that he had missed Otto meant that he probably *was* on his way to getting himself killed. "No, I didn't see him that night."

"Well, I doubt he missed you. Look, Blake." William leaned back onto the couch, crossed one leg over the other. "I've been chasing Otto Albrecht for nearly half my life, with nothing to show for it but a bunch of dead ends. And I'm not the only one.

"You, however, are the only contact we've ever had that's this far into his operation, and to stay alive while doing it. That's saying something. But if you screw it up now, everything any of us has done up until this point will be nothing but a wasted effort. Those paintings will disappear forever. Now is not the time to get out. We're too close. I can feel it."

Blake stared at William. He hadn't realized they had another operative on this job, much less that they had died doing it. He kept his voice steady. "I don't think Otto is a puzzle that can be solved. At least not on the Gardner theft."

William nodded with calculated patience, taking in the city view that was available to him from the couch. "I've been on the FBI Art Crime Team long enough to know that no one is the perfect criminal forever. Eventually, they all screw up."

"Otto may be the exception on that one," Blake said. He knew William's temper must have been on fire under the cool exterior. He'd promised William he would find the paintings and take Otto down in the process. At the time he'd thought he could. But things had changed.

"Did I ever tell you I was a part of a sting where we almost nailed Otto and his former partner—what was her name?" William patted the couch leather, then snapped his fingers. "Carolena. That's it," he said. "She had an ability to spot forgeries like I've never seen before. They made millions together. Chose only authentic pieces on the black market, sold them for a king's ransom. I've never seen anyone beat the system like those two."

Blake crossed his arms. "No, I didn't know that."

"We came this close to nabbing him," William measured a half-inch with his finger and thumb in the air. "I had a portrait by Rembrandt from a private collector that we marketed as stolen. Got the meeting with Otto, who brought Carolena. She spent all of four seconds going over the painting before whispering something to him. They left the meeting without doing the deal, and I never could get another meeting with Otto after that. Somehow she knew we were setting him up. I don't know how. But she knew.

"When she ducked out on their relationship, Otto quit that game. He couldn't do it without her."

"That's when he started the forgeries," Blake said.

"He still does them?"

"Not as much as he used to. Though yes, when something catches his eye. When a client offers him something unique to either appraise or sell, he has it replicated. He keeps the real thing or sells it, and the client gets the forgery."

"Have you figured out who does the forgeries for him?" William asked.

"Honestly, I think Otto does them himself."

"Really," William said like another piece of Otto's puzzle fell into place for him.

"He has quite a few of the forgeries in the vaults downstairs. I recently went through the last of the vaults—doesn't look like he's moved a piece in some time. And the Gardner pieces aren't there," Blake said to the unasked question.

"I figured he wasn't that stupid." William looked at the ceiling and stroked his neck. "But one can always hope. Stupidity is usually a pretty safe gamble with most criminals."

Blake watched William's piercing stare and felt the room go inexplicably quiet. "Otto may not be stupid; however, he's not as careful as he used to be. He's sitting on a lot of evidence. We may not be able to get the Gardner art, but if you're going to nail him, you need to get him on the forgeries. Everything is right there in the firm. I'm sure clients would testify once they knew their art had been stolen from them."

William slowly ran his hand across the oxblood-colored leather couch. His eyes glanced over the broken glass in the corner, and then at the black and white of Blake and Addie. "I can't help but think that you're keeping something from me."

Blake was used to confiding in William, but he needed to go his own direction this time. To protect Addie.

"I'll take your silence as a confirmation," William said.

Blake stayed stone quiet, then lowered his head and gave it a shake. This had to work. He had to get William to arrest

Otto now. Otherwise he would have to figure out how to convince Addie to live a life on the run. "There's nothing else."

"Tell me about Adeline," William said quietly.

"She's innocent. Doesn't have any idea what Otto is really up to."

"That wasn't really what I was asking," William said. "Does he have a use for her?"

Blake tried to swallow the lump in his throat before he answered. "He thinks she may have some of the same usefulness that Carolena did."

"So he has a job planned for her."

Blake nodded.

"I don't know if you knew this, but Carolena disappeared into thin air one day," William said. "We don't know if Otto killed her or if she managed somehow to get away from him. Are you afraid that's what will happen to Addie?"

"I didn't realize. And, yes." Blake thought about how Otto would send Addie the way of the ghost when he was done with her. "But if we can't get Otto put away, then I think she probably should disappear into thin air the way Carolena did. Only on her own terms."

William nodded through his a-ha moment. "An escape. And I'm guessing that you want to go with her?"

"I don't want to go anywhere. But if Otto isn't imprisoned immediately, then Addie needs someone to protect her. This is a dangerous game and she doesn't fully understand what Otto is capable of." Blake lowered his voice. "I've tried to find those paintings and to nail him on the theft in the process." And then he bit out the words he never thought he'd have to say, "I couldn't do it."

"I doubt that. Besides. You're in too deep. Regardless of Adeline, you can't get out now. You made a promise that you would find this art and put Otto in jail. Not just to me and the rest of the FBI, but to yourself."

Blake glared at William. The hatred bubbled.

"If you give up on that now you'll never be able to live with yourself. Do you remember what you told me when we first recruited you?"

Blake's right hand fisted and he had to will himself not to throw it at William's face.

"You told me that you were the only one who had even a remote chance to find the art and to nail Otto."

"And I was right about that," Blake said through clenched teeth. "No one has done better than I have." He knew no one else had his training in art and forgeries, his supernatural ability to push someone, and no one had his undying motivation to see Otto rot the rest of his life in captivity.

Blake had waited a long time to exact his revenge on Otto for the way he had treated his mother. Otto had used her to gain access to priceless works of art she worked with at the Met. Then he exchanged several of them with flawless forgeries. When the Met became suspicious of her she lost her job, after which Otto made her a part of his black market purchases. Her gift for ferreting out the authentic pieces from the forgeries was unmatched. This, along with her weakness for loving Otto, nearly ended her life. Because he refused to live without her, and her unparalleled talents. He shadowed her possessively. And when she tried to leave, he had an associate from the underworld bring her back. They made it clear that, wherever she went, they'd find her. That if she tried to leave again, the penalty would be death.

Blake's plan had been to carefully work his way into Otto's life, become his trusted confidant, find the art, put Otto away, and set him and his mother free forever.

But then, nearly three-quarters of the way through his plan, when the art was within reach, no less, Addie made an ill-timed appearance in his life. She was the woman he'd searched for all of his life. And as much as he wanted to avenge his mother, he now had to make a choice. One that required a painful sacrifice either way. But he wasn't about to let Otto ruin another person's life. Much less Addie's.

"I guess I don't need to remind you what happened the last time Otto thought someone double-crossed him? If you mysteriously disappear now, he'll not take his last breath until he hunts the both of you down and takes you two out like he did the last guy," he said as he inched his face closer to Blake's.

"Which is obviously why I think you ought to arrest him on what you can." Blake leaned his elbows on his knees. "Look, this is not just about protecting someone who's important to me. This is about the best move you've got to catch Otto at anything. The deadline passed. I saw the statement you released that the statute of limitations ran out on the theft. You can't put him in jail on the theft, even if you can link him to it."

"Why don't I take her into protective custody and out of harm's way? Then you can keep looking for the art," William said.

Blake knew that finding this art was William's primary obsession. It trumped his duty as an FBI agent. It probably always would. The hunt for the Gardner art possessed everyone who worked on the case. The case was cursed. It was unsolvable. He also knew that William couldn't protect Addie from Otto. Otto's connections had a long and dangerous reach.

"Because you need to get him out of society. This isn't just about her or the art. This man is a murderer, and who knows what else he's done? We've given this the best shot anyone could. If you pull a killer off the streets, but miss out on the art, then you've made the right choice. He's probably moved the Gardner paintings anyway." Blake sat back slowly. "Who knows where they are? He's probably sold them on the black market already." He held William's stare for a long moment, but when the guilt swam up from his gut he looked away.

If William knew that Otto had invited him to see the art, that he was only inches away from knowing the location of the stolen Gardner pieces, William would probably throw Blake onto some medieval torture device until he agreed to get back in the game and recover the stolen pieces. Then Addie would be sucked into Otto's game, destined to live her life as his puppet, working one scheme after another. When he was done with her, she'd go the same way as the ghost.

"You really are our last chance to find this art," William said. "The department doesn't want to dedicate any more resources to locating the pieces. If you back out now, it's a monumental mistake in every direction."

"You mean, if I back out now, you don't get the credit for the biggest art recovery in history."

Blake's text alarm went off and he looked at the screen. "I've got to go. I'm late for another meeting."

"Promise me you won't do anything until we've had a chance to talk again."

"I can't make any more promises. Not to you. Not to the FBI. I can give you until the end of the day to let me know your decision. And then I've got to start making arrangements." Blake glanced at his phone screen again, then stood with his hands on his hips.

"Then maybe I can't make any more promises to you, either," William said.

Blake froze. He didn't expect this. "I did everything you asked. I honored our agreement."

"You didn't get the art," William said.

"I did everything anyone could on that. No one else was able to do any better."

"Our agreement was that when you got the art, I'd make sure your record was expunged from the system. And you didn't produce the art."

"Our agreement was that I would help you find the art, in exchange for having my record cleared. And I did help you. I won't have my freedom—I can't even travel until you hold up your end of the bargain."

"Maybe if you'll do two more things for me, I'll clear your record."

"And what will it be this time?" Blake threw his hand in the air and let it slap his leg.

"I'll let you know. For now, you need to remember that you're not out. You'll never leave the country for as long as you have that troublesome art theft charge on your record." William stood up.

"You should be more concerned about getting Otto off the street than manipulating me into finding this lost art," Blake said. "There will be another murder if you don't."

William picked up his briefcase and headed to the door. He gave one last warning look at Blake, then left.

Blake walked over to the bar and poured himself a glass of Scotch. He shot the first two fingers, then poured another and killed that, too.

This quiet arrangement with William and the FBI was supposed to give everyone what they wanted. Otto in jail, Gardner art recovered and his record expunged. A little trafficking across international lines that Blake still couldn't believe he got caught doing. That item was supposed to go away with this undercover deal. But he should have expected William would play this card.

Blake felt the hatred shimmering on his skin. He kept his truest feelings about Otto under wraps when he was in public, but in private he let his hatred breathe. The hatred was like a secret identity that needed to be let out once in a while, otherwise it would take him over. Make him do foolish, hateful things.

Like kill Otto.

Something his mother was afraid he would do. He hadn't yet, because up until today he believed he could take away Otto's freedom. Of course he understood William's obsession, because he had it, too. He wanted that art, but not for the same reasons. He didn't live to see it back in its rightful home. And he knew he couldn't put Otto in jail on that crime anymore. He'd missed that window. But the idea of taking something away from Otto that he valued felt too good to his soul. He knew that taking the Gardner art from Otto would hurt him more than if he'd lost his own family.

Blake turned and his eyes stumbled on the black and white photos of him and Addie that William left on the coffee table. The hatred began to lose its momentum. It was her. The woman who had a place in Blake's heart since before he was born.

Saving Addie meant giving up his pursuit of Otto. It meant giving up the art. But would William let him do that?

Blake threw his rocks glass against the wall, and the remnants lay mixed with the broken espresso glass from earlier in the day.

40

———

I came in to the office at 4 a.m. Extremely early. All was quiet, except for an electric hum that came from somewhere down the hall. I settled in to work at my desk and slipped off my shoes. I never could manage to keep shoes on when no one else was around. My office felt a little warm, so I pulled my silk scarf from my neck and laid it beside me on the desk. It slipped to the floor. I'd get it in a minute—for now, I just wanted to make some progress on my research. I flipped open several books and pored through them. The lamp on my desk flickered once, and then twice, and then fizzled out completely. I sat there staring into the blackness of my office.

Without my lamp, the only light coming in was from the portrait lights that illuminated artwork in the hallway. Which wasn't nearly enough. I was now rethinking the decision I made when I moved in to have maintenance unscrew all the fluorescents in my ceiling. But I couldn't handle the constant flickering that my eyes recognized in all fluorescents, so they had to go.

Seemed like there was a light bulb or two that I put in

the bottom of my credenza from my last trip to the supply closet.

I took my phone and opened the flashlight, then knelt down to dig through the bottom drawer. I only came up with two empty cardboard lightbulb sleeves.

I'd have to go downstairs to the supply closet and hope it was unlocked.

And that's when I heard footsteps. What insomniac would be here at 4:15 on a Friday morning other than me? No one was ever here this early.

The footsteps dragged closer, and I peeked over the half wall to see who it was. When I saw Ellen and two hulking men I shoved the phone down into the rug to mute the light, and from the shadows I watched them pass slowly by the windows of my office, which looked out into the hallway. The men wore white, zip-front jumpsuits, and I guessed they were painters or maybe janitorial crew. But it all felt suspicious, and it was still a good idea to stay away from Ellen, so I stayed put until they passed.

I pushed up, and walked into the semi-dark hallway. I looked left and felt the energetic trail that Ellen and the two men left in their wake. Dark and heavy. I didn't want to know. So, I turned in the opposite direction. Down the hall and to the back of the firm, to the supply elevator. I pushed the button for the basement, and tried to be nonchalant about what I'd seen. I didn't need to know what Ellen and those men were up to. None of my business. I was just taking a ride in the elevator, going to get some lightbulbs.

My heart thudded slowly through the next few beats. I had the distinct feeling that once again the perfect world I had imagined for myself was unraveling.

It seemed my senses were ahead of me. From the way my body was reacting I could tell that whatever was wrong with this picture had already registered somewhere within. My conscious mind still had to figure it out.

I stopped on the cool marble floor of the basement, my bare toes wiggling against the chill.

Lightbulbs. Just...lightbulbs.

As luck would have it, the supply closet door was unlocked. Open, even. I was headed toward the small room of office supply bliss when I noticed a light pouring into the adjacent hallway. A vault door was open. My head cocked. An open vault door was an anomaly for a firm so crazed with secrecy. Maybe Ellen and her thug entourage were moving some large pieces. Maybe someone was coming to pick up their art today and Ellen was getting the pieces ready.

I slipped into the supply room and quickly searched the metal shelves for lightbulbs. I needed to get back to my office in case they were on their way back down here.

The elevator bell dinged.

My lungs deflated as I stood with my hand on a four pack of lightbulbs. Five freaking minutes. That's all I would have needed. I debated for one everlasting second if I ought to act casual and clueless. Waltz into the hallway and say, "Hey! I just needed lightbulbs..." No way that would work. Not with people who might have something to hide.

I stepped behind the door and prayed that no one would walk in here to turn off the light, or worse, shut and lock the door. Through the crack at the hinged end of the door, I watched thug one and thug two as they moved the *Madonna and Child* piece I had seen in Otto's office. I stayed frozen. Panic thumped in my chest at the obvious secrecy of the move. Someone had to know that was an authentic masterpiece, and not a copy as Otto told me.

That's the only reason they would move this piece at

four in the morning. And the union rate they must be charging her for showing up at this hour... Cost-conscious Ellen, who knew how many paperclips went out of the firm each month would hardly need help, much less pay over-time, to move a copy. A forgery.

The thought thunked through my brain like a cement block.

Then the idea occurred to me. What if Otto really didn't know? What if the authentic masterpiece in Otto's office was Ellen's doing? Not Otto's?

Otto wouldn't be the first clueless CEO who left the details of running a business to someone else. Lots of business owners left too much responsibility to managers they thought they could trust. Only to end up figuring out the hard way that they couldn't.

Maybe that's what the walls were reaching out to tell me on my first day in the firm. That Ellen was someone I needed to watch out for.

"AFTER YOU HANG THAT ONE, you're going back to the fifth floor, this time to the lobby," Ellen's voice echoed against the painted, cinderblock walls. "Two paintings will be replaced in there."

"Yes, ma'am."

I waited until I heard the elevator doors close, then looked out the door and down the hallway that led to the area with the vaults. No one.

I walked down the hallway that held the four silver doors to the temperature-controlled vaults. One thick door was ajar.

I ran on tiptoe and dashed inside the carpeted vault. I

guessed I had about ten or fifteen minutes max before they returned with another piece.

The right half of the room was stacked with large, wooden crates, some open, others sealed, each one bearing a large, red Fragile sticker. I walked over to one of the open crates and knelt beside the painting that rested inside. I recognized immediately that it was the Bellini *Madonna and Child*.

I gingerly touched a piece of raised paint on the bottom left corner of the canvas. Just as before, visions of the Giovanni Bellini's Venice rushed through me. I pulled my hand back before I lost myself in the artist's world.

I looked at some of the other open crates. I recognized art that had hung on the walls of the firm, and pieces that we had appraised for their owners. Client pieces that I knew we'd returned to their owners since the appraisal or the restoration work had been completed. Only it looked to me like clients didn't get their authentic art returned. They must have gotten a forgery, instead. My breath took up a new pace.

I walked across the quiet carpet to the other side of the room where framed art hung on white wire panels inside a large floor-to-ceiling cage. The panels could move from side to side like curtain samples, or cheap posters that hung on metal planks in a retail store.

I stopped when I saw it: another *Madonna and Child* by Giovanni Bellini.

I slowly reached out and touched the canvas, only this time the story was much different from before. There were no bustling scenes of 1400s Venice, and Giovanni Bellini was nowhere to be found. I jerked my hand away.

I tried to take in air but it dragged up through my lungs, thick and slow. My head spun. The intent of the artist—

these were forgeries. Good ones. If I hadn't placed my hand on the canvas, I would not have been able to tell the difference. I needed to know who did these, why they were here, and if Ellen orchestrated this. I reached toward the canvas—

The elevator bell rang.

They were coming.

41

Ellen directed the two movers to place the framed art in the crated area. "We'll pack them. They have to be logged into our system first."

The movers left the vault at Ellen's direction. She walked to the heavy steel door then paused. She drew the air in through her nose. Perfume. She slowly scanned the vault interior. Then turned around and smelled the air again. It was faint, but she could have sworn she smelled Bulgari.

She grabbed the handle and pulled the vault door shut as she entered the hallway. Outside she punched a series of numbers on the keypad to ensure the vault's security.

42

In the summers of my youth, my grandfather and I, along with my sisters, would collect lightning bugs in glass Mason jars with holes punched in their metal tops. "Let's get home, girls. It's about to get black as pitch out here."

I never fully understood what color pitch was. Until now. Now that I couldn't see my hand in front of my face, and the blackness was claustrophobically close. From my hiding spot between the two crates I rocked back and forth in tiny movements, wrapped my arms around my bent knees, and tried to stop my body from shaking.

It's interesting how a skill like not moving for hours upon end in the dark comes back to you like a natural reflex when the conditions were right. Especially when life had taught you that the dark was not devoid of human life, but rather full of it.

I tried not to notice, but spirits wandered in and out of here constantly. One in particular. I could feel the trails of his energy. His rage had a unique scent.

I worked to focus on something else. Thinking about a ghost could be enough to draw him to you.

With the temptation to panic sweet on my lips, I hugged my legs harder and mashed my lips against my knees. The fragrance of lavender was still on my skin, and my mother's voice traveled on the scent: "Use your gifts, Addie, or they'll use you."

43

Alexa laid in bed and tapped out another text to Adeline. It was too early for most people, though not for Addie. They were supposed to meet for lunch later this afternoon, but she needed to work all day today, instead. Addie had ignored her first text. Alexa was going on the assumption that it hadn't gone through the first time, because Addie could have been in the middle of an epic hurricane and she would have her phone with her, texting her sister about the event.

Plus, Alexa had woken up with that feeling. The feeling she got when something was wrong with someone she loved.

She took a deep breath. She was going to give technology a little more time to work, and then she'd act.

44

———

At 9:30 Ellen glided down the long hallway toward Adeline's office with a hot espresso, its strong essence leaving a fragrant trail. She had walked by Adeline's office earlier and saw her purse on a side chair, so Ellen knew she was around. She was going to drop in unannounced and get her to take the interview with the Stephens firm.

Adeline's enthusiasm for working at the firm almost made Ellen forget how terrified she'd felt to work here these last few years. Adeline's naïveté about the firm's private dealings, and her determination to make her career successful, left Ellen feeling hopeful at times. Hopeful that things would finally change for the better, that she might have a way out some day. Hopeful that Adeline just might pass through this experience unaware and unscathed.

"Why is it so dark in here?" Ellen entered Adeline's office.

It was normally a bright and cheerful space. Adeline took pride in her small office. She'd brought in a deep red and camel-colored rug, colorful pillows for the guest chairs, and kept a fresh bouquet of long-stemmed orchids and peacock feathers on the small conference table. But today it was dark and cool.

Ellen leaned forward to place the cup and saucer on the desk, but stopped mid-air when she saw the open credenza drawer at the back of Adeline's office. She cocked her head to the side, placed the cup down, and rounded the desk cautiously to get a closer look.

Her eyes narrowed as she took in the interrupted scene: two empty lightbulb sleeves—one on the credenza, one on the floor, next to Adeline's shoes. Open books were scattered across her desk, and Adeline's dormant laptop was nestled between them. Her silk scarf and phone had been abandoned on the rug near her shoes.

The hair stood up on the back of Ellen's neck.

Ellen stooped down and pushed the home button. The screen lit up with a slew of unanswered text messages across Adeline's background image of the Venus de Milo. She picked up Adeline's ice blue scarf and brought it to her face. There was no mistaking her trademark scent.

Nausea coated the inside of Ellen's stomach.

"Have you seen Adeline?"

Ellen's entire body shook in one violent jolt at the unexpected sound of Otto's voice. Her heart took off on a high-speed chase. As she stood, she brought the scarf with her and pushed the phone under Adeline's desk with her foot.

"I didn't hear you come in." She waved the scarf and put it on Adeline's desk to signify what she had been doing on the floor. "Ah, no. I haven't, actually. She's around, though." She sounded more breathless than she wanted to, but her heart was giving her a high-impact cardio workout.

"Yes, I smell the espresso." Otto eyed the demitasse cup on Adeline's desk and then looked back at Ellen, who nervously ironed the sides of her French twist with her fingers.

"Look for her, would you? And tell her she's late for a meeting with Charles in his office."

"Of course," Ellen clasped her hands in front of her.

Otto moved to leave, and then turned back around. "And you and I are due to meet in thirty. Are you ready?"

"I'll be there in fifteen." Ellen nodded confidently and hoped he didn't see her heart kicking her chest with the flat ends of both feet.

Otto took off down the hallway, his unbuttoned suit jacket flying behind him like a dark cape. Then he stopped, did an about-face, and walked back into Adeline's office. Ellen had been cautiously listening for his footsteps and was still rooted where he left her. She lifted her chin as he walked in.

"Have the movers gone?" he asked.

Ellen nodded.

"Then you forgot the finial in my office. It was on the list of items to go to the vault." Otto's eyes were clear and focused. "I'll take it down this time. But next time see that everything on the list is taken care of. No mistakes."

"I'll take it down, Otto. It's my fault it was missed. We were focused on the paintings."

"No. I want to see where everything was placed." He looked around Adeline's office with a frown. "It's dark in here. Turn some lights on."

Ellen's knuckles began to turn white in her own grasp as she waited until she heard Otto turn the far corner.

She may not have been able to get herself out of Otto's

labyrinth of deceit, but she needed to at least try to help Adeline. For John. She picked up the espresso, took a shortcut through the kitchen, and tried to rush ahead of Otto to his office. She knew she had to get to that finial before he did.

45

———

Alexa threw a few things into her orange leather hobo and prepared to make the trek across town. Addie never ignored texts. Unless she was sleeping, and Adeline didn't sleep in the mornings. Addie didn't sleep much at all.

Plus, Alexa was fighting a major vibe that something was up.

She reached the door of her apartment and wondered where she needed to go to find Adeline.

Townhome, her gut answered. *Good.* Because she really didn't want to step foot in that firm.

Alexa picked up her phone and sent another text.

I'm on my way.

46

———

In Charles' office Blake sat to the right of Charles in quiet discussion. At ten in the morning the sun was high and still climbing, but in here it was just rising around the left window, casting a soft, golden glow into the room.

Both men fell silent when Ellen walked into the room. Her presence had that effect on most gatherings. "Good morning, gentlemen. Have you heard from Adeline?"

"No, I haven't. She was supposed to join us. Is she around?"

"I think so. I'll find her—she probably just got involved in some research in the library and forgot about the meeting." Ellen flashed a reassuring smile and handed Blake an envelope. "I'm heading into a meeting with Otto. These are the documents you needed earlier. Perhaps you can take a look at them this morning before you get too far into your meeting? I'll be in with Otto for about twenty minutes, and then he wanted to head down to one of the vaults. I won't be available to discuss the documents with you until after that."

"What—?"

Charles's cell phone rang, interrupting Blake's response. "I need to take this call."

"All right. Let's try to reconvene in thirty."

Blake gave a confused look and accepted the envelope. He started to put the envelope in his inside jacket pocket. Ellen gave him a look he couldn't ignore and she walked away.

47

———

My mother had been right.

But use my gifts how?

I dug the heels of my hands into my eyes until I started to see stars.

Starting with the immediate space around me and working my way out, I searched the room psychically. And that's when I saw it. Or felt it. Actually, both.

This wasn't my first time in this vault. I saw the seven-year-old me standing on the far side of the vault with my grandfather. The joy of being with him buoyed me.

I remembered dancing around his office and asking to see what was on the other side of the silver doors on the lower level. He went and got the lady with the blond pony-tail, and she let us in.

My stomach pitched.

Something happened that day. Something I couldn't... quite remember. But it was connected to this room.

Wait.

There were the rippling walls that I encountered in the foyer on my first day.

The walls in here would hold memories, too.

They would have the memories of that day, I was sure of it.

I needed that story.

I inched out of my hiding spot.

I felt the open space with one arm and the carpet below it with the other. Remembering the layout of the room, I moved forward into total darkness. I stood paralyzed with the first step, until I found the courage to take another, and then another, until my outstretched fingertips bumped into the smooth wall.

I stared into the soundless abyss of darkness, keeping my clammy hands connected to the wall. I slid to the floor. My wet palms squeaked on the way down.

I let the energy run from the walls into my hands, and scenes flashed in and out.

Ellen had managed the moving of art for decades. Early on she kept a paper log, and in recent years she began carrying a tablet. I couldn't tell if this scheme was hers alone.

I pushed further into the energetic memories contained in the walls.

Holding my grandfather in mind, I searched for the thread of energy that was strictly his. He had been in this room plenty of times, I knew it. His energy would be in here.

The feel of his energy finally grew stronger until I heard the sound of his laughter. *Oh my gosh.* And finally, there he was—my grandfather, the young woman with the blond ponytail, and seven-year-old me, standing in this room, surrounded by art.

Oil paintings and framed sketches lean against three of the four walls. At least two of each piece of work.

"Now it's your turn," he says. "I've mixed them all up for

you. Show me the original ones, and then show me the duplicates."

I walk around the room, placing the index finger of my left hand in the upper left corner of each piece of work. At the end I walk back to the center of the room and begin pointing. "Original, original, original, and these four are copies." I turn and smile at them.

My grandfather laughs his deep laugh and claps slowly. He puts his arm around the woman next to him and gives her a tug to his side. "See? She's a natural."

I looked at the woman's face. She is much younger. Thinner. Happier. But there is no mistaking who she is.

It's Ellen.

I look to the left, where a man stood unnoticed in the partially open doorway. He's young. His hair was a different color. But I recognize him, too.

It was Otto.

48

———————

Alexa thrust her key in the door of their grandfather's townhome, looked up at the security camera Adeline had installed when she moved in, and pushed her way inside. She punched the code on the security pad and shut and locked the heavy door behind her.

Everything classically elegant as usual. The faint scent of Adeline's perfume hung in the air. A sweet memory scampered across her mind of the two of them in Paris, laughing in the George V gift shop as Addie selected the then-new Bulgari scent. Alexa brought her fingertips to her lips.

She walked purposefully through the townhome and tuned in, sensing as much as she could from the vibrations embedded in Addie's surroundings. She tried to get a feel for what she needed to be looking for, her guidance brought her here for a reason.

Adeline's footprints of energy pulled her into the library, where she paced alongside the book lined shelves, and then finally lowered herself onto the soft, overstuffed couch. She ran her hand along the animal print fabric, felt the sadness rise up from the traces of Adeline's loneliness.

"Oh, Addie."

The copy of Marc Chagall's *Paris Through A Window* tugged at her attention, the mystical two-faced man in the lower corner turned toward her, pulled her in. Alexa thought about how he represented the interior and the exterior, the imaginary and the real. And the realization floated up like a bubble moving through water. The two-faced man was Addie. Ever caught between two worlds, she couldn't trust either one.

"She needs you," the two faces said to her at once.

The faces melted back into the painting.

She would have to go to the firm. A sick sense of foreboding clung to her like a heavy winter's coat on a warm day. She snatched her keys and bag and ran out of the townhome.

49

The scene faded, and the realization that my grandfather knew about my ability to spot fakes began to sink in.

I had forgotten. I was so young.

And Ellen... *She's always known about me.*

And Otto...

In fact, they both would have known about my not so secret abilities on the day I came to interview. Or at least wondered if I still had that ability to discern forgeries from authentic pieces. Wondered if I still used it.

And did they want to use it? Was that the real reason I was hired?

Blake's warning about the art community came back to me, and I wondered if Otto was smack in the middle of my blind spot. I had more than one obvious, foreboding sign on the day of my interview. Not the least of which was the near 10 million dollar Bellini masterpiece hanging on his wall. I scowled at myself in the inky blackness of the room. Otto, or someone in this firm, was involved in a dangerous art scheme.

I couldn't see any of the paintings that surrounded me, but I remembered what they looked like when the lights were on. And too, I could feel their energy. Their stories and true identities beat like audible heartbeats in the dark. I scanned the layout of the room with my awareness. Authentic art on one side, forgeries on the other.

Forgeries in a vault. I scoffed. No one put forgeries in a vault unless they had plans for them. Unless their intent was to deceive. Otherwise they'd put them on view. Like a child's painting on the refrigerator, they'd mount it on the wall and proudly announce: *Look what I did. Look how talented I am. Just like the real artist.*

Just like the real artist—the thought echoed the scene I'd caught while I was alone in Otto's office. His father yelling at Otto when he was a child. "No creativity, nothing original," he'd yelled. The idea hit me in the gut. Otto had learned how to paint by replicating masterpieces. He learned he had a talent for it.

He wasn't putting them on public display as known copies.

I crawled to where I had seen the fake Giovanni hanging on the wire panel. Feeling my way along sharp edges of wooden crates, I found the wire panels. They were still open to the fake Giovanni I had touched earlier.

I perked the antennae located at the tips of my fingers, opened all channels within, and placed my hand against the fake Giovanni. Images and feelings swirled through my inner vision, all of them Otto.

Otto painting the fake Giovanni, his gaze dancing back and forth between the real one and the fake one, getting the details just right. Just as he did in the vision I glimpsed of him as a child. Then he coats the completed canvas with something I don't recognize. Probably something to age it sufficiently enough to fool the expert. He backs away with his hands on his hips and compares the two. "I did it again," he says, pleased and proud.

Ellen rounds the corner and stares at each piece. "I think this is one of your best, Otto."

"I think so, too." He leans close and examines the fake Giovanni.

Ellen pulls a little on her pearl necklace. "How many are you doing?"

"This will be the second and last one," Otto says. "No need for unnecessary risks."

I pulled my hand from the paint. I'd seen enough to answer my whodunit and why question.

My head and my heart battled again. I really didn't want to see Otto in this way.

And why hadn't I seen him for who he really was?

I saw him... I saw him the way he wanted me to see him. I saw him the way...the way I *wanted* to see him. I hadn't wanted him to be the person he is. Just who I wanted him to be.

The fearful are easy prey for the misguided.

I'd tried so hard to build the perfect life for myself.

Somehow I had another scenario where I'd trusted and it wasn't working out well. If I found out that my grandfather had anything to do with all of this forgery mess, I'd.. I'd kill him all over again.

I closed my eyes tight to get a grip. I needed to find out if Otto had any designs on my gifts.

What could I touch in here that Otto would have handled, that he would have spent a lot of time around and it might have absorbed the information I was looking for?

The real Bellini. The frame. It had probably hung in Otto's office long enough to pick up something.

Lowering myself to all fours again, I crawled back to the real Giovanni Bellini masterpiece for data.

When I finally found it, I put both of my hands on the wide, gold frame and searched for a particular strand of Otto's energy. Some story that held his intent for me. My real reason for being here.

"No one is who you think they are," Blake's ghost had told me. Actually, Blake had said the same thing. They dittoed my own thoughts on the subject, and we were all correct.

Meetings with random people I didn't know played before me, endless phone conversations where Otto worked his power connections and enjoyed his game of king of the mountain. I sped through them all until I came to a conversation between Ellen and Otto and I heard my name.

"Adeline will be here at nine tomorrow," Ellen said to Otto.

"Ah, good," he said, then looked up at the frame. "I have a little test lined up for her. Hopefully we'll see that she's the same girl with the same gift we all used to know and love."

Ellen nervously pressed her pearl necklace against her chest and she looked at the Bellini.

"If she is who she used to be, I don't think she'll be able to resist giving it a touch. She used to run through the halls of this firm touching every piece of art in sight. Remember that?"

Ellen nodded. "You don't think that seeing the authentic piece will scare her off?"

"No." Otto's tone was condescending. "I've heard she doesn't have anywhere else to go. She needs this job. If she bites on the Bellini, seeing its authenticity will show me whether she's willing to keep my secret in exchange for the job." Otto rose from his desk and looked out the window at the picturesque view. "Then we can move on to bigger things."

Ellen moved a few steps away from Otto. She posed her question quietly, almost hypnotically. Ostensibly so it wouldn't raise Otto's defenses. "Like the Gardner art?"

"Probably. Philippe will screw that up. I can feel it. And now that John's gone I don't have anyone I trust to authenticate what's there."

Ellen inhaled through lightly pinked lips.

"Other than that, we'll hit the black market again. If all goes well, she'll be my replacement for Carolena to pick out originals. Then we'll sell them on the market or maybe overseas." Otto shifted his gaze to Ellen. "Of course we'll cut you in on whatever we make. Hard to make any of this work without you, Ellen."

Ellen returned his smile graciously.

The scene faded but I kept my hands on the frame.

When the next scene began I released the frame. But not before I heard Otto say, "Develop a steady relationship with her. From the little bit I know, she's spent a lot of time alone lately, so I doubt she'd refuse you."

What?

I fastened my hands to the frame again, but the one thing I didn't want, happened.

50

A cool, motionless breeze drifted across my face, and my chest tightened into a hundred immoveable knots. He was here. I could feel him. And this time there was no way out. Nowhere to escape. In the stillness of the dark, the absence of distraction forced me to take in the details.

It was *him*. Blake's ghost.

His presence spread across the room. When it reached me, my body shivered. The heat of his glare bore down on me from somewhere just beyond the darkness. I was trapped, as I had been in childhood, vulnerable to the bodiless.

He moved past me and behind me, making me dizzy.

I sat frozen, bringing my knees into my chest, curling into a ball. My chest seized, and my breath shrank. No matter which way I turned, I was vulnerable to him.

Memories of several ghosts from my childhood flashed through my mind, one of whom actually strangled me. If my mother hadn't shown up when she did and gotten him off me, I don't think I would have survived. And of course the last time I'd met Blake's ghost he'd nearly killed me the same way.

There wouldn't be anyone to save me this time. There was no way out.

Panic flooded my chest so fast and hard I could taste the fear. I told myself that this ghost was different from the crazier ones I'd encountered when I was younger. But my heart wasn't listening. It was thumping so hard the beat echoed throughout my body.

Then it began, as it always did. The ghost's experiences and appearance, running through me...all without my choice. No barriers. No ability to walk away from it. For now I was his prisoner. My existence reduced to channeling his miseries.

"We meet again, Miss Adeline. Addie... What kind of name is that anyway?"

His anger didn't come from the broken dreams of a middle-aged man. It was a young man's anger at being betrayed and robbed of his life. I was still surprised at how young he was, considering the intensity of the rage I felt from him. Based on that alone, I would have thought him to be twice his age.

A hot, piercing shot ripped through my chest. Hard. A burning, oozing feeling. Then, feelings of betrayal, and shock. I wanted to scream, but I couldn't. There was no voice. No sound. Only excruciating pain, and then blackness.

Murdered. The man was murdered. That's what happened to the ghost. He knew too much, and they killed him because of it. A whole new wave of fear surged through me.

I leaned on the floor, trying to detach from his physical and emotional pain as it ran through my body.

"I was killed for this," he waved his arm at the paintings in the racks. "I was killed for money."

He leaned in too close. My heart clanged in my chest. The heat from his anger burned.

"And now I'm going to make him pay for what he did. They took from me. Now I'm going to take from them."

His fat, frigid thumbs pressed against my windpipe, and my hands flailed at them to move him away. I twisted away from him before he had too firm of a grip, and I went tumbling over a crate, backside first.

He lunged for me and then looked toward the door with a jerk. "I know where you sleep," he said, and backed out of the room.

51

T he sobs welled up from dark places within, from painful wounds I hadn't known still existed. They came from my father's and grandfather's disappearance, from any involvement they had in this forgery mess, from having these abilities and all the problems they brought to my life. From the people who hated me for seeing their secrets, unless they thought they could use me. And from the ghosts, who came and went as they pleased, taking from me what they wanted, threatening and tormenting me. I broke so deep and hard I couldn't stop crying.

Whoever would find me down here, whenever they did find me, would never understand why I was here. And that would be about right since I didn't have an explanation that would sit well with anyone. At least not with anyone in the firm.

Once again I'd found myself staring into the face of people's secrets. Secrets they obviously couldn't or wouldn't have revealed. The fact that I knew about them meant that I would go down, too.

There was no way out. No way out of this room, and no way out of this situation that didn't involve a huge crash and burn.

Maybe this was payback for invading others' secrets. Secrets that unfurled at my touch seemed to take me down along with their owners.

I lay on the cool, carpeted floor.

The keypad beeped and I sat up.

Someone punched in the code.

The lock unhinged.

There was a loud *ka-thunk* and a subsequent pressure release.

52

"**A**lexa, you look as beautiful today as you did twenty years ago." Ellen smiled and kissed her on the cheek.

"Thank you, Ellen." Alexa smiled but kept her defenses sharp. "I'm here to see Adeline."

Ellen smoothed her skirt. "She's here, somewhere. I haven't seen her lately. Was she expecting you?"

"She is. I'm a little early."

"Okay. Well, I'm not sure she's available right now. Can I let her know you stopped by?"

Alexa felt a rush of fury rising. She leashed it before it found words and said, "No, I'll wait. Would you get her for me, please?"

"Of course." Ellen touched Alexa's arm. "May I offer you some tea or coffee while you wait? Espresso?"

"Black tea, if you have it. Thanks."

"Let me get that for you, sweetheart. Make yourself comfortable."

Alexa calmed herself by walking around the lobby and looking at art. She decided she wouldn't start moving through the firm in search of her sister until Ellen had been an opportunity to produce her.

Alexa reached inside her bag and felt the cool steel of her gun she'd left in her purse after target practice.

Ellen returned with a hot mug of tea. Alexa watched the steam rise from the cup. She could use the hot tea as a quick weapon if she needed to. She took it from Ellen and placed the saucer on top of the cup to preserve the scalding temperature.

Ellen sat down beside Alexa on the couch. "Didn't your grandfather call you by another name? Lexie, was it?"

At the mention of her grandfather, Alexa dropped her guard a little. "Lexie, yes."

"I thought so. He was such a good man. I still miss having him here."

Ellen patted Alexa's knee. "Well, let me go and see if I can't find Adeline for you. She's been out of sight all morning—she's got to be reappearing soon." Ellen smiled and disappeared around the corner.

"She's he's hiding something. Because she doesn't want to alarm me," Alexa checked her phone screen again. "This firm is nothing but a coffin of secrets. You should have listened to our mother and grandmother, Addie."

53

I tried to inhale, but my nose was stuffed shut. My eyes were swollen from crying and sensitive from spending several hours in the dark. I had no idea who was standing in the doorway. Otto or Ellen, I guessed.

I hoped I wouldn't get shot the way the ghost had been. I didn't really think I could defend myself against that.

Mascara and eyeliner had melted into my eyes, making it doubly impossible for me to open them. I continued wiping at my face with my hands and sleeves. Footsteps strode closer.

I felt someone kneel beside me, then a warm hand gently on my back. The sheer size of his hand made me feel small and inexplicably safe.

"Are you okay?" he asked in a quiet voice.

I put my hand over my brows to shield my eyes from the bright light.

Blake Greenwood looked at me, projecting comfort with his size and presence.

"Oh Blake." I leaned into him, and he pulled me close, cloaked me in his arms.

"How did you get stuck in here?" His hands caressed my back.

Tears started flowing again. "The lightbulbs...and then there were men in the hallway... I just thought Ellen might be up to...you know...I thought I could— It...[sob]...was strange...[more sobs]...so I ended up seeing way too much [hiccup] as usual...and now I'm in trouble and, I don't know what to do—"

I pressed my face into his chest. "And all this art." I pulled back and waved my hand toward the racks. "Half of it isn't real. They're forgeries," I whispered. "Good ones. I think I've really stepped in it."

Blake lifted me to my feet. "We need to get you out of here." He walked me into the hallway, closed the vault door, and punched a code with his knuckle. We headed for the elevator.

Once inside he used a key, and then tapped another code into the keypad and punched a button. I leaned into him. The elevator started rising and he pressed a soft kiss onto my head.

"I'm going to get you through the firm and out the door so you can head home. People have been looking for you this morning, don't mention what you've seen. Okay? Not until we've had a chance to talk about it."

We stopped at the floor where the kitchen and the bathrooms were located. Taking a sharp right off the elevator, we headed into the ladies' room.

He leaned me against the sink and grabbed a few paper towels from the counter. He wetted them and wiped something off my face. I had to assume my eyeliner and mascara had left my eyelashes long ago.

While he worked on my face, all I could think of was how thankful I was that Ellen stocked the more expensive, cloth-like hand towels in the bathroom, since they were soft on my face. I couldn't process anything I had seen downstairs.

Blake stopped wiping and placed his hands on either side of my face. He brought his face close to mine. "Do you trust me, Adeline?"

I stared right back through bleary eyes. "No. Not really."

He stared at me for a half moment, dazed in disbelief at my answer, and then he let out a laugh. "Well, at least that was an honest answer."

I laughed along with him, mostly out of sheer delirium, though it felt really good to laugh with someone.

I probably did trust him a little, at least right now, because he had rescued me. That, and I didn't have anyone else I could turn to. Which, I guessed, was why I'd spilled the beans about the art.

"I don't really trust anyone right now."

"I understand." He peered at me over the paper towel with intense blue eyes and a sympathetic smile.

Did he understand?

Blake snatched a few more paper towels and held them under the water stream. I turned around slightly and caught a bit of my reflection in the mirror. I looked like something that had crawled out of the well in a horror movie. He grabbed my shoulders and twirled me around so that my back faced the mirror again.

"Let me do this first." Blake smiled and kept rubbing my face with the wet cloth towels. I closed my burning eyes, and surrendered. Any self-conscious ideas I had were gone.

"You know about Otto." I said it as a statement as much as a question.

"I know about Otto," he said.

"How?" I asked softly.

"It's a long story, and we can talk about it later. Look up," he said as he wiped under my eyes. Blake's phone buzzed and he pulled it from his pocket. Then he handed me several tissues from the countertop. "Blow," he said, and looked at the screen.

I did. For someone who I thought might enjoy a steady diet of super-attractive runway models, Blake was bizarrely down to earth.

"Okay, this is good." He put his phone back in his pocket. "Now. Do you trust me enough to follow my direction? This is very important."

I thought about it. He seemed to be telling me the truth, and I really didn't have another choice. "Okay." I nodded.

"Alexa's here."

"What—?"

"Yes, and she's going to take you home." His firm hands gripped the outside of my shoulders. "If anyone asks you what's wrong or where you're going, you're sick and you're going home. You have a stomach virus. Okay?"

"Stomach virus," I repeated.

Blake's features were unyielding and I knew that he understood the seriousness of the situation. Maybe better than I did.

"Don't talk with Alexa about anything that happened today until you're safe at home. Do you understand?"

I nodded.

"Don't answer your phone after you leave here, unless it's me or one of your family members. Understand? No one."

I nodded again. "I don't have my phone with me."

"I've worked that out. Alexa already has your things. Go home and stay there. Can Alexa stay with you?"

"Probably, yes... I don't know."

"Send me a text if she can't stay or has to leave, and I'll come over. Meanwhile, you two stay together at your townhome and wait for my call."

I swallowed on a dry throat at Blake's words. Yes, I would need a plan.

He smoothed my hair down and tucked it behind my ears. "Set your security alarm as soon as you're inside your home, and do not open the door for anyone unless it's me. Not a neighbor, not a friend, no one. *No one, Adeline.* Okay?"

I nodded.

"I'll be by later." His thumb wiped a falling tear from my cheek.

I tried to speak but a double breath escaped when I opened my mouth, so I just nodded yet again. He walked beside me and kept his arm around me. We took the lower hallways then the service elevator—a back path to the front office. We avoided the heavily traveled, carpeted hallways upstairs.

I wondered if I'd ever see my own office again, my little sphere of normal. My heart ached for the typical daily existence that faded.

Blake reached in front of me, put his hand on the door handle that led to the lobby. He leaned next to my ear. "When you walk through this door, you and Alexa need to walk right out of the building. Don't look back. Don't stop for anything or anyone. There's a car out front for the two of you. Get in it and leave, immediately."

Blake opened the door to the main lobby where Alexa stood, holding my vintage Chanel bag and satchel, a few loose files, and my shoes. I walked through the lobby then we went out the front door together. I didn't look back.

FROM THE HALLWAY, through a sliver of the open door, Blake eyed the security cameras in the lobby. When he saw Adeline and Alexa get into his Town Car and disappear, he shut the door the remaining inch and called for another car.

54

———

Blake pulled his pocket watch from his trouser pocket and glanced at the time as he stormed toward the car he'd called for. "Pete, go by a seafood restaurant and get a to-go order of lobster, shrimp, salad, bread, and anything else that might look good."

"Okay, where—?"

"Get plenty. She likes fresh seafood. Just make sure the restaurant is on the way to Addie's. That's where we're taking it."

Blake put the car's privacy screen up, pulled the cell phone from the side console, and dialed William from the call memory. His heel tapped furiously until he heard William's voice.

"I've got to know right now if you're going to go for the arrest. Otherwise I'm taking Addie and we're heading out of town. Today."

"Why? What's going on?"

"Addie got stuck in one of Otto's vaults, she's seen the forgeries, and the security cameras caught it all on tape. The cameras also got me getting her out of that vault, and probably getting her out of the firm as well."

"And Otto reviews those tapes?"

"I don't know. If he's at all suspicious about her not being around today, he might look at them to see how she moved around the firm. He has a lot of secrets to protect. Secrets you need to shine a light on."

"I'll make a call and we'll discuss it on our end."

He said it too casually, Blake thought. As if he were making a note to run by the store to pick up eggs on his way home. Blake ran his hand through his hair in frustration. "You need to get to the firm today, William. If he figures out that Addie has been in that vault, saw things he wasn't ready for her to see yet, he'll assume the worst and will make a move to protect himself."

"Meaning, what, exactly?" William asked after a wide pause.

"Meaning he'll assume that she's on her way to see someone like you. He'll empty his vaults and go after her. And me."

"If I do this, I'm going to need you and Addie to testify."

"Not a chance. I've watched this man kill one person already. If Addie or I testify, he'll come after us both."

"If I storm the firm and come up empty, my case is shot. That means Otto is free to come after you anyway. Best thing you both can do is testify."

"How could you come up empty? The place is full of evidence. Pick a vault. Any vault. As long as you get out there today you'll find what you need. I gave you plenty of warning on this."

There was a heavy silence on William's end of the line.

"If he knows that Addie's been in that vault, has seen his forgeries, he may be moving the evidence as we speak. I've been doing this for a long time, and I will tell you that you rarely succeed in big cases without a back-up plan," William said. "Not that this is all that big of a case anymore."

"I've given you client lists, names and numbers, locations of rooms full of evidence. You've not only got a plan B, you've got plans B, C, and D. Get the clients to testify. You don't need us."

"Over twenty years of experience tells me I do. The two of you can give your statements, leave town until it's time for your testimony, and then disappear again."

Blake stuck his fingers into the wavy hair at the back of his head and pulled. "That won't work. I can't put Addie in that position."

"Then give me your statement. We'll leave Addie out of it. Your testifying was a part of our agreement when you entered into this deal, anyway. Not that this is what we were supposed to be nailing him on."

Blake felt William's jab as forcefully as if William had used his fists. "I can't testify. Not now that she's in the picture. When he finds out I've testified against him, he'll use her to get to me, and vice versa. You're going to have to go with what you've got."

"You're the lynchpin in all of this. You've been in those vaults. You've seen what's there, you've had direct conversations with Otto about his business. I need your testimony to be sure I can put him away."

Blake sat motionless, the car idled at the stoplight. Another two months and he would have recovered the stolen art from the Gardner theft, would have sang like the canary he intended to be, would have let everyone know who Otto really was, and would have put Otto away for the rest of his life. Then, neither he nor anyone else he cared about would ever fear Otto Albrecht again.

But when Addie showed up, that eliminated every promise he had made to William, the FBI, and several others. Including himself. Heat roiled in his belly at the thought of Otto escaping prison time and continuing to endanger those he loved. He dropped his forehead into his palm.

"I get it. I didn't deliver the way I thought I could, and I regret that more than you'll probably ever know. But this isn't just about me and what I want anymore. I have to think about what protects Addie."

"This has never just been about what you wanted. It's been about recovering national treasures. Whatever you feel for that girl has made you lose your focus. If you want your record clean, you'll testify on this forgery case to put him away, or you'll jeopardize the life of the one person you think you can keep safe. Do this voluntarily, or I'll force you to do it. Don't think I won't."

Blake paused. "What's the second thing?"

"What?" William barked.

"When we met in my office you said I had to do two things for you if I wanted my record clean."

"You're going to get me this art."

There was a click on the line and Blake slammed his fist against the seat.

The lavender bath that Alexa prepared swirled around my shoulders. It's warmth swaddled my skin, inspiring me to detach from the events of the day.

I could not yet bring myself to talk about what I'd seen. Thankfully, Alexa was understanding while I sat in catatonic quietness on the ride home.

There was no trace of *I told you so*. Even though she had told me so. Nearly everyone in my family had. Something always seemed suspicious about Otto and the firm to the women in my family. My grandmother had not been satisfied with Otto's explanation of how her husband and son had disappeared. She was certain it was not accidental, though she hadn't been able to prove it.

The police said the disappearances were a fluke. They must have been in the wrong place at the wrong time. Paris wasn't that dangerous of a city, not back then. Especially not for two people who had been there hundreds of times.

Scenes from the vault haunted me as I slipped further

into the tub. Flashes of the forgeries jarred me. This was not what I thought the firm was about. Not what I thought Otto or Ellen were about. And I began to wonder.

"Addie, you okay?" Alexa called through the door.

"Fine, Lex."

She cracked the bathroom door and peeked around it. "You have a text," she said cautiously.

"Oh." I sat up. "Is it from Blake?" I had questions about how he knew to come and get me, how he knew about the forgeries, and what the ghost had said to me.

Blake had gotten me out of there safely. Without him I would still be trapped or worse. Hopefully he was coming over to help, and not to silence me in some way.

Alexa nodded and handed me a hand towel and the phone, and then leaned against the wall while she waited.

Blake: On my way over with dinner and wine. I'll call before I get there. Do not open the door unless I call first, okay?

Adeline: Okay. Thanks.

Blake: You bet.

"Blake's on his way, he said he'd call when he gets here." I put the phone down on the edge of the tub and leaned back against the warmth of the water.

"How far away is he?"

"Didn't say. I'm guessing an hour or so, considering after-work traffic."

"Here, give me your phone before it takes a swim. Would you be all right if I leave for a little while once he gets here? Cocoa is roaming the apartment and hasn't been out all day."

"Of course, take care of your pup. Why don't you bring her back with you?"

"I will. Thanks. Will Blake make good choices for your dinner, or do I need to make a backup plan?"

I thought about how Blake had ordered for me at the restaurant. "He'll do fine."

"Wow." Alexa's eyes got big, and she gave a little laugh as she smiled.

"What?" I looked up at her.

"That's a load of attraction you're carrying around."

"Get out of my head, Alexa."

"I'd love to be out of your reactions, but I feel *everyone's* reactions when I'm this close to them."

I shook my head.

"You've really got it for this guy, don't you?"

"It's complicated."

Alexa let the silence ring loud in the room.

"I'd really rather not feel this way toward him at this point in my life."

Alexa's eyes focused on me and I knew she was about to launch into big-sister-knows-better mode. "I think you're reliving the Jeremy catastrophe too much. Maybe giving Blake some undeserved credit for Jeremy's choices?"

"He has secrets. Also, I think he just feels dangerous to me. I need to watch out for myself."

"You have secrets," she said. Then let more silence bear down on me like a two-ton anvil. "Everyone has secrets. They're not all bad."

I broke the staring contest and looked at the tops of my knees.

Alexa sighed, and her pained expression said tons. "Don't pay too high a price for what Jeremy tind Patti did. It's not yours to pay. Leave the burden where it belongs. With them." Alexa walked further into the bathroom and leaned against the sink. "At some point we all have to leave the past behind, so we can find our future. We're just not sure what it looks like, yet. Which is fine. Because you're figure it out."

I gave a reluctant nod. "Thanks, Lex."

"That's what I'm here for, hon. To shine a light onto the blindingly obvious."

"I don't think that was all so obvious."

"Everything is obvious to me, Addie."

"Right." I sat up and crossed my arms, but I knew no protection was in the cards for me as long as Alexa was around. "You realize that's an annoying quality, right?"

"Are you going to tell me what happened today?"

I stared into Alexa's sea-green eyes that missed nothing. "Yeah." A wave of dread rolled through me. I banged my head against my knees.

"You'll feel better after you talk about it. You need to get it out. And you need to *get* out. You're turning into a prune. Put on a robe and meet me in the living room. Alexa grabbed my robe, threw it unceremoniously over the top of the closed toilet, and put her hands on her hips. "That's your problem. You're always trying to be someone else. Maybe you should just play the cards you were dealt. You are who you are, Addie. You can't change that. You can't outsmart it, either."

Lightning jolted my body, and I froze as I half lifted my body out of the watery bubbles. "You know, a little bit of you goes a long way, Lex."

"We'll figure this out. We're smart. We're Montgomery women. We'll find the right answer to this, whatever it is."

I laughed, and I threw a wet loofah at her. She dodged just in time.

"I'm waiting," she singsonged and backed out into the hall with a goofy grin.

ONLY ALEXA COULD GET a laugh out of me after a day like today.

I bundled the thirsty robe around my still-wet body and stood in front of the fogged mirror. Wiping a clear streak with my sleeve, I stared at my face. Eyelids swollen, nose and lips swollen, skin patchy.

I turned away from the mirror and stood there, leaning against the counter until the walls felt like they were closing in. Everything I didn't know how to deal with or protect myself from was screaming loud. Alexa was right. I needed to talk this out. And I needed to be with my sister. If nothing else, her love would bring comfort.

I met Alexa in the living room, and found her curled up on the couch, two glasses of wine, a half-empty wine bottle of Frey Merlot, and my phone sitting on the coffee table.

"Wow, you read my mind."

"I usually do." Alexa smiled and handed me a glass. "Not the easiest of qualities to be around, I understand."

"Yeah, well. It is what it is."

We both tucked our legs under ourselves and settled in.

MY STOMACH CLENCHED when I thought how the ghost had been killed because of what he knew. I could end up just like him.

"So what happened?" Alexa asked. The proverbial door was open between us, and I found a semi-coherent way to tell her about the movers, my decision to find out if Ellen was behind the original Bellini in Otto's office, seeing the forgeries, getting locked in the vault, seeing our grandfather, how he, Ellen and Otto knew about my gift, and finally about meeting the ghost that haunted Blake and knew about the forgeries and some scheme Otto was involved in, and how Blake had rescued me.

I could see the wheels turning behind her now-luminous eyes. Her champagne-colored hair gleamed like a halo when the sun peeked through the window behind her. She really was my angel. Often a pain in the rear, but my angel, nonetheless. I watched the light through the window and remembered how Ellen had referred to it when she reminisced about being here with our grandfather.

When Alexa picked up a few strands of her halo and twirled them, I realized she was nervous. I expected her to tell me I needed to stop Blake from coming over and that I also needed to start planning my escape from the country.

"This problem is like a room with no doors and no windows," I said.

"I don't know. I think we don't yet have all the pieces to the puzzle," she said.

"What do you mean?" I put down my glass and wished the wine would do more to quell the sick nerves tumbling in my stomach.

"I don't know. It's just what I get. Sometimes puzzles reveal their answers one piece at a time, and there's no way to rush it. This one seems...unfinished. All you can do is put yourself in the best position to see it. We may just need a little time to think about this, that's all."

Alexa put her hand on mine. "I realize that's not very comforting."

"You have some insight or feeling about it?"

Alexa shook her head. "I know we will find a way out of this, because we have to. And so we will." She squeezed my hand, and her strength calmed me.

My phone buzzed on the table and Alexa leaned over to look at the screen.

"It's Blake." She handed me the phone.

My stomach flip-flopped.

"Hey," I answered softly.

"Hey. I'm outside."

"I'll let you in." I wondered how it was that Blake said "hey" like I did. Could he have been raised in the South? I had no idea where he was from. I didn't even know his middle name. It was strange to feel so connected to someone when I knew nothing about him. You can't underestimate the lasting imprints of a past life. I punched a code into the keypad on the wall, and Blake entered through the outside door.

Alexa was already gathering her things. "As our grandfather would say, 'I'm meditating on all of this.' And I am, Addie. When I come back, I'll have answers for you. Or at least I'll be closer to figuring this out." She smiled. "Are you sure you'll be all right while I'm gone?"

"I think so." I nodded as my phone buzzed in my hand.

"Hey. I'm outside your door."

"Okay, I'll be right there."

I had completely forgotten that I was in my robe, my emotions were still overriding my normal awareness of self and appearance. Blake walked in with grocery and restaurant take-out bags. It looked like enough supplies to keep me going for several days without leaving the house.

When I closed the door, I noticed Thomas standing in the hallway in his black suit and sunglasses. My heart bounced to my throat, my stomach, and back again. This man inspired incredible fear in me.

"Thomas is outside," I said to Blake as he moved down the hallway searching for the kitchen.

"Yeah, he's going to help me keep an eye on things."

"Oh," was all I could say. I smiled at Thomas. Though he still didn't return the smile, he nodded. He put his hands in his pockets, and I caught sight of the gun at his waistband before he turned his back against the wall.

56

———

When I walked into the kitchen, Alexa was staring at Blake, her long eyelashes opening and closing like butterfly wings. When he walked away to unpack a few more bags, I pinched her arm.

"Ow," she mouthed.

"Knock it off," I mouthed back.

The dirty look she flashed me had guilt written all over it. All women reacted to Blake this way. Apparently Lexie wasn't immune to his charms, either.

"Right. So, Blake, thanks for lending me your car and driver. I can be back in about two hours. Will you be able to stay with Addie?"

Blake nodded and smiled. "Thomas and I will be here until you return." The seriousness of his mood reached Alexa before he finished his sentence, and she looked at me. Then at him. Then at me again.

She was reading us. *Great.*

"Driver? I thought Thomas was your driver," I said.

"Today he's more in the line of security."

Alexa stood rooted in place until I put my hand on her back to usher her out.

"It was nice to meet you, Blake. Thank you for helping Addie," she remembered to say as she looked over her shoulder. She smiled all the way to the door then turned and whispered like a teenager, "There's history between the two of you—"

"I know. I know. I've felt it."

"You know what it is?" Alexa grinned like a gossiping schoolgirl.

"It's some past life something. I haven't really had time to plow through it all. It's complicated."

"It's only complicated because you don't use your gifts like you should. If you opened yourself up to reading this, you could figure it out."

"It's a little more than that." I thought briefly about Blake's pen that wouldn't speak to me. "But you're not entirely wrong. Let's talk about it when you come back tonight. Don't be long, okay?"

"I won't. I love you." Alexa kissed my cheek and hugged me hard.

"I love you more." I grabbed her arm before she headed out. "I just want to double-check. Do you think I'll be okay while Blake's here? I'll be safe with him, right?"

"I wouldn't leave you here with him unless I had already looked and liked what I saw." Lexie winked, which meant she was keeping part of her insights to herself.

I decided to trust her and not to push it.

Alexa hugged me again. "This is going to be okay."

I closed the door behind her and fought the dread that built inside. With Alexa gone I was now dependent upon someone I didn't entirely trust. Even with her insight and assurances, I hoped I was protected and not trapped.

57

———————

Blake wasn't in the kitchen when I passed by the
door. Instead he was hovering over the coffee table
putting out brie and crackers, sushi, and mini
lobster tails. Leave it to him to lean toward the high end.
Even in a crisis.

He smiled, and walked over to me with a glass of wine in
hand. "Want to sit? I'm sure you need to eat. Have you eaten
anything today?"

I thought about it. "I guess not, actually."

"Come. Sit. Eat. You'll need your strength."

I changed into sweats then sat in front of the table decorated with food but couldn't manage to take any. Blake took
the initiative and picked up a small broiled lobster tail. He
tore off the tail and held it to my lips. I slowly opened my
mouth and took it in.

He picked up my wine glass and put it back in my hand.
I looked at the bottle he'd put on the table. La Marouette.
One of my favorite French wines. One that probably
shouldn't be resisted. Especially in times of trouble.

The food felt good to my body. Blake felt good to my

spirit. He was comforting, encouraging. I felt encircled by feelings of safety. Any concerns I had about not trusting him were waning, just as they had in the vault, and in the limo before that. He may have been pushing, or just caring. Either way, I went with it. I was too exhausted to do anything else.

Lex was right. It was time to move on. Life had a way of slamming doors behind you if you couldn't find a way to move forward. If there was even a remote shot of anything positive happening with Blake, I'd have to quit dragging around this anchor to my past. Otherwise known as Jeremy.

I am who I am. Nothing is going to change that.

And with that realization I managed to eat, finishing most of what Blake put in front of me.

He sat close to me, pulled my legs over his lap, and put his arm behind me.

The power of his presence flowed around me and through me. Where once it had been too much, now it was just what I needed. Blake's protectiveness made me feel that an answer would come. My mind relaxed, in spite of the serious problems at hand. Alexa was right. Somewhere the right answer to all of this existed, and I would find it.

Blake stared out the turret-styled window, I looked up at him, admiring the way his long eyelashes complemented his angular features. I searched for the courage to say what I needed to.

"I'm in serious danger, aren't I?" My heart jumped into my throat.

Blake gazed at the park scene outside the window before he swallowed hard and looked at me. His normally crystal blue eyes were now electric, the evidence of sheer determination and a mind processing an immense amount of information. I had been letting go as I leaned on him, working my way out of overwhelm. He had stayed strong, remaining aware, intact, giving me a safe place to land for a while.

"Yes," he finally answered, and a flash of pain crossed his face. His hand framed my face, his thumb rubbed against my cheek. "We have some decisions to make. And we need to talk about a few things first."

I sat up to the edge of the couch, expecting the worst. "Okay."

"A few years ago, I was approached by an FBI Art Crime Team agent," Blake said. "They knew I did business with Otto, told me they believed he was involved in a major art theft, and asked if I would help them."

He watched my face carefully. I hung on every word.

"I agreed to help."

This wasn't at all what I expected. "The FBI?" I asked. The scene I'd intuited where Blake met with several men in suits and discussed some dangerous assignment came back to me. "Did you meet with them in a conference room at a long table?"

"I did, actually," Blake said, not sounding nearly as confused as I expected him to.

The first wave of relief I'd felt in a long time washed over me. Blake wasn't entirely who he said he was—that part of my insight was true. But his secret wasn't a bad one, just as Alexa had suggested. *Not all secrets are bad.*

"The FBI," I said again. "They've been trying to catch him on a theft?" I thought about the conversation I'd heard between Otto and Ellen while I was in the vault. "The Gardner art?" I asked, not really knowing who the Gardners were, or which art was theirs.

Blake's face took on a solemnness that gave me a chill. "It's the Isabella Gardner Museum theft," he said.

"Gardner." I popped off the couch and crossed the room.

"Gardner. Oh. No. When I heard Ellen say Gardner I thought she was talking about some client with the last name Gardner. Holy cow! I didn't think he wanted to pull me in on the Gardner heist."

"What do you mean you heard Ellen say Gardner?" Blake asked.

"Otto has the Gardner art. I saw him talking about it to Ellen," I blurted and walked circles around the library. "He pulled the Gardner theft. Or he killed whoever did the theft. Or he did the theft with a partner and killed the partner." I was now talking to myself. Trying to figure it out. "And something must be wrong if he wants me in on that."

"When? When did you see him talking to Ellen about this?" Blake rose off the couch and blocked my pacing path.

I realized I had just outed myself.

Panic danced through my nervous system and I thought about leaving. Just walking out of the room. I liked for secrets to stay hidden. My secrets, other people's secrets. They should stay tucked away. Like they're supposed to.

"So, oh wow." I blew out a deep breath. "Well, you weren't exactly wrong about me the other night at dinner. I —" I reached for my wine and took a long sip. "As luck would have it, I do have a few abilities that most other people don't have. And as you suggested, I can get the history—the story—from objects that people have owned. Okay, you probably think I'm nuts. It's called—"

"Psychometry," Blake interrupted. "And I don't think you're nuts."

After an infinite moment I realized my mouth was hanging open and I slammed it shut. "How do you know about psychometry?"

"As I mentioned, I come from a gifted family," Blake said.

"There isn't much about the psychic realm that I don't know. Or that would bother me, for that matter."

Relief mixed with happiness and I felt my shoulders drop. One. Then the other.

Blake chuckled quietly.

"Wow." I was officially speechless.

His smile widened into a nice warm laugh. He put my hands in his. I had the unmistakable feeling I was in the room with a friend.

"Sounds like you're rather gifted." His voice was tender.

"It's a gift that can get in the way sometimes."

"I can handle it." He looked at me intently. "Thank you," he said. "For your trust."

I wasn't sure what to do in this land of open honesty, the land Blake kept pulling me into, and though I was afraid of a good many things, I wasn't afraid to admit that I didn't know my way around this place.

"Thank you for being open. The other night at dinner, you knew, didn't you?"

"I knew," Blake answered.

I rubbed my forehead with my fingertips. "I didn't realize I wore all of my secrets on the outside."

"Only with me," he said.

A lighthearted feeling spread throughout my chest and tingled down my arms. "I think I'm relieved you know."

The orangey-pink of the sunset filled the room and a few birds sang from the park across the street, which gave the room a dream-like feel.

"But how did you know?"

"That night when you were at my gallery. I happened upon you while you were touring the floor. I saw you almost touch the Picasso. I have relatives who are gifted with psychic touch, my mother among them. I've seen her reach out for the story so many times."

I sat up straight. "Your mother is psychic?"

He laughed. "Both parents are. As is my sister. We all have our own gifts."

"Then there really isn't anything I can do that will surprise or scare you?" I asked.

"I doubt it. You inspire me to feel many things, but fear isn't one of them."

I adored this man.

"So *your* specialty would be pushing." I gave him a little push against his chest with my fingertips.

"Maybe I'm the one who wears his secrets on the outside." Blake looked pleased at my discovery.

"Only with me," I said feeling a little smug.

"That would be ideal," he said.

"It was the Jefferson artwork." I softened into the easiness between us.

"Ah, right. Sorry. It's a habit that sneaks up on me sometimes."

"Have you pushed me any other time?"

"No. And you have my word I never will." His lips grazed mine and I wondered about Christie's. "So, that day at Christie's. You weren't pushing me to feel anything?"

Blake shook his head. "Why? You sensed something?"

"Well, I felt something. I thought maybe it had been you."

Blake's smile tipped rather devilish. "Oh, I did have an opportunity to watch you for a few minutes. I wouldn't have expected you to sense that, though. It wasn't as if I was sending that feeling to you."

"I wouldn't have expected to sense that, either. Alexa has

the same gift to push, so I'm pretty immune, even if you had tried. Years of practice."

"She tried it out on me." Blake laughed.

"She didn't get to you?" I smirked.

"No one gets to me except for you. Our connection must be stronger than even I realized."

"You have no idea how happy that makes me."

"Good," he said confidently.

WE SETTLED onto the couch again with the rest of our wine, and I felt like I had found an oasis of heaven in the midst of my hell, a friend among enemies. I told Blake how I'd read the Giovanni frame while I was in the vault, how Otto knew about my abilities, how he wanted to use me to buy and sell art on the black market, pull me onto the Gardner project, and how this had been a setup from the very beginning. "He told Ellen I would be his replacement for Carolena. I don't know who she is but—"

"She was someone Otto used to find authentic pieces of art on the black market. Her gifts were similar to yours, and they made a lot of money together."

"Oh." Otto's misery from the picture in his office revisited me. The one where he and his family stood in front of the Louvre. "Did they have an affair or a relationship?"

"He doesn't talk much about her," Blake said.

"I'm almost positive they did. And I would bet you my left foot that they had a child together."

Blake took a sip of wine.

"His belongings mentioned it to me. Something must be wrong with the Gardner art, though, because he told Ellen he wants to bring me in on that job," I said. "For a girl who can see so much, I sure have a few blind spots."

"Otto's charm has fooled more than just a few bright people. I wouldn't be too hard on myself if I were you."

I shook my head and thought of young Otto painting as a child. I remembered his father yelling at him that his work wasn't original. "He paints the forgeries himself, you know."

"Yes," Blake said.

"They were exquisite. He's quite good. I would never have known the difference between the original and the fake in the vault if I hadn't—I mean, if I hadn't...touched them for their story." I bit my lip and looked out the window. "It's tragic in a way. To have so much talent and end up hiding it."

Otto's father's anger echoed through me and I shuddered. For as much as I feared for my life from the man Otto was, I felt sorry for the child he had been. Maybe he lacked the confidence to paint something original. Or maybe painting replicas was his only talent. Maybe he took those pieces because he craved the great artistic talents those artists had. Maybe it was a revenge of sorts, or perhaps he wanted to forge those paintings to test himself, release the forgeries back into the market to see if he could fool the experts. Show everyone that he was as good as they were. Maybe then he'd feel he finally measured up to his original hero: his father.

"When he said black market, he meant mafia, didn't he?" I asked and I thought about the ghost who had attacked me twice. He seemed so characteristically mafia-esque.

"In Otto's case. Yes, mostly." Blake ran his hand through his hair. "Though he'd sell to anyone for the right price."

"Mafia," I said again. "If he has the mafia on his side, and he really wants to get to me, he will. I'll never be able to walk to a newsstand, or buy flowers at the corner grocery or go to a museum." I stood and began pacing again.

"That's why I've been trying to get the FBI to nail him on the forgeries. The statute of limitations has run out on the Gardner art." Blake strode over to me and placed his hands on my arms to steady me. "I doubt the mafia will do his bidding if he's in jail and no longer has access to art. But the FBI is asking us both to testify to what we've seen in the vault. To help put him away."

"Oh. No." I felt the world slip away from under my feet. "I can't testify. I-I can't sit there in the courtroom in front of whoever his mafia friends are. There's no way. Otto can't know that I know. He'd kill me. I'm sure of it." My mouth and throat went instantly dry and I thought about the ghost in the vault, how he had died.

Blake pulled my hair away from my face. "I understand. I'll tell them it's not an option. They can't make you testify."

"But can they put him away without my testifying?" My voice strained half an octave higher than usual. "I mean, there's a vault full of evidence. That should get him some jail time, right?" My head swam with thoughts of how he probably wouldn't be in jail forever, how Otto would blame me for his going to jail in the first place. So that when he got out he would—

"They can. If they act quickly they have enough evidence without us. And they should be able to get client testimonies. So many of his clients have forgeries now. When clients discover that, they should want to take him down."

"Otto really didn't think this through. Eventually these clients would find out." I couldn't move. Blake seemed to know how I felt and he allowed me space. "It's too bad you and the FBI couldn't recover the Gardner art." I shuddered at the thought of the mafia having possession of Rembrandt, Vermeer, and Degas. I envisioned *The Concert* thumbtacked to the wall of a smoke-filled room. Or worse, rolled up in the corner of a dank, basement closet.

"That was the only reason they brought me in," Blake said, conflict flitted briefly across his features.

"Apparently everyone pays a price when they get close to Otto."

"So it seems," he said.

~

THE SUN SHONE behind Blake and I looked into his eyes, the ones that saw me too clearly, and I saw something I hadn't expected. Or asked for.

Trust.

Given freely.

My walls of secrecy had crumbled and left me feeling oddly safe with this man I hardly knew. Suddenly I hated the idea of having compartments in my life that Blake might not reach, places within me he couldn't touch, things he couldn't understand because I'd held them back. The protective walls I'd clung to all my life felt like weapons against this man I loved.

I thought of the ghost from the firm and Blake's gallery, the one who was all so mafia-esque and I took another long drink from my glass.

Blake rubbed my shoulder with his outstretched hand. "Are you okay?"

"There's one more thing you ought to know about me." I paused to center myself as much as possible. "I see ghosts," I said.

"So, you see dead people?" Blake grinned.

I elbowed him and he nearly spilled his wine. "I do. And there's a wicked ghost that follows you around sometimes. He moves between your gallery and Otto's firm. He breaks glass as a way of making his presence known. He's tried twice to kill me." I gave him my you'd-better-take-this-seriously look.

"The ghost— He could do that?" Blake reached for me slowly, like he was moving through deep water. I laid my hand in his.

"I don't know, actually. I need to speak with my mother and grandmother about it. They're more knowledgeable about these things than I am. But he gave it a good try. He said something like, 'They take from me, I take from them.' He's bent on revenge. I think he's one of Otto's mafia friends."

Blake sat on the edge of the couch, his eyes focused and intense. I realized I'd never actually seen him feel afraid before, and it wasn't comforting. "Can you describe what he looks like?" he asked.

"Brown hair swept to the side, brown eyes, young, like late twenties, I would guess. And he drinks—or drank—a lot. Whiskey. Jim Beam or Jack Daniels. Something like that."

"I thought so." Blake's brows furrowed. "I knew him. And I've seen him. Though I didn't realize he'd been aggressive with you. I'll have a talk with him. Reign him in."

"You can see ghosts?" I asked.

"Not as well as my mother or my sister. Not like you, but Frank, I tend to feel him when he's around."

"Unbelievable," I murmured.

"He's a former business associate of Otto's." Blake made a face that said he used the term lightly. "His name is Frank 'Pretty Boy' Collis from the Pulizzi mob family. His family has purchased most of Otto's stolen artwork since Otto couldn't move it in his own circles. My guess is they used them as collateral for drug deals. But Frank and Otto got a little too close. I think they must have shared some father-son type bond. And I think Frank figured out that Otto had something to do with the Gardner heist. I doubt Otto wanted the Pulizzis involved in those pieces."

"I doubt it's Otto's ethics that keep him from being choosy about his buyers," I said.

"Knowing Otto, he probably knows a collector or two overseas who will pay more than the typical ten-percent of value that the black market yields. If the Pulizzis know he has the Gardner art, they'd pressure him for it. By any and all means."

"Do they know?" I asked.

"I don't know. But I do think Frank knew. I'll bet he knew Otto would kill him for it. Frank asked me if I could help him get out. Next day he was dead. Found in an alley, shot three times."

I rubbed my chest and remembered what it felt like when I relived Frank's death while I was in the vault. "Did he know you were working with the FBI?"

"If he did he never called me out on it. That conversation has haunted me since he died. I was going to get him out." Blake looked away.

"If he didn't know then, he knows now." I spun my sapphire ring around on my finger.

"What do you mean?" Blake asked.

"Because he told me once that you weren't who I thought you were. Unless there's something I'm missing, I would guess that's it."

Blake leaned against the pillows and shook his head in disbelief.

"You can't keep a secret from a ghost," I warned, and downed the rest of my wine. "Stranger things have happened... I think, anyway."

"I knew he was following me," Blake said. "The cold spots in the office, the noises. The broken glass. I'm not replacing the vases anymore." He waved his hand in the air. "I'm sure he blames me for not being able to help him."

"I'm sure he blames Otto for killing him. I'd say he's still here because he needs to wrap up unfinished business in order to move on, but if settling the score by killing me is what's unfinished, then I'd just as soon not help him out," I said. "He's afraid of *you*, though."

"Frank is?"

I nodded. "The two times he tried to hurt me, he backed off as soon as he realized you were on your way."

"Hmmm," Blake said. "The other thing we need to think about—"

"Right now I'm wondering how I live through the night," I leaned forward on my knees.

Blake put his warm hand on my back. "We have to think about the security cameras at the firm. I'm sure they caught your movements in and out of the vault today."

My heart sank.

"I thought about that earlier. And your movements as well," I admitted reluctantly as I sat up. "I'm sorry, Blake. It's my fault you're involved like this."

"Remember I was already involved in this before we met. You don't need to feel sorry for anything." He kissed me on the forehead, but I felt his own worry run through him. His eyes shone with equal parts strength and fear when he looked at me, and I realized I couldn't remember the last time I'd known a man to take a risk for me.

"How is it that you knew where to find me when I was in the vault?" I asked.

"Ellen."

The floor dropped out from under me. "She came in to the vault while I was hidden in there. Something must have given me away. Thankfully, I guess." I held my fingertips to my lips. Ellen went to Blake instead of going to Otto. She held my life in her hands, and at the risk of her own life, she helped me. "I never would have expected her to do that." I thought about the foyer walls of the firm that reached out to me on my interview day. Her voice was embedded in that distinctive wave and now I wished I knew what stories were there.

"I'm going to help you, Addie. We're going to get through this, so don't give up hope." His eyes steeled with resolve, and his pure and untethered emotions poured through me. In this moment, he was easy to read. There was no conflict between his head and heart. I closed my eyes as a wave of vulnerability swept over me.

Like a disease that wouldn't die, thoughts of Jeremy's betrayal knocked against my mind. But then Blake brushed his lips against mine. His tender kiss pierced the protective warnings and reached deep inside me to a place I rarely accessed.

My phone rang.

"It's Alexa," he said and handed my phone to me.

I reached for my wine glass with one hand as I accepted my phone with the other.

"Lex. You okay?"

"Yeah, fine. You?"

"Yeah. Just...finishing some dinner."

"Oh, good, you ate."

Blake walked toward the kitchen.

"Yep."

"Listen, Ad, I don't think I'm going to be able to come back tonight."

My normal hyper-awareness shifted into a higher gear. "Why not? What's wrong?"

Alexa hesitated. "Otto's car is parked down the street from your home."

58

___

"Otto's car? How do you know it's his car? Is he in it?" My heart ran like a hamster in its wheel. *He knows. He knows. He's seen the tapes, he's coming after me.*

"I don't really know. But I think it's him. The back window is down a little, and there's a man with silver hair in the back seat. Does he still have silver hair?"

"Yes. He does. Blake—" I turned around to call for him, but he was standing right there at the edge of the room. "Blake, Alexa thinks that Otto is parked at the end of the street in a Town Car. Or at least she thinks it's him. He knows, doesn't he?" My heart was about to jump out of my chest.

"What are the plates?" Blake asked.

"What are the plates, Lex?" I asked her.

Lexie paused and I could almost feel her squinting. "Um, New York, SJX 4681."

"How close are you to his car?" I asked.

"Not very. Blake's driver has binoculars," Lexie said.

"Oh. Alexa says they're New York plates, SJX 4681," I said.

The air left Blake's lungs, and I felt his energy spin. "That's Otto's car."

"Why is he here? He knows I was in the vault, doesn't he?" I panicked.

"I doubt he's seen the tapes yet. Don't worry, he can't get to you. Not while I'm here. Hand me the phone."

I handed Blake the phone. He left his other hand on my shoulder and I felt his strength run through me. He wasn't going to let Otto near me.

"Alexa, put the driver on, please," Blake said. "Pete, did he see you?... Okay. Are you sure?... Uh-huh. All right. Can you back up and ease out from— Then just take her home. Make sure you're not seen or followed. And make sure she gets inside safely. Then put the car away for the night but don't take it to the gallery. I don't want anyone timing your comings and goings... All right, let me talk to Alexa.

"Alexa, that's Otto's car. I guess you realize it wouldn't be safe for him to see you coming inside. It's better for you and for Adeline if he doesn't see any activity around her home right now, and I'd rather he not have access to you... I appreciate that... I will. Do you want to talk with her?"

Blake handed me the phone and walked toward the foyer where Thomas stood.

"Are you okay?" I asked.

"I'm fine, but how are you? Why is Otto outside your home?" Alexa's voice was tense with worry.

"I think he's fishing. He must suspect something. Maybe he's watching to see if Blake is here. Or to see if I'm really home."

"What aren't you telling me?" Alexa asked.

"That Otto's involved with the mafia," I said.

I felt Alexa's stress hit the roof. "What does Blake say?"

"He's working on it. He's got some outside help, so there's a chance that— Well, there's a chance. Just promise me you'll come visit if I've dyed my hair black, am in the witness protection program and living in South Dakota."

59

———————

I promised Alexa I'd call as soon as I knew something. Then I walked away from the phone and fatigue set in. I hated having more questions than answers, and no plan. And I hated depending on other people. Yet here I was surrounded by people who held my fate in their hands.

Tomorrow would come and my excuse of a stomach virus would expire. Otto was already suspicious. I couldn't think of any other reason why he'd be camped out on my street. If he thought I knew about his forgery scheme, he'd do to me as he had done with Frank—Blake's ghost.

Tingles worked across the upper part of my back, the usual sign that someone was watching me. I turned around and saw Blake standing just inside the room, hands in his pockets while he stared at me.

"Well at least I'm getting better at *that*," I said.

Energy stirred inside me at the sight of him walking toward me, and vulnerability bucked beneath me like a wild horse pushing at me to ride away. But I stood firm, let the sensation wash over me.

"You okay?" he asked, his knuckles grazed the side of my cheek.

"I don't know. I'm tired. I'm tired of secrets. I'm tired of hiding. I'm tired of running."

He waded through the heat between us. I felt his emotion resonating within me before I felt his touch on my arm. It was a feeling of depth and recognition, like an echo to a call I hadn't realized I'd made.

"Then stop running," he said.

Our faces were only a breath apart. Neither of us made a move as our eyes held one another for a timeless moment. And then I wrapped my arms around him.

60

____

We sat on the couch, and talked for hours. Until I fell asleep, snuggled in close against Blake's warm body, my head on his chest, my arm wrapped tightly around him.

When I woke, it was dark outside. Blake stirred when I did, and slipped out to the kitchen. He returned with wine and leftovers—shrimp that somehow we'd missed earlier. The day's events rapped occasionally at the corners of my mind. But I pushed them away. It wouldn't do any good to troll through those details now.

"Is Thomas still out front?" I asked, feeling a little conflicted about Thomas being our bodyguard.

"He's fine. I checked on him. Made him an espresso."

Blake looked over at the candle on the side table and pulled on the knob of the drawer. "Do you have matches or a lighter in here?"

He found and lit the candle, its light flickered against the darkened walls.

We sipped our wine and stared intently into each other's eyes, and then, I watched it happen. Something opened within him. A doorway that offered me passage inside. Only this time it was a refuge and a homecoming.

I accepted the invitation he offered me into his heart and felt my own barriers collapsing one by one as I did. He loved me. He hadn't said it, but even better, I felt it from him. That, for me, was the real litmus test.

I wandered around the space in his heart that was dedicated to me, and I marveled at the space he had made for me. Like a room prepared while he waited for me. Patiently. Waiting. And loving me while he did.

He had been ahead of me, braver than I was. Seeing me —all of me. Before I saw myself. And here I was, at home in his heart, in the place he opened just for me.

I watched Blake's face and colors danced around the edges of him. Colors that had history, our history, that I could read if I wanted to. There was laughter and love and extraordinary happiness that brimmed in the different shades. I opened myself to all of it, and I closed my eyes.

"Adeline, open your eyes."

I did. Lost in the world we had made together, impermeable to distraction, I opened them and saw the crystal blue eyes that had gazed at me from another time.

It was him.

It was Jack.

It was Blake. But it was Jack. I recognized the way he looked at me through those eyes. It was *him.*

"It's *you*," I whispered.

"It *is* me. You remember me?"

"I do remember you. You know who I am?"

"More than you realize, Addie."

"You *did* come for me."

His smile was unmistakable. "How could I ever stay away from you?"

His voice, my new favorite sound, reverberated around me.

I watched his face, his eyes penetrating and intense.

"Is this really happening?" I felt a piece of my heart exchange places with a part of his.

After a near lifetime of feeling like an outsider, I was finally where I was destined to be. I was home.

I was lost in his heart. Lost in the timeless love we shared. "Oh my, you're really here."

"I wouldn't want to be anywhere else."

He leaned toward me, and we kissed each other like we'd never kiss again.

61

___

Wrapped securely in Blake's strong arms, I slept heavily. History worked its way into my peaceful dream state, and nudged me to notice the warm afternoon sun streaming through the gauzy white curtains that hung in the side window. It illuminated the long-ago scene of a young father and his son, sitting on an animal print couch flipping through the pages of a large book of art. The man angled the book so his son could see the pictures clearly.

"This is *Napoleon's Coronation*. Do you remember me telling you about him?"

The young boy looked up at his father, nodding. He had his mother's blue eyes, the shape of her face, even his personality was a replica of hers. The father was nowhere to be seen in the child's features. But he was intent on giving him his love of art.

"This is the painting that has two originals," the boy recited. "One in the Louvre and one in Versailles. Napoleon conditioned them both," he said proudly, his blue eyes sparkling.

"*Commissioned* them. Right," his father corrected with a quiet laugh. "Do you remember what's different about the two originals?"

The boy thought for a minute before coming up with the answer. "The artist fell in love with one of the ladies in the picture when he was painting her, so he painted her dress a different color the second time around."

"Excellent," his father praised. "Remember there's always a story behind the art. That's what makes it so unique and appreciated. It's what people relate to. What makes them relate the art to themselves."

The boy was remarkably bright, he thought. Memorizing whatever he was taught, he seemed innately to understand things on a deeper level. The child's mother had been the love of the man's life from the moment he met her. His passion for her was so intense that he nearly forgot he had a wife and family. When the woman became pregnant, he celebrated their good fortune. And when the boy was born, he promised to give him the world.

He doted on the little one, holding him in his arms, rocking him, and telling him stories of all the great things they would do together one day. When he couldn't be around because of his other family, he lavished gifts on his son to make up for his absence.

Having involved the child's mother in his work, the man felt sure that they would always stay connected. In some way, they would always be a family.

"Are you still going to take me to Paris to see the paintings?"

"Yes. One day soon. I promise." He looked up and noticed the boy's mother standing in the alcove. She smiled at him, but her expression belied her hatred. She was exhausted by all that he put her through, forcing her to use her God-given gifts for his personal profit.

"Run and get the bat and ball I brought you and meet me in the backyard. We'll play a little before I have to go."

The boy threw his arms around the man's neck and hugged him tightly, deepening his home in the man's heart. Then he scurried to get the bat and ball, knowing he might not see the man again for a while.

The mother had been watching from the doorway and the man walked over and kissed her on the cheek. She wondered if he could sense the repulsion she felt toward him. She did her best to hide it when he was around.

"My wife is getting suspicious again, Carolena. I'm sorry. I won't be able to come back for about a month. She wants us to take the kids on a trip to France."

She bristled at the idea of him taking his other children to Paris while their child waited on him for a trip that would probably never come.

"Of course," she said.

"Do you have everything you need?"

"I'd like you to wire the final payment we agreed on."

"I told you I'd take care of you—"

"I know, I know," she soothed him. "It's just that your wife needs you more and more these days. I know you have obligations and—" She smoothed his tie, rubbing her hand against his chest to relax and distract him. "I need to finish out his college fund. He must be educated the way we agreed. They've already paid you for the last piece. I just want to settle my share from it. Then we can start fresh with the next one," she lied.

The money he would give her, she had more than earned. He'd put her life on the line in a way she never would have, if he hadn't threatened to take her son away from her. But it was several million this time, and she would use it to fund their escape, to disappear from him forever. Finally. She'd suffered his rage long enough. She was tired of being his captive, and this was no way to raise a son.

"Okay," he acquiesced. "I'll make a call and have it transferred today." Despite his sense of foreboding, he would honor their arrangement.

When he walked out the door and out of their lives that day, he stared into the eyes of the boy he had helped bring into the world, and his heart cracked. Though he had the ability to compartmentalize his double life, he dearly loved this child. The boy was truly something special.

As he shut the door behind him, the midnight emissary knocked fiercely at the walls of my mind, waking me up with a fright. I lifted off Blake's chest with a start, and I crawled off the couch and across the room to the window. Everything that I had shoved into yesterday's tomorrow was demanding to be figured out. Nausea turned in my stomach triggered by fright, and I leaned against the cool wall.

That man...he was Otto. A younger version, but it was him.

Blake ran over to me, put his hands on my face. The candle burned low but the flame still burned enough to cast a soft light onto the walls.

"Addie...Adeline—"

"It was Otto," I said. "He was in my dreams. And Carolena. He loved her. They did have a child," I said. "But she was—his captive. She was afraid of him. And Otto wants me to replace her? He's never gotten over her. Or the loss of his son." I was rambling too fast to be understood.

He pulled me into him, knowing part of what panicked me. The feel of his arms around me and the scent of his skin calmed me.

"Don't worry about it. Not now," he said as he kissed the side of my face.

"Blake, he wants to own me. I get it now. He wants me all to himself. How am I ever going to get out of this?"

Ever so gently he guided me back to the couch and pulled me against him, my breathing returned to normal.

"I'm here," he said quietly. "We'll work this out. Don't give up hope," he said, and tucked me in closer to him, his kisses landing gently on my head. "Don't give up hope."

"Don't give up hope," I repeated quietly and tried earnestly to follow his mantra.

His warm hands were the healing balm I needed, and as his magical thumb drifted back and forth across my back, I thought...I might just drift off to sleep.

62

———

It was the thumping that woke me.

Thump, thump, thump, thump.

As if I'd been drugged I fought against the noise.

Thump, thump, thump, thump.

I covered my ears with my hands but that only seemed to irritate the source of the noise.

Thump! Thump! Thump! Thump!

I threw the blanket off of my too-warm body, grabbed my silk robe off of the bottom of the bed, and stumbled through the dark toward its source: the front door.

THUMP-THUMP-THUMP- THUMP

In thundering, rapid succession now, the banging was so loud it echoed throughout my body, hurt my head, and sent the room to tilt. Without even stopping to look through the front door peephole, I flipped the locks and grabbed the handle, then flung the front door open wide.

The light from the hallway struck me and I ducked my head as my eyes tried to adjust.

"Addie," the familiar voice said. "Pay attention, love. You need to wake up and pay attention."

"Wha—?"

My eyes struggled against the bright light until two figures stepped up, blocking the sun from blinding me.

"Addie," their voices said over one another.

My father and grandfather stood before me, looking just as they did before they disappeared years ago. I shook my head. "Dad. Grandpa—you're here. Where—?"

I reached out for them but my father pressed his hands onto the outside of my arms and stared hard into my eyes. "Addie. You need to wake up, pay attention to what's going on around you. You're in serious danger."

The thumping started again, and the sides of my head throbbed, along with the pounding.

They backed away and the brilliant light shot through my eyes, effectively blinding me again. "Wait," I said as I rubbed my eyes and tried to find my sight.

When I opened them again I was staring sideways at sun pouring through the Parisian silk curtains that hung in my den, and my mind was mixed against the unfamiliar display.

I found the source of the heavy thumping when my adrenaline-riddled heart shouldered itself repeatedly against my chest, trying to break free. Its heroic efforts reverberated into my head, causing a horrific pain that slammed against the walls of my skull. I closed my eyes again and tried to ignore the pain, suppress the panic, and stem the building nausea.

This was the first time I'd heard from my father and grandfather since they'd disappeared. Only it didn't feel like a ghostly visit, or a visit from beyond. This was a warning. From my subconscious? No, that wasn't it. It was something else. Something I'd never experienced before. The pain surged through my head again.

"Need feverfew," I whispered.

What was I being warned about? Maybe it was just some buried reality about my father and grandfather that was begging for my attention.

Blake groaned. His warm body nudged against me from behind, his thick, muscled arms wrapped securely around me as if he feared I might escape while he slept.

I squeezed my eyes against the panic and the pain, and snugged myself deeper into Blake's embrace. As if he'd sensed the stampede of my adrenaline, a healing balm of quiet and protection emanated from him and seeped through my skin, coating my nerves. The thumping slowed, the pain softened, and I settled even more deeply into him.

Only he could do that.

Blake pressed a kiss onto my head.

I took a deep breath as a sense of safety and goodness surrounded me. I looked down at Blake's arms and smiled.

Scenes from the night before danced across my mind and my heart fluttered with a mixture of excitement, happiness, and hope—emotions I hadn't dared to have in some time. I laid a kiss on his forearm and hoped that what we had started wouldn't find an ending anytime soon.

The text alarm on Blake's phone beeped from the side table. I lifted my head to steal a glance at the wall clock. Holy moly—I'd slept until 6:00 a.m. The last time I slept in until 6:00 a.m. I was... Actually, I didn't remember the last time I'd slept that late.

Blake reached for his phone and tipped the screen.

Unknown: Call me.

I knew who the sender was, though. It had to be the FBI.

Blake put the phone back down and kissed me and pulled me closer. I slowly turned to face him. It had only been a few hours since I'd seen those intense blue eyes, but seeing them in the vulnerability of my new morning sent a shock right through to my soul. They struck a sacred, secreted place within me I didn't think anyone could reach but him.

"Sassy, my love." He stroked my face and my body and mind jerked in recognition of the nickname Jack, the man of my actual dreams, had given me.

"How do you know to call me Sassy?" I ran my fingers through his hair, and drank in a lingering kiss.

"It's how I've always known you. Even before I met you." His eyes glimmered with secrets that yearned to make themselves known.

"But how?" I breathed.

"I just knew. There's not a rational explanation for most things I know. By the time someone has told me something with their words, I've long since seen that information and filed it away," he said.

I drew his hair between my fingers and drank in the scent that rose off of his skin.

"You're the same way," he said. "Even if I hadn't seen you reach out to the Picasso at my gallery, even if you hadn't told me. I've felt it when I'm around you. Your awareness. And I see it in your eyes."

"You do?"

"Awareness shows in the eyes." Blake's eyes locked with my own. "I've known you since before I came into this world. Before I met you I lived with nothing but the hope that you would be here this time. That I wouldn't have to live without you. I was born with the memory of you in my heart, and since then I had to live with the space between us, the painful absence of you that left me searching every face for some sign of your existence. Proof that we might be together again." His fingers outlined my face.

"You knew—"

"I knew the minute I saw you that you were the one I'd searched for. With the intensity of your awareness, you had to know as well."

"Well, you were in my dreams. In this—past life appearance. I've always known him. Loved him. But it wasn't until last night, when the veil broke apart, that I knew he was you. I can't explain it, but you've been with me my entire life. Walking with me, waiting for me."

"Addie, I've never left you. I've never stopped wanting you. Or needing you."

Deeper I fell into an endless love with him, a dizzying plunge into the timeless freedom that only true love can bring.

For the first time in my life, I felt truly alive.

63

The sound of the water splashing into the tub bounced off of the tiled floor and walls and my world slipped into surreality. I sank into the warm water, and panic attack leftovers that began my day, haunted the edges of my mind, and framed my happiness.

My father and grandfather seemed so real in that dream. So alive and present. I'd never experienced anything like that before. They weren't ghosts. It wasn't a message from the Other Side. It was an experience wholly unfamiliar to me.

I sank low into the scented water and thought about Blake, what our future might hold. I had to hope the FBI would arrest Otto and put him in jail for the rest of his life. There was that newfound word that had a tentative root in my vocabulary.

Hope.

The thing that gave dreams their wings.

I wanted to soar with those wings but caution harassed me like Icarus' father and warned me not to fly too high. Warned me that I might come crashing down too hard, since I had so many times before. I pushed the unwelcome warning away.

I dried my hair enough to get the wave out of it, and that's when I noticed: the smell of breakfast. I threw on jeans and a blouse and found Blake in the kitchen, wearing only his dress pants from the day before. He stood shirtless and barefoot at the gas stove making omelets. The window in the library was open and the sound of the singing birds floated in on the scent of a damp, late summer morning.

Oh my, he cooks.

His text alarm signaled a new message. Blake looked at the screen and his face hardened. He stared at it for a minute, typed a response with one hand, and shoved the phone back into his front pocket. I felt his anger spike.

He caught sight of me and his broad smile greeted me.

He strolled toward me, oven mitt on one hand, while I stood stock-still. I was afraid he would disappear before he got to me, as Jack so often had. When Blake hugged me close, I exhaled..

"I hope you like eggs," he said as he drew back slightly.

My stomach growled as we walked to the breakfast table and I decided a little food might not be a bad idea. He placed the eggs and a glass of chilled water with lemon on the small, French table for me. Along with a tiny cup of potent espresso. This was a week of firsts. I never ate at the table.

Blake's text alarm went off again. He looked at the message and gave a heavy sigh.

"Is everything okay?" I knew he was waiting to hear from the FBI about Otto.

"As soon as I get that call that tells me Otto is in jail." He pushed his phone into his pocket again.

"Nothing yet?"

"Nothing final."

I glanced at the door when I suddenly picked up some-one's energy that wasn't Thomas'.

"Where did Thomas go?" Panic kicked up and my chest hurt.

Blake smiled, not needing to ask how I knew Thomas had left. "I sent him home to sleep for a few hours. Pete's outside for us today."

I walked to the door and looked out the peephole. No one was visible, but I could feel him out there. I kind of liked the fact that he was hidden somewhere. Maybe he was hidden to those on the outside as well.

"I'm not that worried about Otto coming by today. I've already checked with Ellen, and Otto has a full calendar of meetings at the office. I don't think he's going to creep around during the day when he would be missed at the office.

"You might want to text Ellen while it's early, let her know you're still sick—until we get word from the FBI."

He clattered around the kitchen while I typed the text to Ellen, even though I figured she knew I wouldn't be in. Appearance was everything in the art world, and I needed to give the appearance of respect.

Adeline: Hi Ellen. Still sick today. Won't be in. Sorry.

Ellen: That's fine. Thanks.

After I'd hit send, both Blake's and my phone rang at roughly the same time. Blake walked into the other room. I stayed where I was.

"Hey, Lex."

"You're safe?"

"Yeah, I'm good."

"Okay." She breathed audibly. "I hope I didn't call too early, I just needed to check on you. Did everything go okay last night? No sign of Otto? I'm sorry I couldn't be there with you."

"No, it's okay, everything has been quiet here. There's been a bodyguard outside the door all night. Blake says Otto should be at the office all day." I wanted to tell her that the FBI was involved and that we were waiting on a call to say that Otto had been arrested, but it wasn't my secret to share.

"So what's your plan? What are your next steps?" Lexi's energy snaked its way toward me.

"We're working on it. Blake has some ideas we're about to talk over."

"You can't talk about the plan now, can you?"

"Basically." I watched Blake pace with his phone to his head.

"Where is he?"

"On the phone in the salon."

"Are you okay?"

"Yeah, I'm fine. It's just—complicated."

"It really is, isn't it? Do you want me to come over? I could take the bodyguard."

"Lex..." I laughed.

"I'm just kidding," she said. "I actually think you're in good hands. It's just killing me that I can't get to my baby sister to protect her."

I could feel Lexie's worry tumbling toward me. "I love you, Lex."

"I love you, too, Add."

I heard emotion catch in her throat. "Is that your shower I hear in the background? Why are you taking a shower so early in the day?"

"Todd's going to be here in about an hour to talk about my show at the gallery. I can cancel him if you need me to."

"No, I'm fine, there's nothing to do right now. Who's

Todd?" I heard hangers sliding against metal rods. She was picking out her clothes. I knew she'd select something to catch the eye, something to impress Todd. Whoever he was.

"The brother of the gal who owns the gallery. I've known him for a while, but lately the chemistry between us is really intense. I think he's the guy I was dreaming about."

"Ohhh," I said. "Have fun."

"I will, but call me."

"I will."

I chuckled. Lex was never happier than at the beginning of a relationship, that glorious time when all the important details were just beyond clear view and made happy endings seem possible.

I looked at the texts on my phone screen and thought about Ellen. Psychically I could tell that indeed she knew far more than she was letting on about all of this. Which actually gave me some comfort. With the FBI about to swoop in on Otto, I worried for the woman who had saved my life the day before.

"How do you think Ellen is going to fare through this?" I asked when Blake returned to the table.

"Ellen has survived all these years in that firm because she's always a few steps ahead of Otto. She doesn't let on about it. Given that she knows you were in the vault, and would have seen a duplicate of every original in there, I would bet she's taken steps to protect herself from any fallout of that."

My thoughts raced along a root system of what-ifs and if-thens. "So, does that mean she warned Otto that I might tell someone? Or is she busy destroying any proof of her involvement with the forgeries? Including the security tapes?"

"It depends if she thought there was enough evidence lying around to really put Otto away, so she can get away from him. Forever. Though I hope she didn't destroy the security tapes."

"Why not?" I asked.

Blake pushed a button and the espresso machine hummed and gurgled. "The ideal would be for her to have pulled the tapes so Otto couldn't see them, but not to have destroyed them. Because if I can show the FBI that you've been in that vault, that's a life insurance policy for you. Otto's going to be less likely to try to do anything to you if his motivation is caught on tape. He'd be the first person they'd finger."

I took a bite of eggs and chewed slowly. "She would give you the tapes?"

"If Otto goes to jail she would. If he doesn't, I'm not so sure. Ellen is hard to read sometimes."

"How long will he be in jail?"

Blake drained his espresso cup, then munched on some toast like he thought about his answer. "Considering the number of pieces he's forged, how many authentic pieces he's stolen from clients, I would guess at least fifteen years. Easily more. Considering he's around seventy now, it's a life sentence."

Blake's text alarm rang out and I waited while he read it. My palms grew increasingly clammy, and silence sat at the table with us while he stared at the screen. "Any word?"

"Yes. They've got their warrants. They're going to the firm today." Blake eased out a breath and waited for the information to sink in with me.

"It's over?"

"Will be soon," he said and he reached for me. "William says they've got one client testimony, and they're going after the rest. That, along with the art in the vault, should be more than enough," he said.

I searched him for some doubt, some reason to believe that this plan might not work. I wanted to be prepared. But I felt bricks of stress dropping from Blake's shoulders and I cautiously followed suit. I decided that it was the abruptness of the news that had surprised me, and my bad habit of anticipating the worst was getting the better of me.

"William said the client they spoke to is pretty mad that they own a nice forgery. He said they're pretty motivated to testify." Something alarming glimmered through Blake's eyes. Something that said he'd stop at nothing until Otto received his sentence and the jail doors slammed behind him. If this effort didn't work, he'd tirelessly continue until he found something that did.

"I owe you a great deal for getting Otto put away," I said. "My life, really."

"You don't owe me anything. Except for maybe a kiss," he lowered his lips to mine.

My stomach did a double flip.

A while later we sat on the couch. I brushed my fingertips across his face, trying to memorize every feature, every angle.

"I'm not going anywhere." He kissed the palm of my hand. "The only way we'll ever be apart is if you leave."

"That will never happen." The fear that plagued me the day before was so far at bay, it was lost. Unable to find me in this guarded bubble we had created for ourselves.

"We still have a few things we need to talk about," he said.

I swam in the endless sky blue of his eyes. "We do? The

FBI will be on their way to the firm soon. They'll find the evidence they need. It's over."

The text alarm on Blake's phone chimed. He ignored it.

"It's never over until it's over," he said. "Even if they find what they need, there still has to be a trial. I have to testify, Addie. But my immediate concern has more to do with you."

"Me?"

"We need to think about how to keep you safe. Since Otto spoke to me about bringing you in on the Gardner work, I've thought it might be better—safer—if you left the country, laid low for a while." He skimmed the backs of his fingers up the side of my cheek. With that stroke I could feel the edges of our sacred bubble beginning to thin. Trending toward a burst.

"Leave the country? Where would I go?".

Blake's text alarm chimed again. He tilted the phone and looked at the screen.

I realized there might not be a place where I was truly safe. At least not until Otto was in prison. "Wait—did you say you're testifying?" The thumping inside my head returned.

"Addie." He reached for me but I stood and walked to the window.

"I just need a minute." I ran my fingers through my hair.

Blake crossed the room, cloaked his arms around me from behind, and I leaned in for comfort. I figured he was pushing me to calm down, and though I objected to his methods, I chose not to care. His comfort was a healing balm unlike any other.

"All I wanted was a job. A career in art. Hundreds of thousands of people around the world work in the art community every day and life just goes on." I said. "And now you're testifying and Otto has connections. You remember that, right? I'm not the only one in danger here."

"It's what I agreed to when I got into this, and I don't think they're going to let me out until I do." Blake tilted my face up to his. "This is not your fault. This is Otto's. And I'm testifying so I can be sure he gets put away."

I nodded in agreement.

"There's a saying that some dreams shatter because we need an open door to escape their collapse," Blake said.

"Like a convenient exit ramp to avoid a bad ending?"

Blake laughed. "Something like that."

Blake's text alarm chimed a third time. When he looked over at it I wriggled out of his arms. "I wish there was something I could do," I said. "I feel so helpless."

Blake's phone rang this time. "Sorry." He declined the call and tapped out a text. Then he grabbed his shirt and buttoned it.

"We don't have any guarantees that Otto's trial is going to go the way we want, and we need to think about your safety. You're going to have to leave town, Adeline. And soon. It's the only way out."

"And what—change my name, my nose, and relocate to Montana?" I laughed but didn't recognize it as my own.

"Something like that." Blake was deadly serious. "Though I think leaving the country is a better idea."

"But, what about my family? What about—what about us?" I rubbed my forehead and pressed at the insistent thumping. "It could be years before he gets his trial?"

"Leaving without your family knowing where you are may be the best way to protect them. I plan to join you shortly. I'm going to give my statement today."

"Lex would never stand for not knowing where I was. And my mother could not lose another—"

The chiming text alarm on Blake's phone interrupted and Blake snatched it.

"I've got to go. We'll work this out when I get back. You know not to leave the townhome, right?"

"Right," I said.

He leaned in and kissed me as if he'd never have the chance to kiss me again. "I'll be back as soon as I can. Pete or Thomas will be outside watching the door. I'll call Alexa and ask her to come sit with you." He turned and began his dash out of the room.

"Blake—"

He turned and took a few steps back toward me, paused in the midst of his urgency, which filled the room.

"Is that saying from a book?"

"What saying?" Blake reached me and ran his hands up and down my silk covered arms.

"The one about shattered dreams offering us a doorway. Is that from a book?"

Blake smiled a patient smile.

"No, it's from my mother. Who should probably write a book."

"She sounds very wise."

"She is."

"What's her name?"

I felt Blake's heart jerk through several waves of inertia, then duck behind a thick wall.

"I'll introduce you some time. I think the two of you would like one another. You okay?" Blake asked.

"Yeah. You really think leaving the country is necessary?"

"Those doorways lead us away from the crash. Without them we would surely get hurt. And yes, I think leaving the country is necessary." Blake held my face in his warm hands.

"I hoped his arrest would be for the Gardner art. But this is where we are. Think Paris."

"Paris?"

"Yeah, I can get us safely lost in Paris for a while. For as long as we like, actually."

"Paris does have the George V Four Seasons. Not a bad place to hide out for a while."

He paused at the doorway and shot me a smile that felt like summer.

Then he was gone.

64

"If you think Otto's connections really are Mafia, then maybe it is a good idea to leave the country until you're sure he's put away. Because if he can call in favors, he could still get to you, and your gifts, even though he's in jail." Alexa reached for one of the scallops wrapped in bacon she'd brought with her.

"It's not just leaving the country. It's leaving the country and staying hidden. Living a life on the run. I don't want to live a life in hiding. Always looking over my shoulder. Wondering if the maid in my hotel room is really there to kidnap me instead of emptying the trash. Besides, have you been to Paris lately? Everyone looks suspicious."

"It's just for a while. I don't think it's the hiding that bothers you as much as it is the being pursued part." Alexa cocked an eyebrow.

"True," I unraveled the bacon and ate it in small bites. It made me feel better. Bacon was a hug from God.

"Being pursued is going to happen no matter where you are." Alexa reached possessively for another heaven-wrapped scallop. "At least for a while. Does Otto know that you and Blake are together?"

"I don't know what Otto knows. The way Blake talks, I think so."

"Because if Otto does know about y'all, then he might use you to influence—"

"Blake's testimony. I know. I've thought of that." I took a long sip of my wine.

"It is Paris. And with a man you love. It wouldn't be all bad." Alexa grinned. "I'd do it."

"You would?"

"With Blake? Heck yeah."

"Lex!" I gave her a shove and she fumbled her latest scallop.

Alexa laughed. "What I mean is that you've both been through a lot and an extended vacation together might not be bad. In the process, you'd be keeping yourself safe." Lex flipped her long hair over her shoulder.

I couldn't really argue with her logic. What else was I going to do with my time? Go back to the firm? Sit around the townhome?

"How did it go with Todd today?"

"Oh my." Lexie rolled her eyes in mock ecstasy. "I don't know why I never noticed him before. We're going out this weekend." She giggled like a schoolgirl and gave an exaggerated sigh. Her face flushed to a tinge of pink.

I grabbed her free hand and gave it a squeeze in the momentary quiet. "If I disappear for a while, you'll be careful? You'll be safe?"

"I'll be fine." Lexie drew out the word fine and squeezed my hand in return. "I have my show coming up, and there's lots to do to get ready for that. I'll send you pictures so you won't miss anything. And I'll be dating. My favorite pastime."

I laughed. She wasn't kidding.

"Shall I help you pack? We'll organize and drink wine. It's the best way to get ready for Paris."

I stared at Lex, wondered if the plan would work. Something could still go wrong with Otto's trial and I'd be living on the run forever.

"It's a good call," she said in all seriousness.

"Okay, then," I said. "Suitcases are in the hall closet."

"I love packing," she sang.

We headed toward my clothes closet, best friends since birth, hand in hand.

"You would, Lex," I said and kissed the back of her hand.

65

Alexa and I talked for another hour about all things Blake. About how he was Jack, that he knew I was intuitive and how I'd never thought I could be this happy. Girl talk, clothes, and wine—Alexa was up to her eyeballs in her element. She had taken over my closet, sorting clothes by Paris-worthiness and then by compatibility with one another. If there'd been a wedding dress in that closet, she would have packed that, too. She was definitely angling for me to have a happily ever after.

"I don't need that much stuff, Lex. I'm supposed to be laying low, remember?"

Alexa pulled four more hanger-clad silk blouses and three long scarves from the closet and dropped them on the bed. The hangers rattled when they collided. "I've already pulled leggings and some blousy tops for you to lounge in. But you and Blake might decide to disappear into a crowded restaurant or maybe on the French countryside. You'll need options." Alexa's eyes were electric with a vision for my wardrobe.

I shook my head with a giggle, decided to leave her to it,

and snuck out to the kitchen for tea. I doubted she'd even notice my absence.

I filled the mug with water from the instant hot water tap, then pulled down the cool-to-the-touch tin of loose leaf rooibos red tea leaves and the tea strainer. Though our troubles weren't over with Otto—we still needed a jury to convict him—I was feeling a bit of peace.

I'd found Jack, my literal life-long love—or maybe it was Jack who found me. I always had the sense that Blake was more than a few steps ahead of me. Even though my faithful dream of having a career in art had died a painful death, I'd gained Blake in the process. So I couldn't complain. There was a man in my life who wasn't asking me to change, who understood me. Plus, the job with Otto never had the future I dreamed it had. If I were honest, it was just another hide-out for me. I was through with those. Well, almost.

I wondered if after Otto was put away and forgotten, if Blake and I might build our own art business. Giddiness ambled through me at the thought. Traveling the world and finding priceless art would be unbelievably fun if we were together. Like a fantasy that wouldn't end.

"Oh!" I spied Blake's wallet on the kitchen bar. He must have forgotten it when he dashed out. I ran my thumb over the soft, black leather and looked around for my phone. I'd call him and let him know it was here so he wouldn't worry.

As if I'd been carried through a cable wire, I ended up in Otto's office. Not the outer office, but Otto's inner-sanctum where I'd interviewed that first day and where Otto had told Ellen about his plans for me. Blake and Otto sat across from each other in conversation:

"I need you to keep a close eye on Addie. Show her interest. Develop a steady relationship with her. From the little bit I know, she's spent a lot of time alone lately. I doubt she'd refuse you," Otto says.

"Doesn't sound too hard," Blake says. "What's your plan for her?"

"I think she could be very useful to the art business I keep on the side. First I want to see if she takes the job. Then I need to know if she has the same uncommon talents she had years ago. You need to keep her close. If anything goes askew between her and the firm, chances are I'll still need access to her. Your job will be to keep that avenue open to me."

Blake nodded. "I'll take care of it."

I shook my head and returned the wallet to the counter. "No. Not right. That was before he met me." I rubbed my chin and paced in front of the wallet.

Sharp-edged bits of doubt poked at my newly-placed trust in Blake. *Maybe this relationship with Blake was his way of using me to get to the Gardner art? To do Otto's bidding? Maybe none of this was real?*

"No," I scoffed. "That's completely wrong." I picked up the wallet again and set my psychic sight to fast-forward past my initial introduction to Blake. Then I searched for the same energetic thread I'd just seen Blake sew with Otto. One that was edged in the vibe of usability.

I knew I wouldn't find anything.

Which made it all the more surprising when I landed in the backseat of Blake's limo. He speaks on the phone, though not one I've seen him use before.

"William," Blake says.

"What did you get from your meeting with Otto?" William asks.

"He's bringing in a new researcher," Blake says.

"No leads on the Gardner art?

"I think she's the best lead on the art. He said he wants to use her for the art business he keeps on the side. I'm sure it's all related. He's asked me to develop a relationship with her, to keep her close. I've got that under control."

"You really think she's a lead to the Gardner pieces?" William asks.

"I do and I'm all over it," Blake says.

"You'd better be," William says.

The tea mug slipped from my hand and smashed on the floor. I dropped Blake's wallet into the spreading puddle of tea.

Alexa ran out of my bedroom. "Ohmygosh. Don't move," she said as she looked at my bare feet surrounded by fragments of porcelain. "I'll get the broom."

Blake's conversation with both Otto and William played over in my head. "Otto knew…I was lonely and…desperate, ordered Blake to…develop a relationship with me, and knew I wouldn't refuse," I said to Alexa as she swept the broken cup into a dustpan.

"What?" She followed my finger as I pointed at Blake's wallet on the floor.

"No, Addie. No." She picked up Blake's wallet, dried it off, and put it on the counter. "There's some mistake. Obviously, it's a misunderstanding." She guided me out of the kitchen and into the salon.

"That's what I thought," I said. "So I looked again." I told her in detail what I'd heard and seen.

"Addie, you don't think that Blake—that this is some kind of ruse?"

"I don't know, Lex." My heart twisted.

"Okay, slow down. And don't be paranoid. You would know. This isn't just some guy, this is Blake. You two have something special. You would know if he weren't telling you the truth."

"Really? And how is that?" I started pacing. "Because I was wrong about Jeremy, I was wrong about Patti. I was wrong about Otto and the firm, I was even wrong about Ellen," I said and I waved my arm in the air. "How would I know if anything with Blake is real? I see everything about people and—still I have no clue as to who they really are."

Alexa crossed her arms, tugged on a lock of her hair and watched me pace around the room. "I really don't think this is a set-up," she said. "I mean, I haven't spent that much time around Blake, but I don't get that he's in cahoots with Otto. And isn't Blake at the FBI testifying against Otto right now?"

"How would I know that? Who's to say that he's not down there right now giving his statement on Otto's behalf? Otto has the Gardner art, and Blake invested years of his life trying to get to that art. Do you know how much that art is worth? Half a billion dollars. That's billion. Blake's dating me—or whatever this is—could be just another way for him to get his hands on the art. Maybe he's secretly in competition with Otto for the art? Did you ever think of that? He's either Otto's pawn or he's out for himself and just using me to get what he wants."

Alexa wisely kept her distance. "I think you would know if he were playing you. You see people really well. You just have a few...blind spots when it comes to—"

"When it comes to what?" I asked.

"When it comes to getting what you want," Alexa said softly. "You can sometimes project what you...want onto the...person."

"And this relationship with Blake wouldn't play into that? Remember what Otto said? He knew I'd been spending all my time alone. Blake is gorgeous and wealthy and he pushes! Otto was right! How could I resist?

"Yeah, I have blind spots. Major blind spots. Blind spots that could block out the sun. Even if I didn't, having a gift for seeing doesn't mean you ever see everything." I stormed off to the bedroom. "Are you through packing?"

"Why?"

"I'm thinking clearly and strictly for myself for the first time in a long while. Is this done?" I asked and looked at the full suitcases spread on the bed.

"All except for your make-up and toothbrush," Alexa ambled in front of me and stared me straight in the eye. "Do not do anything until you talk with Blake," she with her hands on my shoulders. "You owe yourself that. To your point you might not be seeing the full picture here."

Lex's intensity reached me and I gave a shaky exhale. "You think so?"

"I do," she said, nodding confidently.

"You're right," I said. "I'm sure you're right. I'm over-stressed. I've lost perspective. I'm sure I'm just missing some-thing." I grabbed a random handful of eyeshadow, mascara, and face powder, and shoved it into the smallest suitcase.

"Don't do that. You'll mess up my system. I'll do this. You go relax. Have some wine. This is going to work out."

Alexa took over the last bit of packing while I went to the other room and poured a glass of wine. She was right. I needed to relax. Blake would be back soon, I'd tell him what I saw and he'd put my worries to rest.

66

Thomas drove the limo to the front of the firm, and slowed to a stop. "There's no parking," he said. "And there are two police cars and a police van up here."

"Let me out." Blake placed his hand on the door handle, and pulled it. "Wait for me around back. I don't know how long I'll be."

Blake used his access key to enter the building and was immediately stopped by an FBI agent. He pulled off his sunglasses and the agent nodded imperceptibly when he recognized him. He let him pass.

Blake took the small elevator to the top floor then walked the long hallway to the executive offices. The energy in the firm was decidedly different today from how it had always been. Its facade was ripped off. He could feel it. Its elegance was in the process of being stripped away to reveal the nasty secrets beneath that it had held for decades. It was the end of the firm. It was the end of an era.

When he arrived at the doorway of Otto's office he watched an agent break the lock on the mahogany credenza with a small screwdriver. He left a deep scratch on the wood and Blake cringed.

From the open drawer they pulled out a surprisingly small collection of file folders, barely enough to fill one hand. The paltry collection of evidence landed with a *slap* into a cavernous, plastic container on a dolly. It was labeled Evidence on the outside.

Blake's hopes wilted. This might have been a sign.

He cut through a line of agents who wheeled a series of five drawer filing cabinets out of Ellen's office. "I'll bet they don't find anything in there either," he mumbled.

He walked by Addie's former office and saw two agents pack up a box of files. Addie had her laptop at home, and wondered if they would subpoena her for it.

Blake rode the service elevator to the basement and he sensed the energy of a hunt. He knew the real party was in the vaults downstairs and he hoped they were having better luck than the upstairs agents. But there was that nagging feeling that something was off.

When he stepped off of the elevator, everything seemed to move in slow motion. The voices, the agents carrying art into the hallway and packing it for transport. It all moved at glacial speed until Blake saw Otto and Ellen standing at the end of the hallway peering into one of the vaults. They were watching the destruction of the firm, one piece of art at a time. And then Blake knew for sure. Something was definitely wrong.

Otto's clear blue eyes watched Blake with an eerie focus.

"What's going on here?" Blake said when he finally reached him.

"I believe they are looking for stolen art, forgeries, and evidence of intent to sell them." Otto stated the charges like he was talking about plans for a vacation. "Was that every-thing on the warrant, Ellen?"

Ellen nodded in agreement. She crossed her arms, and never took her eyes off of the firm's treasures when they left the vaults. It seemed to Blake that she was too scared to move.

Otto leaned nonchalantly against the wall and gave Blake a look that said he was neither surprised nor concerned. "They're trying to find enough evidence to arrest me, I would guess."

Blake stepped closer to him. "This is bad, Otto. Have you thought to offer them something that might interest them more than this?" It was Blake's last-ditch effort to get Otto to cough up the Gardner art. He just hoped Otto didn't recognize it.

"What would that something be?" Otto asked.

Blake felt unprepared for the certainty in Otto's look. "Whatever you have that might negotiate your release."

"Perhaps the last project we discussed is the thing you're thinking of." Otto's lips spread into a gracious smile, but his eyes glistened cold and soulless. "Is that it?"

The game had changed. And Blake realized it too late to plan for it. He studied Otto quietly.

"You know I find tests to be ever so useful. You lay them out as elegantly as afternoon tea, and people take them without even being told to do so. Then, as the test scores come in, you get to see exactly who that person is. What they're made of. What their agenda is," Otto waved his hand along the scene that played out in front of them.

Blake blinked. He'd been set up. And he'd missed it.

"I've often wondered if you were really an ally. True allies are quite hard to come by, and I figured you were too good to be true. But I had to determine how to test you. To find out for certain."

"Test me?" Blake's breathing picked up pace.

Otto ignored him. "And then our friend Addie Montgomery walked into my office. The moment the two of you shared on that first day gave me my answer. The fireworks were so extraordinary they probably saw them in Long Island." Otto sighed in mock affectation. "All I had to do at that point was let nature take her course."

"I didn't have anything to do with this, if that's what you're saying." Blake nodded toward the agents who continued to examine and catalog paintings.

"Are you sure about that? Because I find my tests are quite accurate." Otto paused, and Blake tried but couldn't speak.

Ellen stepped away from the two men and walked into the vault with the agents.

Otto leaned forward with a whisper. "I mention the Gardner art to you, and Addie's usefulness to me. Then suddenly I'm being investigated and Addie has disappeared. You don't find that to be just a little uncanny? Because I do."

Blake was silent for a moment. Then he said what he'd wanted to say for a very long time. "You're screwed, Otto. It doesn't matter what you think. If my count is right they've walked six paintings out the door since I've been here. As long as they keep this up you'll be sending out Christmas cards from federal accommodations for the rest of your life."

Otto laughed so loud that everyone turned and looked.

He lowered his voice and tilted his head close to Blake's ear. "I'd rethink that if I were you, my man. No one has been able to put me away yet, and this time won't be any different. I'll be free a lot sooner than you think. You'll never get your hands on the Gardner art, and one day you'll be without your precious Adeline as well, because she'll be with me."

Now it was Blake who laughed. "Addie has you figured out, Otto. You won't fool her anymore."

"Oh, Addie will be with me. As an ally, and a team member, and who knows what else?" Otto patted Blake on the shoulder.

"Good luck with that." Blake removed Otto's hand from his back. His right hand balled into a fist.

"Actually, you might want to hang on to that luck. You may remember that it doesn't work out well for friends who have betrayed my trust. This really was rather foolish on your part." Otto tsked three times and shook his head slowly. Then he grinned pleasantly as if he were at the social event of the season.

Blake's anger finally peaked. He pushed close to Otto's face. "Your days of calling the shots are finished. Before the end of this day, your reach will be limited to a small room with no view. So, don't threaten me. Or Addie."

"Oh, I'm not threatening," Otto said pleasantly. "I'm telling you where you got it wrong. You see, I gave Frank the same benefit before I put a bullet in his heart."

"We found it," William said from inside the vault. "Both of these paintings match the client's description of his art. Arrest him. Take her down to headquarters and question her."

Otto turned his face in the direction of William's voice. When he looked back, Blake took a step and let his fist fly. The crack of Otto's nose filled the semi-quiet and the pain in Blake's hand gave him a warm, satisfied feeling.

Otto fell to the floor. "Ah," he said with blood dripping over his smile. "Let the games begin."

67

———

"You have the right to remain silent..."

Blake's eyes followed every move of the two black-jacketed, FBI agents when they cuffed Otto, read him his rights, and scuttled him out of his own firm. But it was a hollow victory. One that came with a price Blake never expected to pay: the forfeit of a deep-rooted dream.

He watched them escort Ellen out as well, and was grateful when they forewent the cuffs. She wasn't the real problem in all of this, she was just a fly trapped in Otto's web.

He felt Otto's presence in the firm waning toward emptiness for the first time. As if the roots to the poisonous plant had been hacked, and its slow death had begun.

Somehow the employees would find out that the firm was closing. Maybe Ellen would have the chance to inform them before they showed up at work the next morning to discover their keys no longer worked.

William walked out of the vault with a laptop held firmly in the clutch of his large hand.

"What are your plans for Ellen?" Blake asked.

"They'll question her, search the evidence to find out what she knows. But I wouldn't be too worried. She just negotiated a deal for herself."

"How so?"

"While you and Otto were having your tete a tete, she walked in and quietly asked if she could help us find what we were looking for. Said she had familiarity with some of the clients' work since she logged it into the system when it was brought into the firm."

"Was she able to help you find the client art you were looking for?"

"Yep. As I mentioned on the phone we found a client who agreed to prosecute if we found evidence that his art had been forged. I gave Ellen his name and the title of his painting. She went through the wire racks and picked it out. We found its match on the other side of the room. It had been sealed in a crate. Did you learn anything from Otto?"

Blake offered up the only thing he had left for William. "At a price. The Gardner art is in New York."

"All of it?"

"So he says. Hard to know without actually seeing it. He referenced a seller. That could be his partner. Or that could be a cover for the fact that he's the only one who has the art. He had a partner in this firm years ago. A founding partner, John Montgomery."

"We're aware of him. He went missing a few years ago."

"So, he might be involved in this from a distance some-how. Or maybe Otto killed him off, too."

"What was the price for the information?"

"My cover is blown," Blake said.

68

Even though I'd told myself to chill, the episodes between Otto and Blake and William and Blake were stuck on repeat in my head. I stared blindly out the library window while I occasionally sucked down large gulps of wine. A water buffalo could have pranced by and I wouldn't have seen it. I couldn't see anything beyond the conversations in my head.

I'd studied the scenes from every possible angle. I'd crawled into Blake's mind of that moment to see if maybe he had lied to Otto. But he hadn't. In fact, he'd been game to meet this new gal Otto was bringing in to the ruse. "Maybe she'll be cute," he'd thought. "A distraction." I'd crept into his thoughts when he was talking with William. Indeed he had been telling William the truth. Still, Blake deserved the benefit of the doubt. And certainly, I'd missed the mark before. Maybe this was just one of those times. I hoped, anyway.

I heard the front door open and close. Blake's appearance was fierce and uncompromising, his jaw was set and determined, and I could tell he'd been doing battle. The suit he wore was not the one he'd worn when he left earlier. He must have stopped at his home or office and changed. Tiny dots of something that looked like blood dotted the front of his white shirt and I quickly scanned his face but didn't see any injuries. I was unreasonably relieved.

"Where's Alexa?" Blake asked.

"She headed home when you texted that you were on your way. She has a lot of work to do for her show, and I wanted some time alone to collect my thoughts."

Blake took the glass from my hand and swallowed a healthy serving of wine.

"What are these?" He gestured toward the suitcases with the glass..

"I'm packed," I said. "For Paris."

"You're open to leaving?" He asked.

"Yes." I walked away from him and sat down. "Alexa talked me into it." My tone was far more serious than I intended. "Tell me." I said and slipped on a pair of leather driving shoes. "How much, if anything, of everything we shared was part of the set up between you and Otto?"

Blake squinted. "What are you talking about?"

"The arrangement. Between you and Otto."

Blake was quiet and his perfect lips drifted apart.

"The one where he told you to develop a relationship with me. He told you I was lonely. That I wouldn't resist you. You said that didn't sound so hard. You even told William that I was a lead for the Gardner art and you were—how did you put it? All over it."

Blake swallowed visibly. He opened them again, but nothing came out. He walked over to the library window and stared at the darkening sky.

This was not the good sign I had hoped for.

He ran his hand through his hair and gave it a frustrated squeeze.

A man of too many secrets.

"Your wallet." I said softly. "You left your wallet, and it... spoke to me." The house was quiet excepting the white noise in my ears. Inky shadows formed on the walls and I thought it a fitting display for what apparently would be the close on this short-lived, lifelong dream. "Was this...a setup? From the very beginning? Just tell me, Blake. I'll find out eventually, anyway."

He turned and all I could see was the soul of the man whom I thought had sought me out from another lifetime.

"Blake." I stood.

"You're right, Addie. This was a setup. And I'm sorry. I shouldn't have let things get this far."

I stopped sick in my path, his betrayal tore a hole through my heart like a bullet. "What?"

He stood firm, with his hands on his hips. I tried to read him, to feel what he was feeling. However, something dark and solid dropped over his energy and I couldn't get in. I stared at him and felt my dream of a future together ignite and burn.

"I'm sorry you found out this way."

"How was I supposed to find out?" I asked.

"I guess I didn't think you would. I'm pretty good at keeping secrets. I'm even better at getting people to believe and feel what I want them to." He stared at me with dead eyes. "You felt happy. You felt loved. I never heard any complaints."

"Devastation dragged on my heart. "Are you serious?"

He nodded.

"Why?" I asked.

Blake stayed quiet.

"The Gardner art," I finally said.

"The Gardner art." Blake sat in the white armchair near the library and tapped his fingers on the armrest.

"I thought you were supposed to be helping the FBI?"

Blake gave a half shrug. "I don't have any loyalties. I'm a hired gun. I work for the one who has the best offer at the time."

"And what— I was just the idiot pawn in the game?"

"I tried to warn you when we had lunch together on the day we met. No one is who they say they are in this community. That was your chance to walk away."

I felt Frank, Blake's ghost, enter the room behind me. When he passed by, his deadly chill brought goose bumps to my arms, as did his eerie sideways glance. He circled behind Blake.

"You see?" Frank said. "I told you." He started to drift toward me but Blake raised his hand and stopped him.

"Stay back, Frank," Blake said. "She's been through enough."

Frank did as he was told and stood sentry behind Blake.

I couldn't believe what I was seeing.

Both of them stared at me without moving, and I had my answer.

"You're still going after the art, aren't you?" I swallowed hard.

Blake nodded slowly.

Everything hurt.

"I have a job to do" Blake looked at me intently.

After a boundless moment, the text alarm dinged on my phone, and I was grateful for a reason to pull my eyes away from Blake's face. It was Lex. I tapped out a text to tell her I hadn't been wrong and asked her to call me a cab. I was leaving tonight.

"I left your wallet on the counter," I said without looking at him.

I grabbed my suitcases and walked out the door.

69

———

It was cold on the plane. First class was only half-full and of course, night had fallen.

After take-off it was easy to cover up and close my eyes and to be left alone. I didn't cry. I was still too stunned to cry.

Fatigue carries me into sleep, one that's deep enough to dream. Jack rounds the corner, then shakes his head as he looks at me.

"I thought we agreed never to leave one another," he scolds me gently, then runs the back of his fingers down my cheek.

"I'm not leaving—I'm here." I struggle to sit up.

He gives me a reproving look. "Then why are you running from me?"

"I'm not running," I say.

"Are you sure?"

My eyes flew open and saw only that I was alone among my flight-mates.

I filled the rest of the plane ride to Paris with movies, and I kept the volume off. The drone of the plane's engines was better background for the noise in my head. For as much as my head had tried to keep me away from Blake when we were together, now it questioned everything I had done. *Had I read the wallet correctly? Did I overreact by leaving so quickly? Should I call him when I get to Paris to talk things out?*

My hopes that the wine might have sedated me at some point on the plane ride were dashed by the ache in my heart. It was too strong, too afflictive. The admonishing visit from Jack certainly didn't help. He might want to check in with his current day self once in a while. If only to get his story straight.

So, I selected the closed captioning feature on the TV, read the words across the pictures on the screen, and drank wine until the commentary in my head developed a slur.

When I finally walked through the wide, glass doors of the Four Seasons George V Hotel, I was immediately enveloped by a familiar cool, shielding sensation. A protectiveness I'd always felt when I stayed here. It was a home, of sorts.

This was my first time in the hotel alone. I'd stayed here several times with family. Most recently with Alexa. I missed her. I'd thought several times about asking her to stay with me for a couple of weeks. She was busy preparing for her new show.

The bellman tried to show me around my suite but I was so tired I could barely maintain civility.

"Thanks, I've got it," I said when he showed me how to adjust the thermostat. I gave him several Euros and ushered him out the door, just before I collapsed on the bed in a lump of utter exhaustion.

70

Blake awoke at 3 a.m. to the vibration of his phone rattling on his desk. He had fallen asleep in the armchair of his home office, Scotch glass in hand. He got his bearings, fumbled his phone and looked at the screen.

"Maman," Blake said. "Is everything okay?"

"I haven't heard from you in several days."

Blake gave a heavy sigh, told her how Otto had been arrested, that the charges weren't all he had hoped for. Then he told her about his conversation with Addie and how she had taken off for the George V in Paris. Or so Alexa had said when they ran into one another outside of Addie's building.

"Forget the art," she said.

"No."

She cursed at him.

"Then go after her," she said.

"William won't clear my record." Blake ran his hand across his tired face and bleary eyes.

She cursed again.

71

———

On the third day of hiding out in my hotel suite, I woke up crying.

Again.

The tears didn't even wait until I'd opened my eyes.

I couldn't stand it anymore. I had to get myself together and get out of the room. I was starting to offend myself with the constant crying and moping.

I took a hot bath, washed and dried my hair. I cried through the entire process and had to dry my hair while sitting on the vanity chair. Much as I wanted to, I didn't think I could do anything to stop the fits of grief.

I was crying for the loss of Blake. The loss of Jack.

I cried for the loss of a career that I'd very much wanted. For a long time. Longer than I'd realized. And, although I didn't know if any clues were even possible, I cried because I didn't think I'd ever find out what happened to my father and grandfather.

Healing would come when I was ready. I couldn't force it.

For now I needed to get out. I was sure I'd cry less if I

were in public and had plenty of distractions. I could go to a museum. Paris was full of them.

The Louvre? No, too crowded. Maybe the Musee' de l'Orangerie. I could sit among the murals painted by Monet and let them soothe my emotions.

I flipped open my suitcase and stared into a heap of clothing. They were a wrinkled mess. My lips pulled into a grimace. I grabbed a weighty chunk of items on hangers, dragged them to the closet, and hoisted them onto the rack. Progress. Organization of one's things could create order in the mind.

When that task was finished I put the folded clothes into drawers. Alexa wouldn't be happy with my lack of a system, but it would do for now. I went back for the shoes and noticed something stuck inside my favorite pair of ankle boots. I reached in, my fingers graced the outer edge of the item, and I knew the vibe immediately.

I pulled out his empty wallet with the pinch of my index finger and thumb, dropped it on the bed, and guarded myself against any information that might start singing. Nightmares were hard enough the first time around. I didn't want a second showing.

I took the other boot and turned it upside down. A coiled up belt tumbled onto the floor. It was Blake's. He'd taken it off when he'd stayed with me until morning. He'd obviously forgotten it.

Alexa had shoved Blake's wallet into my suitcase because she wanted me to check my facts. She must have found his belt and tucked it in on the off chance that I might get a different point of view. Of course that was before she knew Blake admitted our relationship was just a ploy.

Rubbing my palms against my robe, I walked back and forth in front of Blake's belt and deflated wallet and felt the haunting ache of how much I still cared for him. Hope was a dangerous thing, sometimes, and I had no reason to invest in it today. He'd been very clear with me. His most important priority was the Gardner art.

I had no interest to see what else the belt and the wallet held, and I walked away from Alexa's challenge. Instead I ordered espresso, eggs, and ham from room service, then got dressed. This was the longest I'd gone in three days without crying, and I didn't want to buck the positive trend by scrounging around in Blake's life. I wanted to be stronger first. In case I saw the same story again. Or worse. I couldn't let him wreck me twice.

I sat in the next room and ate breakfast, all the while staring into the bedroom at the two borrowed items that lay on my bed. With each sip of coffee, with each bite of eggs, I weighed the pros and cons of reading these leathered possessions.

Finally, I couldn't stand it any longer. I wiped my mouth and hands with the textured cloth napkin and walked into the bedroom. I stood with my hands on my hips and stared at the both of them. Now it wasn't a matter of *if*, it was a matter of which one I'd tap into first. I would read his things, just to confirm what I already knew. That would help me move on.

The belt, I decided. I'd go back to when he and Otto were meeting that morning, when Otto first told him to develop a relationship with desperate me.

I inched up the soft bell sleeves on my sweater and reached toward Blake's belt. Nervous sweat prickled, and the espresso amped up my senses. My fingertips hovered two inches above the leather and I felt the aura of Blake's energy emanating from the belt. The essence of him leapt off the belt like a flame and coursed through me, like he knew how hungry my heart was for him. I leaned into his vibe, but the shrill ring of the hotel phone shook my concentration and brought me out.

I stared at the belt until the ring seemed to get louder, I finally answered. "Hello?"

"Ah, allo, Mademoiselle Montgomery, pardon, but you have a guest in the lobby."

"A guest?"

"*Oui*, Mademoiselle. She is waiting in the lounge area for you."

She. My heart sank. Not a he. It was Alexa.

"*Merci beaucoup*. Tell her I'll be right there."

"*Oui, merci.*"

I quickly slipped on a pair of ballet flats and headed toward the elevator. Of course she wouldn't let me know she was coming, lest I say no. Alexa was here to take care of her baby sister for a few days. And now that I'd gotten through the first few days of crying, I would let her. I needed someone to help me get out. Out of my room, out of my head. With her support nearby I could go back to the belt and the wallet and woman up. I would read what was there. Whatever it happened to be.

Once off the elevator I walked past the exquisite flower displays that the George V was so famous for and looked for Alexa. When I couldn't find her I asked at the front desk.

"She is in the lounge, Mademoiselle," the man behind the desk said. He walked me around the corner and toward a thickly carpeted area that held cushioned chairs and couches and a baby grand piano. "Just there." He directed me toward a dark-haired woman wearing off-white from head to toe, a chic scarf tied elegantly to the side of her neck. I'd never seen her before, but when she turned, it was apparent to me who she was. It was a subtle likeness, in the frame of her jawline, the color of her hair, and the shape of her smile.

As she looked in my direction she extended her arm to welcome me.

"*Bonjour*, Addie." Her French pronunciation placed the accent on the second syllable of my name. "I would have known you anywhere." Her smile was as gracious and affecting as her son's. Her sleek, dark hair parted carefully on the left, its blunt edges graced the shoulders of her ankle-length, off-white jacket. She looked as though she'd stepped directly from the cover of Paris *Vogue,* and I was a little star struck.

"*Bonjour*, madam," I said and fought the impulse to curtsy.

"Addie. Call me Carolena," she said in her lilting French accent. "I feel we are family." She kissed me firmly on each cheek and looked me over. "You are more beautiful than I imagined. *Tres magnifique!*" she exclaimed.

"Oh, thank you—I—?"

"Won't you join me for some croissant in the garden? I've everything arranged." Without waiting for my response, she ushered me to the door that led to the central conservatory, an area I didn't realize was even open to hotel guests. Toward the middle of the glass-encased room, a table for two was shrouded by large, elephant-eared trees and flowering plants. It was set with a basket of fragrant chocolate croissants, a chilling bottle of sparkling wine, and a crystal vase of red roses.

"Baptiste." She waved her hand and a waiter appeared. "*Si vous plait.*"

He placed our napkins in our laps, then poured us each a glass of the Alfred Gratien Cuvee Paradis Brut, the name fitting to our surroundings.

"*Merci*, Baptiste," she said, and he disappeared with a bow. Carolena seemed the know the hotel and its staff quite well. She'd obviously been here more frequently than even I had.

"Carolena," I said. "You must be Blake's—"

"I am Blake's mother," she quickly confirmed and she leaned close. "I realize he's never told you about me. I'm afraid there are some rather good, though unfortunate, reasons for his denying our relationship." One by one, she loosened the fingertips of her biscuit suede gloves and placed them on the table.

I remembered my dream about Otto, Carolena and their son, and I recalled the story from the photo in Otto's office. The heartbreak he suffered and the child he missed. "So, that would mean that Otto is..."

"Otto is Blake's father." She said it clearly, and while looking me in the eye. Blunt and sincere. I had the impression that she didn't have time to waste, least of all on a misunderstanding.

I took a deep breath, the shock quickly giving way to odd relief, like the missing pieces of the puzzle just snapped into place.

"I didn't know—" I started.

"No, of course not. Blake wanted to protect you from Otto. And knowing this information would have made the both of you too vulnerable." She leaned her elbows on the table, her fingers laced under her chin. "I understand from Blake that Otto found a personal use for you."

My head swam with the prospect of discussing these things aloud. "Yes," I said.

"Let me guess. He fooled you into thinking he was a kind someone he is not, and you didn't see this until you were too caught up in it."

"Apparently," I answered.

"He did the same thing to me." Carolena shook her head in disgust. "Do not feel stupid about this. You know Blake's father can push, yes? He is too good at it much of the time."

"Otto...pushes," I said. "My Goodness. I never saw that."

"*Mon Dieu, effectivement!*" She leaned closer to me and whispered, "He is better at it than anyone I have ever seen. Blake is powerful, but Otto's ability is deadly. Like a snake. He uses his gift to charm hypnotically. Then, when your defenses are low, it's easy for him to make you see what he wants you to see. Before you realize what's happened, he has wrapped himself around you, squeezed the very life from you while he gets what he wants."

"Oh." I exhaled and leaned my forehead onto my fingertips. "He certainly did that to me," I said, and thought of how my life lay in a muddled heap.

"Unfortunately, Blake's father is a very dangerous man. He's...unpredictable at best. At worst, well, he's a thief...and a murderer. Those are just two of the many reasons why Blake has been trying to put his father in jail." Carolena casually offered me the pastry basket, and I chose a croissant, though I didn't think I could eat. Then she took one for herself. "I was young and stupid. And in love." She shrugged.

I managed two swallows of the champagne, then smiled. "I guess we've all been there."

"I can't complain. I've a reasonably good life now. And he gave me Blake. From the rest of it I learned valuable lessons."

"I have to ask," I said after a moment, "How did you find me? I didn't think anyone knew I was here."

"No one is hidden well enough, if at least one other person knows your whereabouts." Carolena arched one perfect eyebrow as she said this, as if I should heed this wisdom. She tore off a piece of croissant.

Tele-phone, tele-graph, tele-Alexa. I nodded slowly. If Carolena knew where I was, then Alexa must have told Blake first. It was the only logical flow of intelligence. He knew, but he wasn't here. I gave a painfully slow exhale of disappointment. I was not used to the idea that we were done. Wait—

"Is...Blake...with you?" I had to ask.

"Blake is experiencing a little trouble with his passport. Unfortunately." Carolena rolled her eyes up in disgust. "So, *non.*"

I was sure there was a story there. More mystery from a man who was already an infinite puzzle. "Pardon my forwardness, but... Why go to the trouble to seek me out and tell me all of this?"

Carolena dabbed the corners of her rouged lips. "I adore my son, Addie. More than life. But sometimes men need a little help from a woman. You understand this, no?"

A short laugh escaped before I could catch it.

"He is a brilliant man in so many ways. I admire his strength, his talents, his extraordinary courage. But... He is too stubborn. Too headstrong for his own good. Like his father."

The phrase *like his father* sent a chill traveling through my body.

"I will tell you, when Blake was young, I kept him so close to me. I was always afraid that Otto would find us. So we lived in different cities around Europe, moving constantly. Paris, yes, but we also lived in Venice, Austria, Switzerland... I had not yet told him why we moved so often. But one day when he was about nine or ten, he said to me, 'Maman, when I grow up I will make sure that you and I will live a free life. We will live in one happy place for the rest of our lives. And you will not be afraid.' He knew. He is so intuitive I think he always knew. So he is fighting this battle, still. I am afraid his determination to put Otto in jail is consuming him. He has lost sight of what is most valuable to him." She gestured her hand in my direction. "I fear that soon he will have become exactly like the man he wants most to destroy." She was unable to keep the worry out of her voice.

Carolena sipped her wine and waited for my response. But I couldn't offer her any help for her son. Blake didn't want me in his life. He didn't want me at all. "I don't think—"

"He loves you, Addie. There is no doubt of that in my heart. He has loved you since he was a boy."

The tears welled up and traced my cheeks before I could stifle them. "Everything has changed. We're not...seeing one another anymore. I don't know that we ever really were..." My thumb pressed and rubbed against my palm under the table.

"He thinks that by sending you away, that he is protecting you. He thinks he is doing the honorable thing. But, he is being an idiot."

My laughter burst through my tears and resounded off of the glass around us.

Carolena chuckled too. "I can say this because he is my son, and I know him as no one else does." Her knowing smile was contagious, and the mother's love she had for Blake brought some light and warmth to shadowy places in my heart.

"You must call him. Talk to him." She reached across and placed her hand on the table in front of me. "You two belong together."

"No, I don't think I can. He has...other priorities." I wiped my cheeks. I decided not to mention the Gardner art. It didn't sound as though she knew about Blake's agenda.

Carolena waved her hand, though I couldn't tell which part of what I said she was dismissing.

"Talk with him," she insisted.

"I can't," I said resolutely.

The quiet grew between us.

"Perhaps you bring too much of your past into your future. You must fight to move beyond that and to see the truth."

I scoffed. "He was very clear with me about where he stood," I said. "There's no future for us."

She finally gave one head shake and I felt her back off.

"I'm sorry," she said. "I am not here to push. Or blame."

We both took a sip of wine until she finally spoke again. "Blake told me that you read his wallet."

I nodded.

"Seeing secrets is a disappointing business," she said. "You and I don't have the ability to pretend that people are someone they are not, as everyone else does." The melody in her French accent made the harsh truth sound more beautiful than it was. "But people have so many facets. We have to remember that."

She caught sight of my ring and reached out. "Like your ring. So beautiful." She held my hand and tilted the ring for a better view. "Such a powerful history. Though a difficult one." Her eyes gleamed like Blake's did when he knew more to the story than he revealed. It felt to me that she knew the epic tale within my ring.

"I found it at an antique store here, in Paris, years ago." I paused while she gazed at the ring. She was reading it for herself.

I thought of her love affair with Otto and what it must have been like for her when she learned the truth about him. I understood what she meant by facets. "It's particularly hard to see some of those facets when it's someone we love."

Carolena agreed with a slow nod. Her blue eyes were so close to the color of Blake's that it was hard to look at them for too long. She released my ring and I felt her energy return effortlessly to her body.

"Sometimes what is held in one facet can ruin the entire person, certainly the relationship. But occasionally we must see other angles before we can judge."

"Maybe," I said.

The text alarm went off and she skillfully ignored it.

She placed her hand gently on the top of mine, and her heavily jeweled bracelet rested against my fingertips and jangled against the glass topped table. On its contact a movie threaded my vision—a young Otto and Carolena dance closely. The small orchestra serenades them as if they performed only for this one couple in the crowded dance hall. So fiercely in love with one another, they are oblivious to the world around them. "I love it," she says and she pulls her right hand from his lead and focuses on the bracelet. "*Je t'aime*, Otto," she says before they kiss. The vibe within the bracelet lead me back to the current moment.

"Otto gave you this bracelet?"

She suddenly donned the same unreadable expression I'd seen Blake wear. "A long time ago," she said. She pulled her hand away, cleared her throat as she shifted her position. I had the distinct sense she'd never stopped loving Otto.

Carolena stretched one glove over her hand, and then the other. "You know sometimes wisdom arrives in the form of fear. It warns us, keeps us safe. But sometimes our fears can push away the wisdom." Carolena let her words move through the air while she looked at me. "We must discern which is which. Oui? You'll find the right direction in all of this." She picked up her purse as she glanced at the phone screen.

"I must go," she said. "I am meeting someone."

I fumbled for something to say as I stood up with her. "Do you live in Paris?" I asked.

"I'm sorry. Now I am the one who must keep a few secrets." She smiled and kissed my cheeks. "Otto still looks for me. So I keep the location of my home a secret."

"Oh," I said. *Blake really was fighting for his mother's freedom from Otto.*

Carolena kissed both of my cheeks. Her gloved hands squeezed mine when she smiled at me, her bracelet carefully tucked away. "There is a reason for everything." Carolena hugged me. "I hope you'll remember that."

The fact that she echoed my mother's advice wasn't lost on me.

72

———

The Eiffel stretched tall against the rose-colored sunset. I propped my feet on the balcony railing and sipped a glass of cabernet. Shawled in a soft blanket against the cool of the early autumn air, I wandered through the colors of the evening sky. Carolena's words tumbled across my brain. I tried sifting the different elements of her visit into separate bins to organize my thoughts, to make perfect sense of them. But they wouldn't stay where I put them. Like mischievous children they jumped back and forth, refusing to stay sorted. My questions fueled their agitation even more.

I looked at my ring and thought of the facets she'd mentioned. Yes, we all had our facets. Looking at just one was informative, but not always the full picture. I got that. Still, one really bad facet ruined the entire thing.

Blake was Otto's son. What an odd piece of truth. And yet it explained Blake so clearly— his motivations, his behavior, even the sealants in his office.

But instead of bringing any clarity, I thought this new information convoluted our relationship even more. What did he really feel for me? And did it even matter when I factored in the Gardner art?

"Seeing secrets is a disappointing business," Carolena had said.

It was. It always was. My hands wanted to touch, my head needed the story, but my heart struggled with what I saw.

I looked at Blake's belt and wallet that lay on the bed. I was certain that they held secrets I hadn't yet seen. What if Carolena was wrong in thinking that Blake loved me? Mothers didn't always know their child's mind.

I turned toward the Eiffel again.

If nothing else, I knew what Blake had told me. The Gardner art was his priority and his focus. I sipped my wine and tried to push Blake out of my heart once and for all.

But a cool breeze touched my face and I remembered what I'd felt from him.

He loved me.

And I knew that he was Jack.

Was Carolena right? Did he encourage me to leave so he could protect me from Otto? Or was he simply choosing his lifelong goal of destroying his father over how he felt about me?

I didn't know. Maybe because I hadn't seen enough? Maybe that's what she had been telling me about facets? I probably ought to look into it further. If only to be prepared.

I was right when I told Carolena that I was just trying to be smart with all of this.

Or was I trying to outsmart this? Alexa had accused me of doing that. In addition to dragging my past into my present. *Was* there a reason for everything? And if there were, was that reason always the result of some higher power guiding us to a better place? Or was it more like karma where I was reaping what I'd sown somewhere along the way?

I pressed my fingers against my forehead.

I understood now why other women chose relationships based on convenience or what a man could provide. I had refused to settle something so commonplace and believed instead for genuine, special, meant-to-be. I'd believed for Jack.

Perhaps I'd been foolish.

The wine glass slipped, and emptied all over my leggings. "Argh!"

I sprinted through the suite and searched the bathroom for a clean towel, but all the towels lay in a neat pile on the floor. The Do Not Disturb light on my door had kept house-keeping at bay for the last three days and my towel supply had expired.

I rang for more towels. Then I put my wine-christened outfit in the hotel laundry bag for dry cleaning, and called that request in as well.

"Dry cleaning, Mademoiselle?" He emphasized the word cleaning. "We'll be right there."

I would let housekeeping do their work tomorrow. I needed to get out for a while anyway. Maybe I'd work out in the hotel gym. Or finally get to that museum.

After changing into another of the several pairs of leggings Alexa had packed for me, I stood in my too-quiet room. Blake's wallet and belt stared at me from their spot on the bed. I stared back.

Maybe just a tiny touch. To ease the absence of him.

Blake's energy radiated a few inches from the wallet, and I dragged my fingertips through it. My senses filled with all things Blake.

The doorbell rang loud. I startled. Opened my eyes and jerked my hand away.

I was alone in my room. Not with Blake. I felt so foolish.

I snatched the laundry bag off the floor and headed toward the front door. After floundering with the latch, it finally came undone and I dragged the heavy door open.

"*Merci'*," I said flatly and passed the bag through the doorway.

Blake took the bag and smiled. He placed it on the floor beside him.

He was all warmth and kindness and I had no words.

"I'm an idiot," he said with his hands fixed on his hips.

My immediate laughter came with tears, the kind that only pure joy and an opened heart could create. My palm covered my lips.

"I should never have let you go," he said, "I shouldn't have said the things I did. I'm sorry."

He took a step toward me and we met in a heated kiss. Our combination bore a powerful alchemy that made the rest of the world and every possible concern fall away, and I leaned into it with every fiber of my soul.

He lifted my legs around his hips and pulled me against him. "I love you," he said between our kisses. "I can't... remember...a time when I didn't. I am such an idiot."

My body shook with a giggle. And then our laughter danced together, loud and clear.

73

———

We sat on the white couch in the main living area, a cool breeze drifted through the open patio doors. "That's the third time today I've heard you referred to as an idiot." I left out the part where I was rather enjoying it.

Blake smiled with a shade of vulnerability I didn't often see in him. "My mother mentioned that she paid you a visit, and that a few of my secrets are now out of hiding."

"At least two of them. Maybe more, I don't remember." I felt an impish smile on my face.

Blake leaned forward. Our laughter quieted into seriousness.

"Are you okay?" He was once again the attentive soul I'd known him to be, ready to respond to whatever I needed. Still, something of a mystery.

"I think so." I said.

We sat together in the silence. Ten or fifteen seconds ticked by while I mulled over the questions that competed with one another. He had to know they were coming.

"It's a relief, actually, to know more," I said. "I think I'm finally finding my way through this maze that began when I met you."

"I'm sorry," he said. "It was never my intention to mislead you. Or hurt you. I only wanted to protect you. I went about some of it in the wrong way."

I nodded. "So your mother said." The doors to my balcony were still wide open and Gothic cathedral bells rang in the distance, echoing the understanding and the forgiveness I felt.

"She's a beautiful woman," I said. "She loves you very much."

"Sometimes you remind me of her." His touch on my cheek was so gentle, it traveled a path direct to my heart. "You're both so gifted, so elegant in the midst of an unfair world. I feel I'm here to protect you both."

"I would tell you to let Otto go, that you're ruining your life by pursuing him. But I guess that wouldn't do any good."

"Probably not." A steeliness rose to his face. "After all these years Otto still chases my mother, and now he'll chase you. My life will never be my own until he's dead or rotting in a jail somewhere."

"I understand," I said. And I did. Blake was not the kind of man who could move on with his life while his loved ones were in danger. I couldn't say I was disappointed about that.

I thought about Carolena's worry that Blake would become like his father, and I crossed my legs over his and scooted closer, face to face. "I need to know," I said. "The truth, please, whatever it is I just need to know. Okay?"

"Okay," he said willingly.

"Were you using me at any point in time? To get to Otto? Or to get to the art?"

His blue eyes never blinked. "I planned to," he said calmly. "I guess you saw my meeting with Otto—I don't know how much of it you were able to see. When he suggested I build a relationship with this woman he was bringing in that day, I agreed to do it. I figured he had some plan for you that involved the Gardner art, and I needed to know what that was. But when we met, at first glance, I knew who you were. And that changed everything."

I nodded and took a deep breath. "How far were you planning to take it with this woman, before you knew she was me?"

"I wasn't going to pursue anything romantic, if that's what you're asking." Blake took my hands in his. "That's not really my style. I can get information I need just by pushing. Usually, anyway. And my goal was to find out Otto's plan for her. For you. But Otto ended up revealing that.

"I never used you. Not by developing a relationship with you or any other way. The connection we shared was never a set up. Ever. I'm sorry I put that suggestion in your head. I just thought you would be safer away from Otto, away from me. But as my mother so directly pointed out to me—by sending you away, I had simultaneously increased Otto's chances of getting to you, while forfeiting my lifelong dream of being with you."

Blake's humility brought a smile to my face. His kiss brought a warmth to my heart and a comfort to my soul I knew only with him.

He drew me to him and held me close.

"Our situation is complicated and it won't get any easier now..."

"Life is complicated," I whispered against his chest. "I won't keep running from that."

"It will be harder now that Otto is after the both of us. He knows I'm not his ally, and he knows about your gifts."

"I don't understand his need for me." I pulled away. "I

mean, surely there are other people around who could help him discern forgeries from authentic pieces. And there must be plenty of people who would help him with the Gardner art."

"It's simple, really. He's fooled so many experts with his own forgeries that he doesn't trust experts anymore. Carolena is the only resource he's ever found who couldn't be fooled. He's been looking to replace her since the day she left him. You're the only one who ever compared."

The truth of what he said washed over me and I suddenly realized what this meant for my life. "So, I'll be living my life as a fugitive."

"We both will, at least until the trial is over and we know how long Otto will be in prison. I lived the first half of my life evading Otto, though. So, I'm well practiced at it, and I'll keep you safe."

And then I remembered. "I thought Carolena said you were having trouble with your passport?"

"Oh, that was a stupid…art trafficking incident from years ago." Blake dismissed that piece of information with his hand.

I shook my head. "Another secret."

Blake spread his arms wide, palms up. "I'm an open book to you now. Read what you like. What you see may not be pretty, but I've nothing to hide. At least not from you."

"Is that supposed to make me feel better?"

"Not necessarily, but you deserve the truth. And I can give you that."

No answer could have been more perfect. "Thank you," I said and ran my hand across his cheek.

"I made a bad call by carrying a piece of stolen art out of the country," he offered to my unasked question.

"Stolen," I said, and pulled back a little.

"It was a stupid mistake. It's how William and I met, actually. William was supposed to erase it from my record in return for my help to nail Otto. But he's mad that I didn't get him the Gardner art, so he withheld his part of the deal."

"How did you manage to get here?"

Blake looked down briefly. "I had to make another deal with William."

My heart wilted. "What kind of a deal?"

"I have to find the art for him," Blake said.

"He owed you your freedom."

"I could bail on the deal, but I don't really want him chasing me around the world. And he would."

"I understand," I said, and I knew William wasn't his only motivation for going after the art. "Does he know you're here?"

"Yes. Though he made it clear that my record was clean on a contingent. The entire art crime team is pretty angry that we didn't get the Gardner art. I have to go back and help when they need me. Otto ought to go to trial in about six months."

"You still have to testify?" I asked.

"I'll do whatever it takes to put Otto where he belongs," he said.

"A new deal with William and the FBI," I said. "I don't think I trust them."

"I don't either. But I wasn't going to let anything keep me from you." He stared into my eyes. "I love you, Addie. I can't remember a time when I didn't. You're the heart to my soul, the breath to my life, you're the guiding thought in everything I do."

I threaded my arms around his neck and delivered my response in a kiss.

74

———

The night air sparkled with energy that was uniquely Parisian. It was a rare concoction of love and passion, art and mystery, ladled over centuries of French history.

"Oh, Blake." I placed my purse next to one of the black rattan couches on the rooftop garden. "The view!" The Eiffel was lit up in brilliant lights that gave the feeling of celebration. "When did you reserve the penthouse?" I turned and saw him smiling at my amazement.

"When I was on my way,, I wanted you to stay someplace special. Whether or not you forgave me."

I looked across the city and noticed several other famous architectural images—the American Cathedral, the Sacré-Coeur Basilica and the roofs of the Opéra, the Madeleine, the Pantheon, and Les Invalides. "It's breathtaking," I sighed. I welcomed the change and was happy to be away from the bed where I'd spent three days crying.

"You didn't bring Frank with you, did you? I noticed the two of you had become quite close, and I'd really rather not have to share this with him." I gave Blake a questioning look and I brushed the arrangement of hydrangeas that sat on the iron table. Several plates of appetizers and a bottle of wine with two glasses surrounded fragrant candles that flickered in the breeze. I tilted the bottle and looked at the label while I waited for Blake's answer.

"Frank and I have reached an understanding." He walked over and picked up the wine opener. "He's agreed not to harm you again. And in exchange, I'll let him help me give Otto the justice he deserves."

A chill shivered down my body. "And if he doesn't uphold his end of the agreement?"

"Then I'll have Carolena cross him over to the Other Side," Blake said and he slipped off his leather jacket and put it around my shoulders. "I gave Frank a quick lesson on how karma works, so he's not real excited about heading home just yet. He knows that Carolena's not afraid to kick his rear across that cosmic line when called to."

"Why not just have her cross him over anyway?"

"Because he knows more than Otto wants him to." Blake opened the bottle of LaFleur merlot.

"He's your ally now?"

"I want to see if he can help me find the Gardner art. He's very motivated by revenge."

"I noticed. Any word on Ellen?" We sat together on the couch.

"Interestingly." Blake handed me a glass of wine and clinked his glass to mine in a toast. Dark berry flavors spilled into the air. "Otto told the investigators that Ellen was removed from the critical parts of the business. He said he mostly kept her on as a favor because she had been with the firm for so long. He told them she handled basic functions like billing and scheduling, ordering office supplies. But nothing else."

My eyebrows made a slow climb to my hairline. "There isn't anything in that firm that doesn't bear her fingerprint in one way or another. She had to have erased her trail as she went along each day." I thought about the iPad Ellen used to catalog the contents of the vault. "Otherwise they would surely have found proof of her involvement."

"Which is kind of amazing when you think about it," I added. "I mean, to CYA like that every day."

"Ellen is always a few steps ahead. She knows what's at stake. She also offered to help William with some of the art in a way that didn't incriminate herself. So, that is helping her."

I breathed a sigh of relief. It was no small aside that she had saved my life, protected me at her own risk when I had no other way out. But she was also one of the great loves of my grandfather's life, and if only for that, I wanted her to be free from Otto's tangle. "Why do you think he said that to them?"

"I've been trying to figure that out. He probably needs her to take care of unfinished business. The FBI might not have gotten all of the artwork. Or, she might know where the Gardner art is and will keep an eye on it while he's... away. What I do know is that he couldn't do much without her. She's far more useful to him on the outside."

"It's too bad she can't orchestrate a way out," I said.

Blake placed his wine glass and pocket watch on the side table, stretched confidently against the couch, and crossed one leg over the other. The air around us was starting to fill with potential, the scent of new beginnings.

"She's probably afraid to leave. She has to know who Otto's connections are. They have a long reach and a taste for settling scores."

"Hopefully those connections don't reach to Paris," I said.

"They won't as long as we're hidden well enough," he said.

"Are you staying in the George V as well?" I asked.

"In one of the secondary bedrooms if you're okay with that."

I studied his sincerity, then nodded. I stared out at the Eiffel in all of its sparkling glory and wondered if Ellen had ever traveled here with my grandfather. "All that time I spent at the firm, I wish I had been able to uncover at least a clue as to what happened to my father and grandfather. Do you think Ellen knows what happened to them?"

"I think it's worth a shot to talk with her about it," Blake said.

"I'm going to do that," I said. "Maybe she knows something."

Memories of my life in New York filtered through my view of Paris. Those lonely, ghost-filled days and nights had lost their power to haunt me. Not because my life was flawless, but it had become perfect in a way.

"You're smiling," Blake said.

"Hm?" I felt Paris cast its magic around us.

"You're smiling," he said. "Actually you're glowing."

"I was just thinking," I said softly. "When you and I met, all I wanted was a normal life. I saw my gifts as a problem, the hurdle that stood in the way of the lifestyle I wanted. But I've realized my gifts are not a preoblem." I let out a deep exhale, and the last of the anxiety I felt about my identity left on that breath. "Not perfect by any means. Certainly not normal. But suddenly I have no interest in a normal life." I wondered if awkward would land between us. But it never showed up.

"Good," Blake said. "Normal is a highly overrated pursuit."

I laughed quietly. "I'd much rather be here, in the City of Lights, surrounded by the most priceless art in the world, and with you, the love of at least two of my lifetimes. It's not at all the life I thought I wanted, but I am happy."

"Truly?"

"Completely."

His hands, confident and strong, caressed my back and pulled me to him. I rested my brow against his and his thumb traced my spine.

I ran my hand along his neck. "You've always been with me, haven't you? Even when you were only in my dreams you were watching over me. Walking with me and guiding us together again. I love you, Blake. My gosh I've loved you for so long."

"You're my heart and soul, Sassy." Blake spun the sapphire ring on my finger. The connection of Blake's and my touch on the ring at the same time jostled a memory loose from my soul.

Jack holds me in his arms as he spins me around. My laughter fills the room, his piercing, blue eyes dissolve into the same brilliant eyes that gazed up at me today. Feelings of home, belonging, and never-ending love surged and rocked between us in the present.

I eyed Blake's pocket watch, which sat on the side table, and felt the familiarity of our history swimming within it. It didn't surprise me, though I didn't yet want to relive that part of it. I'd have to one day. I could feel it. "It's funny that my ring and your eyes are just as they were in our 1920s life together. Like breadcrumbs to help us find our way to each other again. Perhaps there really is a reason for everything."

"Clues, in case our memories failed us," Blake said.

I rubbed my fingers up alongside his face, and the tips of his light beard pricked at my sensitive fingertips. "Were there other clues that triggered your memory that we were to be again?"

"Several. Though one rather big one." Blake grinned with more secrets yet to share. "I'll show you when we're back in New York. For now, we'll enjoy Paris."

Paris. Plans for the future. As he spoke of them, hope and excitement danced with one another at the tips of my toes and swirled together, upward through my body like a coil, growing stronger with each turn until I thought my heart might burst.

"I can't remember a time without you," I said as scenes from our lives together ran collectively in my memory, past and present.

"Perhaps there's never been a time when we were without one another," Blake suggested.

"Perhaps there never will be," I said. And I kissed the man my soul refused to forget.

SOMEWHERE IN TIME

BOOK 2 IN THE FINE ART OF DECEPTION
SERIES

Cloaked in Blake's button-down dress shirt, I crept barefoot through the darkened salon of his New York penthouse apartment. His scent laid heavily on his collar and I brought it to my nose. I breathed it in deeply as if the aura of him could protect me when he was away.

I stopped at the floor-to-ceiling windows where the cold, winter breeze disturbed the long, white curtains. Searching the twinkling cityscape, just as I'd done every night for the last twenty years, I wondered where my father and grandfather might be. Their presence or the trails of their energy couldn't be sensed anywhere and my heart ached from their absence.

They were out there. Somewhere.

Were they were warm and being fed well? Were they in good health? Were they hurting? They appeared well when I'd seen them just a few months ago, but I didn't know how much of that vision I could trust. It had been so unusual.

The surrounding walls of my fortress inched into my view. Along with it crept the concern that being safely tucked away and being a prisoner were too much of the same thing.

Blake stirred in his bedroom.

Blake Greenwood. My protector, my defender, the love of at least two of my lifetimes. In our last life together we were Jack and Sarah, star-crossed lovers from the 1920s. In this life our names were different, but we were the same souls, in love with one another even before we met, happiest when we were together. Nothing and no one could get to me when he was near.

I wasn't sure if it was his intent or some energetic force-field he created, or the effect of his endless love for me. I was pretty sure I could lie naked in the middle of Central Park at midnight and no one would bother me if Blake were nearby.

Strangely, this all-encompassing love didn't bring me peace or confidence. Because when the love of my life finally appeared, the flip side of that reality became crystal clear. I knew that if I ever lost him, that loss would be insurmountable. And that insight left me on the ridge of a double-sided coin, stuck between fear and gratefulness. I could easily pitch to either side.

Blake snuck behind me, gently drew me to him, and that was all it took. I was surrounded by love. Total protection. If only time could stand still.

"Going somewhere?" Tired-eyed and pillow-haired, Blake's voice was thick with sleep.

"Definitely not." I spun in his embrace and snuggled against him. Typically, the gentle rise and fall of his chest was the steady cadence that comforted me and set my world to right. Though not this time. Not when worries played with one another in my head like caffeinated children on the playground.

Soft and slow, he kissed the top of my head, "Can't sleep?"

"I gave up. I was on my way to the kitchen to see if you had an espresso machine."

Blake leaned back and gave me strong "don't be ridiculous" smirk. "Wouldn't be home without one."

He led me by the hand to the small kitchen where broad, cream-colored cabinets and dark wooden floors greeted me with surprising warmth. Most of the New York penthouses I'd visited were chilly with sophistication and excess, but this room breathed comfort. There was also a shielding sensation I noticed when we first stepped inside the apartment late last night, and I knew I was safe here. At least for the moment. The outside world rang with chaos, but in this home, there was peace.

With only Blake in residence, the kitchen wasn't quite the center of his home as it was with most abodes, the steady pulse of its heart beat beyond the far wall. Whatever room that was, that was where Blake had spent most of his time, dreaming, thinking, living.

"I miss Paris." I sipped the hot espresso and it heated me from the inside out. Memories of endless museums by day, outdoor cafes for lunch, and remarkable dinners laced with jazz that lingered until wee morning hours danced between us. With only a visit, Paris seeped into your soul. "And I miss our quiet life in the country, too."

Blake leaned against the counter and savored his own cup of espresso. "Then we'll go back. Just as soon as Otto's trial is over and he's in prison. Where he belongs. We'll stay as long as you like." He kissed my neck and the corners of my mouth rose. "We just need to get through these next few days, then we're on our way."

My smile slid into a grimace and I tried to hide the fact that my heart had taken a shot of adrenaline. I didn't want to think about Otto Albrecht's trial. Or testifying in it.

AUTHOR'S NOTE

What a joy it has been to write Blake and Addie's story. And what a story it is—spanning several lifetimes and three books! The entire trilogy has been released and you can read their full story back to back with SOMEWHERE IN TIME AND LOST IN TIME. (Both are free through Amazon's Kindle Unlimited) I do hope you enjoy reading these books as much as I enjoyed writing them!

After I finished LOST IN TIME I fully planned to continue writing in that world. Until the idea for THE HAUNTING OF ALCOTT MANOR landed on me. Sometimes stories choose their author and that was definitely the case with this one!

When you've finished THE FINE ART OF DECEPTION SERIES, you might want to try THE HAUNTING OF ALCOTT MANOR Series. It's a contemporary gothic romance that's full of mysteries, twists and surprises!

I love to hear from my readers and you're welcome to get in touch with me at AuthorAlyssaRichards@proton mail.com or via my website. While you're there, sign up for my mailing list so I can let you know when I have a new title.

I hope you enjoy your journey through time with Blake and Addie!

Alyssa Richards

THE HAUNTING OF ALCOTT MANOR

It was the wind that stopped her.

Not the force of it, but the message it carried on its course. Cold air tumbled over warm currents, whipping around her legs and across her chest. It swirled about her body like a lover who simultaneously promised what was next and took control to make it come about.

Seventies rock blasted in her ears and she slowed her run. Her feet stopped their rhythmic pounding on the packed sand of Stinson Beach.

Her beach.

She tried to catch her breath and searched the deep lapis waves that rode toward her. It was cold air that blew over the warm, a pattern her mother said meant that upheaval rode on the appearance of calm.

"No," Gemma said between gasps for air. Her voice was low. Determined. Firm. "Not again."

She pulled the earbuds from her ears, stared at the waves that rolled over the depths of the ocean, and the wind settled as though backing down from her challenge. It switched to a sun-warmed draft that caressed her face and neck.

Something tingled inside of her from it, like the effects of a possessive kiss. An awakening, a calling. The result of an event already put into motion.

She tried to cast aside her mother's Native American wisdom, especially because it had proven itself right more often than she liked.

"Stay away." Her voice held no mercy and no patience. She fit the earbuds into her ears again and cranked up the volume.

The gray shingles and glass of her house were in her sight now. She ran toward it with all the speed she had left, along with the sinking feeling that this wind pattern was signaling yet something else she couldn't outrun.

ALSO BY ALYSSA RICHARDS

THE FINE ART OF DECEPTION SERIES

THE FINE ART OF DECEPTION, UNDOING TIME

SOMEWHERE IN TIME

LOST IN TIME

THE FINE ART OF DECEPTION, BOXED SET

THE ALCOTT MANOR SERIES

THE HAUNTING AT ALCOTT MANOR

A MURDER AT ALCOTT MANOR

A STRANGER AT ALCOTT MANOR

THE CHASING SECRETS SERIES

CHASING SECRETS

FORCED PERSPECTIVE

Be the first to know about Alyssa Richards' next novel, sign up here: www.AlyssaRichards.com

and follow her on Amazon or BookBub to receive a new release alert!

ABOUT THE AUTHOR

ALYSSA RICHARDS is the USA TODAY BESTSELLING AUTHOR of romantic suspense and mystery thriller novels. She loves living in the South with her husband and two children. She also loves good espresso, her rescue dogs, magnolias and gardenias, and, of course, reading a great book. She grew up running barefoot in the Blue Ridge Mountains of North Carolina, where her favorite weekly adventure was a trip to the library with her mom.

Sign up for Alyssa's newsletter at www.alyssarichards.com to receive special offers, and news about her latest releases.

For More information
www.AlyssaRichards.com
Contact Alyssa at:
authoralyssarichards@protonmail.com

instagram.com/alyssaauthor
amazon.com/Alyssa-Richards/e/B00S1IGJ9O
bookbub.com/authors/alyssa-richards
goodreads.com/alyssarichards

ACKNOWLEDGMENTS

My heartfelt gratitude ...

...to my husband for his unending support and encouragement.

...to my boys, for being such bright lights in my life.

...to Yvonne for so graciously reading the early versions and for sharing her honest feedback.

...to Diana Young for her kind support and expert advice.

...to Libby Murphy for editing the manuscript with such a gifted eye.

www.ingramcontent.com/pod-product-compliance
Lightning Source LLC
Chambersburg PA
CBHW072020110726
47910CB00005B/1818